CUPCAKE DIARIES

SIMON SPOTLIGHT

An imprint of Simon & Schuster Children's Publishing Division
1230 Avenue of the Americas, New York, New York 10020
This Simon Spotlight bind-up edition November 2016
Emma All Stirred Up!, *Alexis Cool as a Cupcake*, and *Katie and the Cupcake War*
copyright © 2012 by Simon & Schuster, Inc. All rights reserved, including the right of reproduction in whole or in part in any form. SIMON SPOTLIGHT and colophon are registered trademarks of Simon & Schuster, Inc. For information about special discounts for bulk purchases, please contact Simon & Schuster Special Sales at 1-866-506-1949 or business@simonandschuster.com.
Text by Tracey West and Elizabeth Doyle Carey
Chapter header illustrations by Laura Roode and Ana Benaroya
Design by Laura Roode
Manufactured in the United States of America 1016 OFF
2 4 6 8 10 9 7 5 3 1
ISBN 978-1-4814-8438-1
ISBN 978-1-4424-5079-0 (*Emma All Stirred Up!* eBook)
ISBN 978-1-4424-5081-3 (*Alexis Cool as a Cupcake* eBook)
ISBN 978-1-4424-5374-6 (*Katie and the Cupcake War* eBook)
These titles were previously published individually by Simon Spotlight.

CUPCAKE DIARIES

Emma
all stirred up!

Alexis
cool as a cupcake

Katie and the cupcake war

by coco simon

Simon Spotlight

New York   London   Toronto   Sydney   New Delhi

Emma
all
stirred
up!

CHAPTER 1

Little Brother, Big Problem

My name is Emma Taylor, but a few weeks ago I was wishing it was anything but! I was pretending that the little boy who was outside the school bus, wailing that he did not want to go to day camp, was *not* my little brother, Jake Taylor, and that those desperate parents who were bribing and pleading with him were *not* my parents, but rather some poor, misguided souls whom I would never see again.

In fact, I was wishing that I was already an adult and that my three best friends and I—the entire Cupcake Club—had opened our own bakery on a cute little side street in New York City, where none of my three brothers lived. The bakery would be all pink, and it would sell piles of cupcakes in a rainbow of lovely colors and flavors, and would cater mainly to movie stars and little girls' princess birthday parties. That is my fantasy. Sounds great, right?

But oh, no, this was reality.

"Emmy!" Jake was shrieking as my father gently but firmly manhandled him down the bus aisle to where I was scrunched down on my seat, pretending not to see them. I could literally feel the warmth of all the other eyes on the bus watching us, and I just wanted to melt away. Instead I stared out the window, like there was something really fascinating out there.

"Emma, please look after your brother," said my father. How many times have I heard that one? My older brothers, Matt and Sam, and I take turns babysitting Jake, but somehow the bad stuff always happens on my shift. My dad gave Jake one last kiss, reached to pat me on the head, and then dashed off the bus. I wished I could've dashed with him.

A counselor sat on the end of the seat, scrunching Jake in between us, so he couldn't run away. Jake was wailing, and the counselor—a nice girl named Paige, who is about twenty-one years old and probably wishing she were somewhere else too—was speaking in a soothing voice to him. She looked over his head at me, smiled, and then said, "Don't worry. This happens all the time. We always get one of these guys. He'll settle down within the week."

The week?! I wanted to die, but instead I nodded and looked out the window again. I also wanted to kill Jake that moment, but it was only seconds later that his wails turned to quiet hiccups. Then he slid his clammy, chubby little hand into mine and squeezed, and I felt a little guilty. "It's going to be okay, Jake," I whispered, and squeezed his little hand back. He snuggled into me and looked up at me with these really big eyes that get me every time. It's not the worst thing in the world to have a little someone in your life who looks up to you.

I sighed. "Feeling better, officer?" Jake is big into law enforcement, so it usually cheers him up if we play Precinct. At least he wasn't crying anymore. Paige gave him a pat on the head and then went to help some other kids get on the bus. But Jake wasn't feeling better. I could tell just by looking at him.

"I feel sick," he said.

Oh no. Jake isn't one of those kids who fakes being sick. My mom always says on car trips that if Jake says he feels sick, we pull over, because he *will* throw up, 100 percent of the time.

I jerked the bus window open and quickly flung

Jake over me, so that he was sitting in the window seat. "Put your head out the window, buddy. Take deep breaths—in through your nose, out through your mouth. We're going to start moving soon, so the wind will be in your face. . . . Deep breaths."

I rubbed his back a little and looked up to see if anyone I knew was getting on at this stop. My best friend and co–Cupcake Clubber Alexis Becker was going to the same camp, but her parents were dropping her off on their way to work. I fantasized about them driving me, too, and leaving Jake to his own devices. Ha! As if my parents would let me get away with that! At the very least, I did have our Cupcake Club meeting to look forward to later today. Just quality girl time, planning out the club's summer schedule and reviewing the cupcake jobs we had coming up. Chilling with my best friends— Alexis, Katie, and Mia—and brainstorming. It was definitely going to be fun.

A bunch of little kids streamed on and sat mostly in the front of the bus. Suddenly I spied a familiar shade of very bright blond hair, and my stomach sank. Noooo!!! It couldn't be.

But it was.

Sydney Whitman, mean-girl extraordinaire and head of the imaginatively named Popular Girls

4

Club at school, came strolling down the aisle, heading straight for the back row, where only the most popular kids dared to sit. I quickly looked out the window and pretended I hadn't seen her. But no luck.

"Oh, that's so cute! You and your little brother sitting together! I guess that's easier than trying to find someone your own age to sit with?" She smiled sweetly, but her remark stung just as it was meant to.

Jake hates Sydney as much as I do, if not more, so when he turned his head to look at her, he began to gag. Sydney's eyes opened wide, and her hand flew up to cover her mouth. "Oh no! He's going to—"

Luckily, Jake turned to the window just in time and hurled the contents of his stomach out onto the road.

"Disgusting!" shrieked Sydney, and she fled to the back of the bus.

I didn't know whether to laugh or cry. It's just one more nail in the coffin of my possible popularity, not that I ever really stood a chance. And not that I really wanted to. But it was also kind of hilarious to have Jake take one look at Sydney and then throw up. Definitely not her desired effect on men. I made a mental note to tell the Cupcake Club later. They'd love this.

Jake barfed a couple more times and then sat back down, looking as white as a sheet. The good news about Jake's car sickness is that after he's done throwing up, he's always fine. I pulled a napkin from my lunch bag and gave it to him to wipe his face. Then I cracked open his thermos and gave him a tiny sip of apple juice. I felt sorry for the poor guy. I hate throwing up.

Jake smiled wanly. "Thanks, Emmy. Sorry."

I laughed. "I feel the same way when I see Sydney Whitman." I wasn't sure I would have been so psyched about going to this camp if I'd known Sydney was going—or at the very least that she'd be on my bus. It definitely put a cramp in my happiness.

Jake rested his head back against the seat and promptly fell asleep. In a minute his head was resting, sweaty and heavy, against my shoulder. First days can be hard for anyone, especially little kids. At least tomorrow we wouldn't have the same problem. I said a silent prayer that Sydney wasn't in my group.

At camp, we got off the bus and a crowd of cheering counselors with painted faces was there to greet us. My mom must've called ahead to tip off someone, because one really pretty counselor was holding up a sign, like people do at the airport. It read OFFICER JAKE TAYLOR. That at least allowed me to peel him off and hand him over to the counselor, so I could go with my group, Team Four, to our rally zone (whatever that was) at the arts-and-crafts center.

The boys and girls have separate areas at camp, so I wouldn't see Jake again all day, thank goodness. And thank goodness again, because Sydney headed off with Team Five in the opposite direction. I didn't have a minute to review who was on whose team. Anyway, I didn't know a lot of the kids, but I did know that wherever Alexis was, she and I would be together. (We requested it, and my mom promised me she had spoken with the camp director.) That's all that matters.

As I headed across the green lawn to the arts-and-crafts center, I heard someone calling my name. I turned, and, of course, it was Alexis! I had never been so happy to see her in all my life.

"Thank goodness!" I cried, and threw my arms around her, like a shipwreck victim who has finally been saved.

Alexis isn't much for big displays of affection, so she patted my back awkwardly, but I didn't mind. In any case, she just saw me a few days ago.

7

"What's going on?" she asked as we separated and followed our counselor.

"Jake drama. Screaming, puking—the whole deal." I lowered my voice. "And Sydney Whitman saw the whole thing."

Alexis waved her hand in the air, as if to say *whatever!* That is just one of the many things I love about Alexis. She doesn't care at all what other people think. "Too bad he didn't puke *on* her," she said with a laugh. "Or did he?" Her eyes twinkled mischievously.

"No such luck. But the good news is, we aren't on the same team as her."

We'd reached the log cabin that was the headquarters for our team. On its porch stood two teenage counselors—a guy and a girl. As the crowd amassed in front of them, I counted twelve campers: all girls, of course. Yay! Finally! A break from all the boys in my life!

"Hello, people! Listen up!" The guy counselor was clapping his hands and kind of dancing around in a funny way to get our attention. Everyone started laughing and listening.

He bowed and said, "Thank you, ladies! My name is Raoul Sanchez, and this is my awesome partner, Maryanne Murphy."

Maryanne did a little curtsy, and we all clapped. She was pretty—short and cute with red hair and freckles. Raoul was tall and thin with rubbery arms and legs, and his face had a big goofy smile topped off by black, crew-cut hair. It was obvious neither of them was shy.

"We are going to have the most fun of any team this summer! Raoul and I personally guarantee it!" Maryanne said enthusiastically.

Raoul nodded. "If this isn't the most fun summer of your life, when camp is over I will take you to an all-you-can-eat pizza party, on me."

There were cheers and claps.

"Okay, we have a lot to tell you, so why don't you all grab a seat on the grass and get ready to be pumped!" said Maryanne.

Raoul and Maryanne then proceeded to tell us how we'd get to pick our own team name. ("Team Four" was just a placeholder, they said.) They told us about all the fun activities we'd do: swimming, kayaking, art projects, team sports, field trips, tennis, and more. Then they told us about the special occasions that were scheduled: Tie-Dye Day, Pajama Day, Costume Day, Crazy Hat Day, and finally, the best day of all . . . Camp Olympics, followed by the grand finale: the camp talent show!

Ugh. The camp talent show? Getting onstage in front of more than a hundred people? *So* not up my alley. I made a face at Alexis, but she was listening thoughtfully, her head tilted to the side and her long reddish hair already escaping its headband. She was probably wondering if there was any money to be made here; business was mostly all she thought about. In fact, her parents said if she did an outdoor camp for part of the summer, she could go to business camp for two weeks at the end of the summer. Sometimes I wonder how we are friends at all; our interests are so different!

"Thinking of signing up?" I whispered.

"Myself? No. But you should," she whispered back.

I laughed. "Yeah, right. What's my talent? Babysitting?"

Alexis raised her eyebrows at me. "Maybe. But I'm sure you can come up with something more marketable than that."

Right. I can't even keep the kid I babysit for from throwing up.

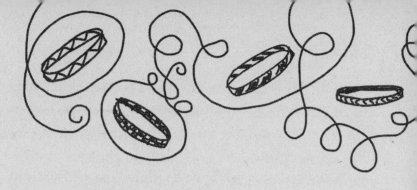

CHAPTER 2

Meet the Hotcakes!

First we played a getting-to-know-you game called Pass the Packet. We had a mystery brown bag filled with something, and we each took turns holding it and telling the group about ourselves and then said what we wished was in the bag. (I told the group I had three brothers and I wished the bag had tickets to a taping of *Top Chef*.) When it was Alexis's turn, she told the group how she, Mia, Katie, and I had a Cupcake Club and about all the business we do, baking cupcakes for special events. The other girls in the group thought it was so cool. I felt great, and Alexis and I promised to bring in cupcakes for the group.

At the end, Maryanne opened the "packet," and it was filled with these awesome friendship bracelets for each of us. We all grabbed for the color we wanted. I, of course, grabbed a pink one.

Then we got down to business, naming our team.

A very pretty girl named Georgia, with light red hair and dark eyes, suggested we be "Rock Stars." I thought it was a great idea, but because it was the first idea, everyone still wanted a chance to make their own suggestions.

A girl named Caroline, who turned out to be Georgia's cousin, said, "How about the 'A-Team,'" which everyone thought was funny. Alexis suggested "Winners," because the power of positive branding would intimidate our competitors. I had to laugh. Then a girl named Charlotte—with bright blue eyes and dark, dark hair—suggested that since we would be having cupcakes a lot (she laughed and looked at me and Alexis when she said it), we should be the "Cupcakes." Right after she said it, a funny girl named Elle said, "No, the 'Hotcakes'!" and that was it.

"The Hotcakes! I love it!" cried Raoul. He and Elle high-fived. "Let's take a vote, girls! All in favor of the 'Hotcakes,' put your hands in the air!"

Everyone screamed and waved their hands high,

and that was that. Maryanne announced it was time for the Hotcakes to change for swimming, then lunchtime.

Alexis and I grabbed our backpacks and headed to the changing rooms.

"This is superfun, don't you think?" I asked as we walked across the central green.

"Yes, *and* I think we have the best group," said Alexis in a sure voice.

I laughed. "How do you know?"

She shrugged. "I counted how many girls we have versus the other two teams in our age group, then I evaluated how many of our girls are nice and smart. As a percentage, we have the nicest team by far. I would also venture that one hundred percent of our team is smart, and with Sydney on Team Five and stupid Bella on Team Three, their intelligence rate is at least ten percent below ours."

"Alexis! You are too much!" I shook my head. "The only bad part is, I wish the others were here."

She knew who I meant. Katie and Mia from our Cupcake Club were doing different things from us this month. Alexis frowned thoughtfully. "Yeah. But we'll see them plenty. And maybe it's good for us to branch out a little. It will generate some new business strategies and connections!"

I swatted her. "Is that all you think about?"

She pushed open the door to the locker room with a grin. "Pretty much!"

"I just hope they don't replace us with new friends."

Alexis shrugged. "Maybe they're thinking the same thing."

I thought back to last fall, when Katie had been dumped by Callie, her old best friend, so that Callie could hang with Sydney and the Popular Girls Club. New friends and old: a tough thing to balance. I sighed after just thinking about it.

When I came to the open house they had in March, one of the things I liked about this camp was that they have private changing rooms in the locker room, so you don't have to strip naked in front of strangers. I could never change in front of other people. Forget about being naked and getting into a bathing suit—I can't even change into pj's at a slumber party or try on clothes at the mall if someone else is in the room. Except for Mom. It's just a personal thing. I am very private about my body. Maybe it comes from being the only girl in a family of boys or from having my own room, but I just like privacy.

Alexis and I changed in rooms next to each other, and were chatting through the opening at the top of the dividers.

"Wait till you see my new suit!" she said. "It's so cute!"

"Me too! My mom brought it home as a surprise!"

We came out and took one look at each other and then started laughing our heads off. We had on the exact same bathing suit! They were tankinis, navy blue with white piping and a cool, yellow lightning bolt down either side. Alexis is kind of muscular from soccer, and I'm kind of thin (I play the flute, but that doesn't exactly build muscles!), so the suit fit us way differently. We couldn't stop giggling, though. We looked like total dork twins.

Georgia and Elle, and Charlotte and Caroline all gathered around, and we admired what everyone was wearing. We all had on new suits. Then one girl named Kira, who was shy and superpretty, came out. She had her towel draped around her shoulders, and she wasn't smiling.

"Let's see!" said Elle, clapping.

Kira shook her head. "Uh-uh." She bit her lip, and we instantly realized we shouldn't push her.

She looked like she might cry at any second.

"Okay!" Alexis said quickly. I could tell she was desperate to make Kira feel better, but couldn't think of how. Suddenly she hoisted her towel across her shoulders, to cover herself like Kira. "Capes it is!" I was so proud of her right then for her idea.

Everyone followed suit. Georgia yelled, "The Hot*capes*!" and we all hooted. I glanced at Kira and saw relief on her face, and we all marched out to meet Maryanne and Raoul, who were waiting outside to walk us to the huge pool. I had to wonder how bad Kira's suit was, though.

We sat for a water safety lecture by the lifeguard and swim director, Mr. Collins, a really nice gym teacher from the elementary school whom I recognized. The safety talk was a little boring (yeah, yeah, don't run, no chicken fights, no diving in the shallow end, swim with a buddy), but then we were in the water for free swim, and it was heavenly! The water wasn't too cold and the pool was huge, with a supershallow end and a superdeep end with a diving board!

In my excitement to get in the water, I had forgotten to check out Kira's suit, but I stole a glance the first chance I could. She was kind of cringing in the shallow end, and her suit was a one piece with Hello Kitty on it, and it was way too small for her. I felt terrible. It was babyish and it looked bad. I wondered why she didn't just swim to the deep end to cover it up.

"Okay, people! Now it's time for some fun!" Mr. Collins blew a whistle and beckoned us all over to the wall in the shallow end. I love to swim and I'm pretty good at it, so I did a loopy backstroke, kind of hamming it up, and Alexis did her old lady breaststroke, where she keeps her head out of the water the whole time. We cracked each other up.

Once everyone had reached the side of the pool, Mr. Collins whistled again to get our attention, then he spoke. He had a very kind voice, and was very quiet and patient.

"Okay, kids, today we're going to just get a feel for skill level and what we need to work on with each of you. One of the great things about Spring Lake Day Camp is that you will all leave here swimming really well by the end of the summer, and you'll have fun learning! So let's break you into four groups of three, and we'll have each of you swim a length of the pool in three heats. Count off by threes, then come down to the shallow end and we'll get started."

Alexis and I swam stood next to each other in the lineup, so we would be on the same team. I was first, and Charlotte was the third in our group. The other girls arranged themselves, and Maryanne and Raoul followed, walking along the edge of the pool. The counselors were in bathing suits, but I guess they didn't have to get in the water since Mr. Collins taught this part of camp.

"Okay, girls. Everyone settled? Any stroke you like, no rush. We're not racing. On your marks, get set . . . *bweeet!*" He blew his whistle hard, and I took off, swimming freestyle, all the way to the deep end. I knew we weren't racing, but it felt good to try hard and swim fast. I hated knowing people were watching me, but at least three other girls were swimming at the same time as me, so the bystanders weren't watching *only* me the whole time, which made it okay.

I got to the deep end and slapped my hand against the wall. First! (Not that we were racing!) I hung on to the wall and watched Georgia, Jesse, and Caroline come in right after me. I was breathing hard, but it felt good. Next up was Alexis, along with a girl named Tricia, a girl named Louise, and Kira in the fourth group. Mr. Collins blew the whistle, and they were off.

Alexis is a great swimmer too. Just what you would expect: efficient; not show-offy; fast, clean strokes. Tricia and Louise were doing fine too. But . . . uh-oh. Kira wasn't.

She had pushed away from the wall fine and was gliding, but then when the water got deeper and her glide wore off, she started to flounder. She put down her feet and tried to push off again, but that only got her into the deeper end, to where she couldn't stand. She started to sink.

Mr. Collins was in the water in a flash, as was Raoul. They both dove from opposite sides of the water and reached her at the exact same moment. I was frozen to the spot, watching as they grabbed her and hauled her toward the side of the pool. *Oh my goodness,* was all I could think. Kira can't swim!

When they reached the wall, Kira was sputtering and coughing. They each had an arm around her, and had towed her to the side in a flash. Mr. Collins lifted her onto the deck and pushed himself up and out of the water. Maryanne came running over with her own towel, and put it over Kira's shoulders. Kira started to cry. Tricia, Alexis, and Louise had reached the deep end's wall (they'd been oblivious to what had happened), and now everyone was just silent, watching.

At first, we were all scared for Kira, and then as it became clear that she was okay, we were all really embarrassed for her.

Mr. Collins quickly established that Kira was not hurt or in danger, then stood and called out to the group, "She's fine! Just a little rusty, like the best of us after a long winter! Everything's okay. Just swim for a minute while we change our plan." He and Maryanne and Raoul chatted in whispers, then Raoul jumped back into the pool and swam to the shallow end.

Mr. Collins called out again, "Now is there anyone else who'd like a little extra practice with Raoul? It's fine! Just raise your hand." He looked around. No one was raising their hand. But then Elle, who was still in the shallow end, raised her hand.

"Great! Go with Raoul to the corner and you'll work on it a little. Kira"—Mr. Collins reached down and patted Kira's head—"just come on over and join Raoul and . . . what's your name, young lady?"

"Elle," called Elle.

"And Elle while they practice at this end, okay? The next group, get ready to swim."

In a few moments Kira was back in the water

with Elle and Raoul. Now, if there is one thing I noticed when we were having free swim, it's that Elle is an amazing swimmer. After what she did for Kira, I knew she'd make an amazing friend, too.

CHAPTER 3

New Friends, Old Friends, and Old Enemies

Sydney Whitman sat at a picnic table next to us at lunch. She must've been bragging to her group that she knew a lot of kids at camp, because she had walked right over to us and acted really chummy. (She was obviously going for quantity over quality since we're not friends.) We weren't falling for it, though, and anyone could see she was really just doing it for show.

"What, no cupcakes?" Sydney asked, with a big fake smile as she inspected our lunch.

Alexis shook her head. "Nope." She continued eating, as though Sydney wasn't even there. The rest of our table (Charlotte, Elle, Georgia, and Kira—Elle's new best friend) just looked blankly at Sydney, probably wondering who she was.

Sydney was floundering. She tried a different topic. "So what's your team name, girls?"

Georgia, who was so sweet, was perplexed. She clearly felt uncomfortable with Alexis's rudeness, while I for one was loving it.

"We're called the Hotcakes," Georgia said politely.

Sydney laughed meanly, but she had a kind of surprised look on her face. "That's so . . . like, young. Like Strawberry Shortcake or something. We're Angels, like *Charlie's Angels*. Gorgeous and powerful, get it?" She flipped her hair.

Georgia and Elle looked at each other, then at me, like *Who is this person?* I just had to shrug.

"I heard someone in your group almost drowned today," Sydney said next, really casually.

I looked at Kira and saw her face turn a deep red. I wanted to throttle Sydney. Instead, I thought about what Elle did earlier and how brave and kind she was. I decided to copy her.

"It was me." I shrugged.

Sydney's hand flew to her mouth, and she started to laugh in surprise. "Really! You can't swim?"

"Actually, it was me," said Alexis.

Sydney looked confused. "Wait, what?"

Georgia was laughing now. "It was me. I fell into the pool and drowned."

"No, me!" said Elle. Now we were all howling. Even Kira was giggling a little.

Sydney looked at us, one to another, then she got a mad look on her face and gave a slight shrug. "Whatever. I'm just trying to be a concerned citizen." And she stalked back to her table. That last line really got us going. While I know it isn't nice to laugh at other people, it felt good to be part of this group and laughing for a good reason. The very idea of Sydney Whitman as a caring, concerned individual was truly hilarious to me. Of course, when we stopped laughing, Alexis and I explained who she was and why she was such a villain. There's nothing like a common enemy to unite a group. That's when Alexis spontaneously promised to start cupcake Fridays for camp, and I wholeheartedly agreed.

The first day of camp seemed to last forever. It was only four o'clock when we all piled back onto the bus, but it seemed like I'd left home weeks, not hours, earlier.

Jake was sticky and muddy and tired when I met him at our bus waiting area. He promptly handed me his grimy, mud-caked towel and wet backpack to hold for him, thereby killing my happy first-day-of-camp glow. At least Alexis was on the bus ride home with me. But as it turned out, Jake wouldn't let her sit with us. He pitched a fit that he wanted to sit with only me, so Alexis sat in front of me so we could chat on the way home. And after all that, Jake fell asleep as soon as the wheels started turning. Apparently he only pukes on the way *to* camp.

Alexis and I spoke in whispers as we reviewed the day, kind of free-associating.

Me: "Mr. Collins is really nice."

Alexis: "Yeah, that was scary."

Me: "Very cool of Elle to pretend she needed help."

Alexis: "I'm psyched for cupcake Fridays at camp, too."

Me: "I wish SW wasn't here."

Alexis: *(Moans. Pretends to puke.)*

We laughed.

But then Alexis grew serious. "You know, I learned more about Kira, because Louisa went to school with her. I feel really bad. Her mom was sick for a few years, and she died about eight months ago. Kira has three much older sisters, but none of them live at home anymore, so she just lives with her dad. He's, like, much older than our dads and kind of clueless and sad about his wife and everything."

"Wow. That is so sad. Poor Kira."

Alexis nodded. "I know. So that kind of explains the lame bathing suit. I guess her dad didn't know which kind to buy her. And maybe her mom just wasn't well enough to teach her to swim, and maybe her dad didn't know you had to know how to swim to go to this camp."

"Bummer. I felt terrible for her."

"Yeah, but at least she's really nice," said Alexis.

"And superpretty," I added, feeling generous. I made a mental note to make an even bigger effort with Kira. Even though my mom isn't around a lot, it would be really hard if she was gone for, like, forever. I couldn't even imagine it.

We had reached Alexis's stop, so she hopped off. We were having a Cupcake Club meeting at her house at five thirty, but I was going to go home and shower first. I'd see her again soon.

Just before our stop, I nudged Jake awake, and when we arrived, I half carried, half dragged him and his disgusting gear off the bus. He was so dirty, I considered hosing him down in the yard, but instead I talked him into a bath by promising him that he could use one of the fizzy blue bath bombs I got for my birthday. His gear I would have to hose off.

I spent a lot of time babysitting Jake earlier in the year, when my mom had to switch jobs for a little while. It was hard work and kind of a bummer because Jake is not the easiest kid to babysit. Also, it cut into a lot of my own activities. Now that my mom is back at her old job, things are a little better. During the summer, I have to take Jake to and from camp, and two days a week I stay with him until 5:15 p.m., when my mom gets home. The other days my older brothers, Matt and Sam, take turns watching him.

After Jake's bath, I got him into his pj's and settled him in front of the TV, and then I showered and cleared out my lunchbox and backpack. At 5:10 I was ready. At 5:20 my mom had not yet appeared. At 5:30 I called Alexis's house to say my mom was running late. At 5:40 she pulled in. I was waiting in the driveway with my arms folded and my bike all ready to go.

"Honey, I'm so sorry," my mom said as she clambered out of the car with all her grocery bags. "The checkout line was horrible, and it took longer than

I'd planned, plus, they were out of the good tortillas for the quesadillas Dad likes, so . . ."

My blood was boiling. I was all ready to start yelling at her about how I'm always left stranded, always ditched with Jake; how no one ever considers my schedule, and so on. But suddenly I thought of Kira and how hard it must have been for her to lose her mom. I took a deep breath; kissed my mom on the cheek; yelled, "See you later!"; and took off.

I was twenty minutes late for the meeting. I needed to be home by six thirty for dinner, so that only gave us forty minutes to meet.

"Mia! Katie! You are a sight for sore eyes!" I said, and it was true. Because even though I saw them yesterday, it felt like a year ago. And it was so exhausting trying to make new friends that it was a great relief to relax with old ones. I just sat and smiled at them like an idiot for a minute.

"Ookaaay . . . ," said Katie, and giggled. "We missed you, too."

Alexis had filled them in on camp, but then I had to give my version and they had to tell me about their day. So it was 6:10 by the time we finished, and we only had ten minutes for club business—fifteen minutes if I biked home really fast.

28

"First order," said Alexis in her official voice. "I need someone to take over my deliveries to Mona on Saturdays. I now have a summer golf clinic on Saturday mornings."

Every Friday we bake five dozen mini cupcakes for our friend Mona, who owns a bridal store called The Special Day. We met her when Mia's mom got married and we were all bridesmaids in the wedding. We bought our dresses at Mona's store. The store is so beautiful and peaceful and girlie (so unlike my house!), and Mona is so nice. I waved my hand in the air.

"I'll take over!" I said. "I will, I will!"

Everyone laughed.

Alexis beamed. "Great. Thanks. Next, Jake's birthday."

I groaned. "What color cupcake would 'annoying' be?"

Mia loves Jake (it's mutual), so she protested. "No, they have to be really special. Our best work for that little mascot of ours!"

Katie asked, "What about P-B-and-J?"

"Nah, peanut allergies in his class," I said.

"Triple Chocolate Fudge Explosion?" suggested Katie.

"Why don't we just ask him?" asked Mia.

"Fine." I wrote it on my to-do list. (I am all about lists.)

"What else?" asked Alexis.

"Well, I was wondering if we should try to mix things up a little for Mona. Maybe try a different flavor?" asked Katie.

"Yes, but it has to be white," reminded Mia. Right now we baked only white cake cupcakes with white frosting because Mona can't have anything chocolate or, like, raspberry in a store full of white, white, white bridal gowns!

We thought for a minute.

"Cinnamon bun with cream cheese frosting?" I suggested.

"Ooh, I love those!" said Mia enthusiastically.

"Or coconut?" suggested Katie.

Alexis made a face. "Not everyone likes coconut," she said.

"Also maybe allergies, right?" I said.

Katie looked kind of bummed, so I said, "Why don't I ask her on Saturday, okay?"

Alexis made a note in the meeting minutes, and I added it to my to-do list. Sometimes being in this club is about balancing people's feelings as much as it is about baking and making money. It can be hard work.

"So Friday night, we're on, right? My house?" I said.

Alexis and Mia nodded eagerly. They have crushes on my older brothers (Alexis on Matt, Mia on Sam), so they always want to come to my house. And ever since I bought my own pink KitchenAid stand mixer, it's gotten much more efficient to bake at my house too.

I wondered if Alexis and I should mention that we're baking for our new friends on Thursday, too. I glanced at Alexis to see if she was thinking about it, but her face betrayed nothing. I decided to wait.

It's weird having other friends. I wondered if they'd become as close as my old friends. I really couldn't picture it!

CHAPTER 4

A Secret Celebrity!

So, when I thought Jake's crying and barfing were just first-day jitters I was dead wrong! They were *every day* jitters! My mornings were exhausting and mortifying. Seriously, every morning he got himself all worked up, he cried, Dad made me sit with him, and then he puked. It was completely, totally unfair.

I tried to go on strike and get a ride with Alexis, but my parents insisted I take the bus so that I could watch over Jake. The only good thing was that because I did bus duty (and maybe because instead of freaking out at my mom when she was late that time from picking up groceries, I was nice!), my parents declared that I didn't have to babysit Jake anymore when we got home! Now it was all up to

Matt and Sam (and my mom). Yay! Freedom!

Needless to say, the bus was still a major bummer. And Sydney made a big deal of sitting really far away from us and bringing perfume that she sprayed in our direction when she got on. That perfume was probably what was making Jake sick, if you ask me. Either that, or it had just become a bad habit for him. Or maybe the sight of her really did make him gag.

Anyway, besides the bad arrivals and departures, camp was awesome! I loved, loved, loved it! And what's really weird was that I'd grown so close to my Hotcakes teammates so fast. I mean Elle, Georgia, Charlotte, Caroline, and Kira. I felt almost as close to them as I do to Mia, Katie, and Alexis. It's weird. I guess it's because we spent so much intense time together, and we chatted all we wanted (unlike at school, where we actually have to shut up in class and learn!). I think Alexis feels the same way.

Oh, and it was true that we had the best team. We got Raoul and Maryanne to admit it. Sydney's team was the worst because according to her counselors, by way of *our* counselors, every day she made a different girl on her team cry. Can you believe it?

The week seemed really long because of all the newness, so by Thursday night I was pretty wiped out, but Alexis and I had to bake for camp's Cupcake Friday. The other bummer was when Mia called to see if we wanted to go to the movies. (Her stepfather, Eddie, was treating.)

Now, the thing about the four members of the Cupcake Club is that when one of us proposes an activity or a plan, the only thing that really prevents us from doing it is if it's something random, like a sibling's birthday or someone's grandma is visiting. Because we all know one another's schedules so well, we don't even bother proposing plans unless we know all four of us can make it.

So Mia and Katie knew Alexis and I were technically free Thursday night. Except that we weren't. Because we were baking for our new friends. Ugh.

When Mia called I was speechless. Of course I wanted to go, but I also didn't want to let down our new friends, especially when everyone had made such a big deal about our cupcakes. I mean, our team was basically named after our cupcakes! So I ended up kind of lying and telling Mia I was really tired and couldn't go, but that I could do it Friday after we baked. But Mia said we really wouldn't have time to do both. She was kind of bummed and a little annoyed when she hung up. I'd never turned down a plan before.

I wanted to dial Alexis to warn her, but I knew I'd get busted, what with Mia calling at the same time. (I could just picture Alexis: "Oh, hang on, Mia, I have Emma calling on the other line." Yikes!) So I sat by the phone and waited for it to ring, which I knew it would.

"Hi," I said, drumming my fingers on the kitchen counter. I could see from the caller ID that it was Alexis.

"Whoops," she said.

"I know. Major whoops. What did you say?"

"I said we had relays today and I was tired, but I could do it tomorrow."

"Me too! I said basically the same thing!" I love Alexis. She and I have just always been on the same page, ever since we were little.

"Phew," she said. "But I think she was mad."

My heart sank, remembering. "I know."

We were quiet. Finally I said, "Oh well, when are you coming over?"

Alexis said she'd be over soon, so I hung up to await her arrival, and began making bacon for my trademark bacon cupcakes with salted caramel ribbons. It sounds gross, but they're one of our bestsellers. I always make extra for Matt and Sam, because they love them.

I busied myself in the kitchen until, at last, Alexis came in. She took one look at me and flung herself dramatically across the kitchen table.

"What?" I asked. My heart was thumping. Had the others found out?

"They know," she whispered.

"Whaaaaat? How?"

"I confessed," she whispered again. It was almost like she didn't want me to hear her.

I sat down heavily in a chair. "Why? How? When?"

"I called Mia back and said we wanted to bring in cupcakes to camp tomorrow—I didn't say who asked us—and that maybe if they wanted to come to your house tonight, we could all bake them together." She cringed.

"So does Mia know we weren't telling the truth before?"

Alexis nodded.

I put my head in my hands. "We shouldn't have lied."

"I know." Alexis sighed. "Honesty is always the best policy. Especially when it comes to friends. But they are coming. We decided we'd bake the samples and the usual batches for Mona tonight and go to the movies tomorrow instead." She grinned at me.

"Alexis! You tricked me! So they aren't mad?"

Alexis shrugged. "A little, but I think they understand. I offered to let them take some cupcakes with them for tomorrow, too."

Katie was taking an intensive cooking class at the Y (it was actually for older teens but they made an exception for her because of her skill and passion and, I think, the Cupcake Club). Mia was working as an intern for her mom, who was a fashion stylist on photo shoots. Very glamorous. She'd go to sleep-away camp later in the summer.

"Wow, you are some negotiator," I said.

Alexis beamed and did a fake Sydney-esque hair flip.

"I'm not thrilled about delivering two-day-old cupcakes to our best client, though," I said.

"I know, but every once in a while we can make an exception," said Alexis.

"I guess. But let's pinkie promise not to do it again for a really long time, okay?"

Alexis stuck out her pinkie and hooked it with mine, and we shook our hands from side to side. "Okay."

It was a little awkward when Mia and Katie came, but I apologized and explained, telling them why I'd felt nervous to admit our plan. They were mad at first and told me so, but we made up and then it was fine. One of the great things about old friends is they can forgive and forget. Little incidents become tiny in the scheme of longer friendships.

We made new samples for Mona, baked up her minis, and made the frosting, putting each into separate Tupperware containers to keep them fresh. I'd assemble them Saturday morning before I dropped them off. Mia teased me and said it was my punishment for lying.

The cinnamon bun cupcakes turned out delicious, and I knew Mona would love them. I couldn't wait for her to try them.

I was up early Saturday morning, putting the finishing touches on Mona's delivery, even though I was a little tired. The movie the night before had been awesome, and we'd run into a couple of girls from camp. It was actually fun introducing Mia and Katie to Charlotte and Georgia and watching them chat, like two different worlds mixing! Mia and Katie were really pleased when the Hotcakes girls made a big deal about the Cupcake Club and admired how the Cupcakers were such best friends and moguls-in-training. I think then that Mia and

Katie realized Alexis and I will always love them best, even if we have new friends at camp. I would always choose my old friends over my new ones. No matter what.

After Mona's cupcakes were ready, my dad gave me a ride to The Special Day on his way to drop Matt at soccer practice. He was going to round-trip it and then wait for me downstairs. I was looking forward to my trip to Mona's and to some time alone in that all-white plush palace of hers, even if it was for just a half hour.

I was surprised to see that all the assistants were already there. Usually, the few times I'd gone with Alexis to make the delivery (like, if I'd slept over at her house the night before), it was really quiet. The store stayed open late Friday nights to accommodate people with busy work schedules, and Mona didn't open to the public until ten on Saturday mornings.

But today, the store was buzzing, even though it was only nine o'clock. Patricia, Mona's number-one assistant and store manager, came whizzing over to greet me. It was weird. She seemed like she was kind of in a rush to get me out of there. She looked outside the door to make sure no one was behind me, then she locked the door after me. It was like she was nervous other people might be trying to come in.

I said, "Hi, Patricia! I have our delivery, and we also—"

Patricia, who was normally supersweet and patient, interrupted me. "Thanks, Emma. Okay, then, we're all set. Let me just get your money. Wait right here. . . ." She took the carriers from me and headed to the back of the store. Usually we carry them back to the counter, and they pay us out of the register. I stood there in confusion.

"Do you need help?" I called lamely after her.

"Got it!" she kind of whispered back at me.

What on Earth was up?

Just then Mona stepped out of the largest and fanciest of all the salon rooms (called the Bridal Suite) and pulled the door tightly closed behind her. Was there a client in there already? Mona was really dressed up, even for her, and she looked even busier than usual. She strode over to a rack to select something, and then she spied me.

"Emma!" she cried, putting her hand to her chest, like I'd given her a fright.

"Hi," I said, smiling awkwardly.

"Is Patricia helping you?" she asked urgently.

"All under control," Patricia trilled nervously.

"Um, Mona, we brought some new kinds of cupcakes for you today, on the house. We were just thinking you might be tired of the usual order, okay? So just let us know . . ."

Patricia came bustling back to me with the cash. "Okay, then, we're all set. Thanks so much." She took my arm and steered me to the door.

"Patricia, is everything okay?" I suddenly got nervous that maybe they were being held up at gunpoint or something. I'd seen that on a TV show one time, where the robbers made the store employees carry on as usual, even while they were holding one of them hostage in the back of the store. "Are you being robbed or something? Should I call 911?" I asked under my breath.

Patricia stopped in her tracks and took a good look at me, then she collapsed in laughter, her hands on her knees. Mona rushed over.

"What is it, Patricia?" she asked.

Patricia was trying to catch her breath. "Oh my," she said, wiping her eyes with a tissue from one of the many boxes in the store (brides' families always cry when they see the brides in their dresses for the first time). "Just an attack of nerves," she said, still mopping. "Emma, you are too much. No, we are not being robbed. We are fine." She glanced at

Mona, seeming to ask a question with her eyes.

Mona stepped in and spoke in a low voice. "We have a very exciting, very private client here this morning. We opened early for her, so she could have the place to herself. It's just a little nerve-racking, but very good. Thank you for your concern, sweetheart." She turned to Patricia. "Isn't this one just divine?" she asked.

"Divine," agreed Patricia.

Just then the door to the Bridal Suite opened, and out walked the biggest surprise of my life.

"Oh my goodness!" I gasped.

CHAPTER 5

Me, Model?

Our town has only ever produced one major celebrity, as far as I know, and it made a doozy. It's like the town saved up its potential star power, and instead of launching a handful of B- or C-list one-hit wonders and soap stars, it stockpiled all its fairy dust for one lucky young lady: a gorgeous, blond Academy Award–, Golden Globe–, *and* Emmy-winning actress named Romaine Ford.

Every girl in America wanted to be her and every guy wanted to date her. Every father wanted his son to marry her, and every mom approved. She was twenty-nine years old, wholesome, smart, beautiful, talented, and reportedly very nice. She did charity work all over the world, recorded hit songs with famous costars, and was a Rhodes Scholar—

whatever that is. I'd only seen Romaine Ford once in real life, when she came to town to be the grand marshal for a parade a few years back. I knew, of course, like the rest of America, that she was now engaged to the devastatingly handsome heartthrob, actor Liam Carey, and that she planned a wedding in a top-secret location for late this summer. She was just about the last person I ever expected to see here this morning.

"Hi!" she said, friendly but a little reserved. She was wearing one of the white velour robes The Special Day gives you to put on in between dresses, and white fluffy slippers.

I was speechless. I think my jaw was actually hanging open.

"Yes, Ms. Ford, what can we do for you?" said Mona, hustling over to her side.

"I just had one thing I forgot to tell you. Um, my niece, who is also my goddaughter, is going to be a junior bridesmaid for me. I'm supposed to find a dress for her, and I wonder if you could help with that, too."

"Of course, we will bring in a selection immediately. Patricia!" Mona all but snapped her fingers at Patricia, who was standing, like me, frozen, like a deer in the headlights. Patricia came alive and started across the store to where the bridesmaids' dresses were.

Romaine was still standing there, actually kind of looking at me. She was so beautiful, I couldn't help staring. Her hair was long and thick and yellow-blond (natural, supposedly), and her eyes were wide and blue. She had a huge, almost goofy smile, and big white teeth, with a big dimple in her left cheek and freckles on her nose. She was tall and thin, in great shape, of course (she climbed Mt. Kilimanjaro last year to get ready for a part, and she did orphan relief work while she was there. Thank you, *People* magazine!), and very graceful.

Mona spoke to Patricia again. "Patricia! Emma!" She gestured at me.

Patricia smacked her forehead hard. "Right. Sorry." She doubled back to let me out of the store first. She went to unlock the door, but Romaine interrupted the silence with one word.

"Wait!" she said.

We all turned to stare at her.

"Sorry, but . . . that girl looks a lot like my niece. And I was wondering, maybe, would it be possible for her . . . I mean, do you have the time, sweetie? Would you be able to try on a dress, so I could see what it actually looks like on a girl?"

Would I? I looked at Patricia, who looked at Mona. Mona seemed to weigh the options, then found herself in favor of the idea. "Certainly. Emma, come."

"Do you have time?" asked Romaine as I started across the expanse of white carpet toward her.

I didn't trust myself to speak, so I nodded, wide-eyed, as if I was in a trance. As if I wouldn't have time for *anything* Romaine Ford asked me to do!

"Oh good!" she said, sighing. "Being a bride is a lot of work. I wouldn't want to fall down on the job and not get the junior bridesmaid's dress right!"

I couldn't imagine Romaine Ford not doing everything perfectly. I also had a hard time picturing any girl not being so happy to be in her wedding that she just wore whatever Romaine told her to. Like a trained puppy, I followed Patricia to the rack, where she selected a few dresses and wordlessly held them up against me to see if they'd fit. Finding four, she led me to a dressing room and gestured that I should go in.

"Call out when you have one on, and I'll come pin it if need be."

I looked at myself in the mirror in the dressing room. Was I dreaming? Had I imagined all this? Was I really going to model dresses for

Romaine Ford because she thought I looked like her niece?

I pinched myself—actually pinched myself—to make sure I wasn't dreaming, then I put on the first dress, quickly but carefully. I know from being a bridesmaid before that these dresses are very fragile and very expensive, but I knew I had to be fast, for Mona's and Patricia's sakes.

"Ready!" I called. Patricia flew into the room and started pinning wildly.

"There!" she declared, taking a long appraising look at me in the mirror. "Let's put up your hair. It will look much neater." Then finally she said, "Okay. Ready."

Patricia led me out into the salon and then knocked on the door of the Bridal Suite.

"Come in!" Mona trilled, and we entered.

Huge fluffy wedding dresses hung from every available rod and pole, and others were draped over the white sofas and chairs. Mona's fanciest silver tea service was laid out on the white lacquer coffee table. There were four women gathered around the table, sipping from fancy china teacups.

"Oh my! You really *do* look like Riley!" said an older blond woman who must've been Romaine's mother.

"I told you!" said Romaine proudly. I smiled shyly.

"Ladies, this is Emma Taylor, our cupcake baker and former client. She has a few dresses to show you, so let's see what you think. This first one is a hand-crocheted lace from Belgium. It truly is one-of-a-kind and, as such, one of our most expensive junior bridesmaids' dresses at eighteen hundred dollars."

Eighteen hundred dollars! I nearly fainted! My bridesmaid dress for Mia's mom's wedding had cost $250, and I thought that was a lot! But Romaine and her group seemed unfazed by the crazy price. I remembered Romaine had earned ten million dollars for her last movie, a big drama where she played a famous queen from the sixteen hundreds. Talk about earning power! *Alexis, eat your heart out,* I thought.

"Very pretty," said Romaine's mother.

Another lady (her grandmother? Her agent?), who was older than the woman who spoke earlier, said, "Yes, and you look lovely in it, dear."

Romaine was looking at me with her head tilted to the side, considering. "Yes, you look fab, and the dress is so pretty. I wonder . . . Would you think I was rude if I asked to see you with your hair down, like it was before? I'm sorry. I just think with the hair up, it's more of a mature look. . . ."

I nodded and looked to Patricia for help. She took right over. "Absolutely. Of course. So right. A natural look is always much better for this age," she said, and she hurriedly undid her previous work and fluffed out my loose hair with her fingers.

"Ahh! So pretty!" said a girl Romaine's age. I think it could have been her sister. According to *Us Weekly* magazine, she has three sisters and a brother.

As the minutes wore on, I thought I'd explode if I had to wait any longer to tell my friends about this. I kept my composure, though, turning this way and that as they admired the dress. A few minutes later they were ready to see the next dress, and I returned to my fitting room to change.

Patricia undid the back of the dress for me and tactfully left the room. I wouldn't be able to do this if I had to change in front of everyone, but as long as I could do it privately, it was okay. I called Patricia back in to help with the buttons, and we did the modeling all over again.

Between dresses number two and three, I rushed to the phone to call my dad to tell him I'd be late. I didn't tell him why. It wasn't that I thought he'd call the paparazzi or anything, but I wanted the experience to be complete before I started blabbing. Maybe it wouldn't end well, or maybe it would. Who knew? It was still just a private event, though.

My dad was fine with a later pickup, and in the meantime, Patricia stood behind the counter and organized the cupcakes on a beautiful silver serving tray to take in to the ladies.

"Remember," I said, "some are different. We included cinnamon bun cupcakes with cream-cheese frosting. Mona hasn't approved them yet."

"Oh, I noticed that some of these looked different than usual," said Patricia. "Well, let's give them a whirl. Maybe they'll be a huge box-office hit!" She popped one into her mouth, and chewed. "Oh, Emma! These are just . . ."

"Divine?" I offered.

We laughed, and she delivered the cupcakes while I changed dresses again.

In dress number three, I took a hard look at myself. This was not such a pretty dress. Even I could see that it was too grown-up for me. The dress was made from a slinky material, with a low-cut front and a slit up the leg. I wasn't comfortable in it at all.

Patricia returned. "Hmm," she said. "It's not right for you. But you know how people dress in Hollywood. I think we should show it, anyway."

She pinned it into place and then led me back into the room.

"NO!" said Romaine as soon as I walked in.

I was taken aback, and it must've shown on my face because she hurried to apologize.

"Oh my gosh, I'm so sorry, sweetie! I scared you!" She jumped up and came over to pat my arm sympathetically. "I just have really strong reactions to young girls dressed inappropriately. I just hate it. I was reacting to the dress, not to you. You poor thing! I forgot for a moment that you're not a professional model! Are you okay? Did I scare you to death?"

I composed myself and laughed a little, but she *had* shaken me. It must be hard for models and actresses to remember that their audiences aren't reacting to them personally, but rather to the outfits or the performances. It would take me a while to get used to that.

In the meantime, Patricia passed around the platter of cupcakes. Romaine scooped one up (from my kitchen to Romaine Ford's mouth! The Cupcakers—not to mention my brothers—would die, just die, when I told them!) and popped it into her mouth.

"Oh my gosh! What are in these cinnamon ones? I love them! They're so insanely delicious!"

Mona looked very pleased. "Emma made them, as I said earlier. She and her friends started their own business baking cupcakes."

"You do?" said Romaine. "That's so entrepreneurial! I was like that at your age." Alexis would love to hear that!

Back in the fitting room, I changed into dress number four. It wasn't much of a hit either. It was kind of *Little House on the Prairie* style, with long sleeves and a smocked front. Kind of country. Romaine didn't like it.

Mona was all business. "We have a trunk show scheduled for next Saturday, with all sorts of new dresses and accessories coming in this week for it. They are absolutely gorgeous and all brand-new, never-before-seen designs. We could arrange for you to come in at the same time and have a private showing, if you're available?"

Romaine's group all consulted their Black-Berrys and iPhones, and agreed. Mona turned to me. "Emma? We'd love for you to return, if you're free?"

I nodded happily. "Sure. No problem. I can come. I'll bring the cupcakes, too."

"Yum! Thanks!" said Romaine. She came and gave me a hug good-bye, careful not to squash the dress. "See you next week," she said. "Thanks for all of your help! You were a doll!"

On my way out, Mona asked me not to mention next weekend's plan to anyone. She said it was fine to say what happened today, but they wouldn't want any gawkers hanging around next weekend if word got out. I felt really privileged to be in on the plan, so I promised I wouldn't tell.

I couldn't believe the morning I'd had.

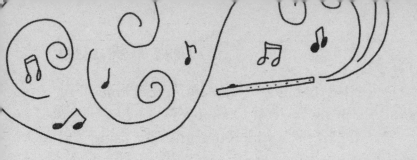

CHAPTER 6

Now *I'm* a Celebrity!

Okay, so start again from the beginning, when you first saw her open the door. How did you know it was her?" Katie asked.

Mia, Katie, and Alexis could not get enough of the story.

"No, tell about when she said she was entrepreneurial like us when she was a kid!" begged Alexis.

I had told the story three times already today, and I knew I'd tell it again to a very receptive audience at camp on Monday. I almost wanted to stop now, to keep it fresh for the Hotcakes girls. I just laughed.

"It was amazing," I said, shaking my head. It was like a dream.

"I can't believe you didn't get her autograph!" said Mia morosely.

"I can't believe Mona didn't pay you!" said Alexis.

"Oh my gosh, I probably would have paid her!" I laughed.

"You are so lucky," Katie said with a sigh.

"Do you think you'll ever see her again?" Alexis asked.

"I hope so," I said. I was dying inside since I couldn't tell them about the plan for next weekend.

"If they call you back, maybe we could all go?" asked Katie.

I laughed again. "Let's cross that bridge if we come to it."

"*When* we come to it," said Alexis. "Confidence sells!"

Monday morning at camp was almost more fun than Saturday morning at The Special Day. All the Hotcakes were riveted as I told the story of Romaine Ford. Even Maryanne and Raoul. Raoul kept asking if she was as pretty in person. And Kira was so excited, it was crazy.

"Oh my gosh, she has been my idol ever since I can remember. You are so lucky, Emma. You know, she lived on my block when she was in elementary school. I've always felt like she was my soul sister or something. She's been my role model and my inspiration! She's just an amazing and generous person, and the fact that she is from here, that she went to the same schools as me! I just worship her."

No one noticed Sydney Whitman until it was too late. "What are you Hotcakes yapping about?" Sydney managed to sneer whenever she said the word "Hotcakes."

"Just that Emma modeled for Romaine Ford this weekend," Alexis said.

Sydney's head whipped around. "No way! You? Modeling? That can't be true!"

I nodded, never happier in my life than while seeing this bomb being dropped on Sydney, despite her disbelief that I could ever model.

"Wait, *the* Romaine Ford?" Sydney was still incredulous.

"Uh-huh!"

"Oh, wow! I can't believe it! I'm going to *be* her in the talent show! I'm singing 'Sweet Summer Love,' that duet she had with the country singer, old what's-his-name, you know! I'm singing that!"

"Wow," I said. "Small world." Leave it to Sydney to make it all about her.

"Everyone says I look a lot like her, you know.

Everyone says I'll grow up to be just like her." Sydney posed while we all stared at her like she was an alien.

"Really," said Alexis finally, more like a statement than a question.

"Yes!" said Sydney. "Really!"

"Well, good luck with that!" I said cheerfully. I wasn't going to let Sydney "Horrible" Whitman ruin my day by taking over my story and making it about her.

Maryanne came over to tell us it was time for softball, so we ditched Sydney to follow her to the field.

"Listen, what is everyone doing for the talent show?" asked Maryanne as we walked.

"I'm using a Hula Hoop!" said Elle. She was such a cutup. We all laughed. "No, really! I'm serious. I'm great at it! It's my little-known talent!"

"That will be great!" said Raoul enthusiastically. "I can help you with music and choreography if you like." He was a big dancer. The two of them started scheming and laughing.

Charlotte and Georgia were going to do a gymnastics routine, and Caroline was going to sing. She was in her church choir and, according to Elle, was so good that she regularly sang solos. A few other girls, like Tricia and Louise, told us their plans, and then Maryanne looked at me and Alexis.

"How about you two?" she asked. "What about a bake-off?" Our cupcakes had been a huge hit on Friday. I think she was just angling for more to sample.

"We'll definitely bring some cupcakes, but as for the show, I'm not a talent myself. But I am happy to be a talent manager," said Alexis affirmatively.

"I don't have a talent. Anyway, I'd die of embarrassment up there," I said.

"How about the flute?" Alexis suggested. She turned to Maryanne and the others. "Emma's really great at the flute. She plays in the school orchestra. You should do that, Emma."

"I'm not that good. And, anyway, I don't play alone. It's one thing to be part of a big group when you're onstage, but *alone*? No way."

Alexis turned to Maryanne. "I can see I've found my first client. Don't worry. I'll get her to do something."

It was not going to happen, but I didn't want to embarrass Alexis by not letting her at least pretend she could convince me.

"Just remember," said Maryanne, "there are three qualities they're looking for in the talent show: *Talent*, like how good you are at the thing you're doing. *Presentation*, like, are you confident, is your act polished, and did you think through your moves and your program? And finally, *charm*. This is how appealing the crowd finds you. Do you have that certain charisma audiences love? Each performer is rated in each of the categories on a scale of one to ten. Whoever has the most points wins overall, but there's also a winner in each of the three categories."

Alexis leaned back and whispered, "We're going overall, baby. Shoot for the moon."

She was already talking like a Hollywood agent. I laughed and hit her playfully. "Get real!" I said.

"Oh, I'm real, my friend. I am really real."

The bus ride home was one of the more annoying rides of my life. For starters, Alexis would not back off from the idea that I was going to play the flute in the talent show, and she decided that on this bus ride, she would convince me she was right. In the course of one mile, she moved from asking to demanding I do it, and she was only half joking.

To make matters worse, Sydney asked if I'd brought any baby wipes to sanitize things after Jake threw up. Jake yelled, "I'm not a baby!" and then started to cry, so that was fun. *Not*.

Alexis decided to cheer up Jake by asking him what kind of cupcakes he wanted for his birthday. But he couldn't make up his mind. First he said, "Vanilla, with vanilla icing. That's what my friends and I like."

But, annoyingly, Alexis couldn't leave it at that. She said, "Oh, come on, Jakey, make it a little harder for us. Don't you want a fun topping? Or a cool design? What's your favorite, favorite thing on Earth to eat?"

So Jake moved from one flavor to the next: chocolate, banana, s'mores, cinnamon bun, and caramel. They discussed Oreo topping, marsh-mallow frosting, SpongeBob colors, police badge designs, and on and on. By the end of the ride, Jake was more confused than when we started. As she stood up to leave the bus, Alexis promised, "Jake, these will be the yummiest, best-looking, coolest Jake Cakes anyone has ever seen. I person-ally guarantee it," and I wanted to scream at her for setting his expectations so high.

And then, walking backward down the aisle, she called out, "An announcement, everybody: Emma Taylor is playing the flute in the talent show. Emma, practice your piece tonight! Bye!" Then she ran off before I could actually kill her.

All the kids on the bus turned to look at me, and I had to kind of smile and nod and acknowledge what she said. I wanted to die with all those eyes on me.

There was no way I'd play in that talent show!

CHAPTER 7

Shoved into the Spotlight

The weekend couldn't come soon enough! All week I felt butterflies in my stomach every time I pictured going back to The Special Day, but I couldn't tell if they were happy butterflies or nervous butterflies. It was like I dreaded and looked forward to it the same amount. On Friday night at our cupcake meeting/baking session, I couldn't stop thinking that we were baking for Romaine Ford!

We finished the cinnamon bun minis for Mona, and the extra vanilla/vanilla minis. Then it was time to bake samples for Jake.

"I had a great idea for Jake's cupcakes, so I went ahead and brought the supplies," said Mia, pulling a plastic grocery bag out of her tote. "Are you ready?

Dirt with worms!" She held up a package of Oreo cookies and a bag of gummy worm candies.

I groaned. "Gross!"

"He'll love it!" said Katie, clapping.

We had some extra batter from Mona's minis, so we baked up a few full-size cupcakes, and Mia set about crushing the cookies.

Alexis said slyly, "We have a talent show at the end of our camp session, and Emma is going to play her flute!"

I rolled my eyes. "I am not."

"Oh, Emma! You should! You're so good!" said Katie.

"Why wouldn't you?" asked Mia.

I started ticking off reasons on my fingers. "Well, for one thing, I'm not that good. For another, I have nothing to wear. Third, I hate getting up in front of people, and I also hate having people look at me. And fifth, I don't have any 'charm,' which is another thing they score you on, so all in all, I'm not doing it."

My three friends stared at me. Then Mia said, "Wow! You've got it all figured out, I guess. But why are you so down on yourself?"

"I'm not down on myself. I just know what I'm good at and what I'm not good at."

"Well, couldn't you practice a piece? Isn't there anything you know well enough?" Katie asked.

"That's not the point!" I said. I crossed my arms to show I was annoyed. I felt like they were ganging up on me.

"The other reasons are just silly," said Mia. "You could wear the bridesmaid dress from my mom's wedding. That looked amazing on you, and then it wouldn't be just hanging in your closet until you outgrow it."

Annoyingly, she was right. I wished she hadn't solved that problem so easily.

"And you obviously don't hate getting up in front of people that much, since you did it for Romaine Ford last week, for goodness sake!"

"That's different," I said, blushing.

"Why? Wouldn't you think a professional performer is a tougher critic than a bunch of parents who think you're adorable and little brothers who are just waiting for the show to be over so they can eat some cupcakes?" said Mia, laughing now.

I hadn't thought of that either. "But what about charm? I don't have any charm!" I insisted.

Alexis interrupted. "That is something I can take care of for you. That shouldn't worry you one bit. Anyway, it's not like you'd be trying to win *all three* categories. No one does."

I thought you said we were to "shoot for the moon," I wanted to remind Alexis, even though I didn't want to encourage her. Instead, I huffed and looked away from my friends. They were making it really hard to keep refusing. And now that they'd sort of solved all my qualms, a tiny part of me was starting to problem solve the rest, and think about how I could do it. But . . .

"How can I compete against Sydney Whitman? I know she's going to win, anyway, so why bother?"

Mia pressed her lips into a thin line of disapproval. "That is just a bad attitude right there. You're way more charming than she is, for one thing. Anyway, what is she doing?"

"Singing that Romaine Ford country song," I mumbled.

Katie burst out laughing. "Have you ever heard Sydney *sing*? Wake up, people! I am here to tell you that she was in my music class last year, and the girl cannot sing a note! It was like listening to a dying hyena!" Katie started howling tunelessly, and we all began to roar with laughter.

We finished our samples for Jake, packed up Mona's minis, and cleaned up. By then it was time for the others to go home.

Mia gave me a hug good-bye and said, "You've got to do the talent show, Emma. Even if it's just to beat out Syd the Hyena. Do it for us. Do it for the Cupcake Club!"

"And don't forget to let us know what Jake thinks of the dirty cupcakes!" added Katie.

I laughed and shut the door.

Upstairs, I looked for something to distract me from the butterflies that had returned, and I spied my flute, lying in its case on my desk. I sighed, then crossed the room, picked it up, and set it up to play. I have to admit that as I played, a whole hour passed before I even realized it. I really do love playing the flute. Just not in front of a crowd.

The next morning, I was up at the crack of dawn to shower and blow-dry my hair. Mona had e-mailed to confirm the timing (I had to be there at eight thirty, cupcakes and all), and she reminded me to appear "natural," meaning no makeup, no fancy hairstyles or anything. It was hard to resist the temptation to tinker, but I managed.

Down in the kitchen, I discovered Jake eating worm cupcakes for breakfast. He loved them so much, he tried to hug me, but I dodged him—chocolate crumbs and all.

My mom dropped me off, leaving my dad in charge of the boys. She asked me if I wanted her to wait outside and read a magazine, but I knew I couldn't let Mona down by spilling the beans (not that my mom would call the paparazzi, but still). I told her I had some work to do with Mona, to choose the flavors for the next month, and that she should come back later.

When I reached the store, the door was locked, so I rang the bell. I could see all the attendants bustling around inside. Patricia was putting big vases of white roses on every available surface. The two other ladies were dusting tables and fluffing sofa cushions. Mona heard the bell and made a beeline for me at the door.

"Darling! You look divine! It's so good to see you and your tiny cupcakes! Come in, come in!" She shooed me inside and locked the store's door tightly behind me, just as Patricia had done last week.

I brought the cupcakes to the counter, and she paid me and then led me to an even larger changing room than before.

"Now, a few things before we begin," she said. "First of all, I have this for you." She handed me a full-length nude-colored slip.

"Put this on to wear for the whole time. It will give you a clean line under the dresses and make the fabric move right, and it will protect your modesty. This way Patricia can be in the room arranging the next dress as you take one off."

That was a good idea. I wondered how she knew I hated to change in front of other people?

"Everyone hates to change in front of other people, darling," said Mona, reading my mind.

"Next, some tips. Stand up straight, straight, straight. No slouching. Let's see . . . Hmm . . ." She pulled my shoulders back and tipped my chin up into a kind of awkward pose. "I know it feels strange at first, but it looks wonderful. See? Divine!"

I looked in the mirror and saw that she was right. The pose made my neck look longer and kind of elegant.

"Now don't forget to smile, darling. Smile so your eyes sparkle. Let's see it."

I smiled, but she didn't approve.

"No, that's more like a grimace. Think of a princess or a movie star, how their eyes kind of light up. Lift your eyebrows a little. Be happy! Try again. Yes. Better." She turned my face to look in the mirror. Then she did different smiles next to me while I practiced.

"Good. Better. Yes, much better. Now, most important of all, don't forget to breathe. Just take deep breaths and think your happiest thoughts. Think about cupcakes and your divine friends and all the fun you'll have this summer. All right?"

I nodded and mentally reviewed her list of directions: stand up straight, shoulders back, chin up, smile with sparkly eyes, breathe, and think happy thoughts. Okay!

I heard the doorbell ring, and Patricia trilled, "They're here!"

Mona and I looked at each other with excitement. "Good luck, darling. You'll be smashing!" And off she ran.

Smashing. Divine. Oh my gosh! Here we go!

CHAPTER 8

Hard Work and a Good Deed

*D*id I mention that modeling is really hard work? You have to do all those things Mona said, plus you're wearing a dress that might be itchy or heavy or too big or too small or loaded with pins that could stab you anytime. You have to get used to people saying they think what you're wearing is ugly or too expensive, that you should take it off immediately. Also you can get hot and hungry and even bored, no matter if your audience is a major star who is beautiful, nice, and interesting.

But I still had a blast!

Romaine was even nicer this time, if that is possible to believe. First of all, she remembered my name. She said, "Hi, Emma!" when I walked in, and jumped up to give me a double kiss, like they do in Europe. Then she ate a bunch of my cupcakes and complimented me on them, even pretending to faint when she took a bite.

Patricia helped me in the dressing room the whole time, and we got to chat about everything. I told her all about the talent show and how the Cupcakers want me to do it and that they told me to wear my bridesmaid dress. She thought I should totally go for it, and was surprised when I said I didn't have the guts.

"But you're so poised doing this! Why wouldn't you just treat it the same way? It's like work. You just go out, you do your little routine, you turn around, and you leave the stage. That's it! It's great practice for real life, because when you're an adult, you do end up having to get up in front of people and perform, for all different occasions and reasons."

I thought about it while I twirled around the Bridal Suite in a tulle-skirted dress that made me look like a ballerina. Romaine tried to get me to do ballet poses, and we started joking around. It was really fun. She'd make a good teacher.

Mona hustled me back to change, though, whispering we were running out of time to keep the store closed to the public. I loved all the dresses I had tried on, so the time had flown. I was sad when I put on the final dress, and I think Patricia could tell.

"It was fun, right, honey? Kind of like being a princess for a day? That's how brides feel when they come in too." She gave me a little pat on the back and sent me into the Bridal Suite for the final time.

Romaine walked over to me to inspect the dress. Meanwhile, in the background, her mom and her aunt were talking. My ears perked up at the word "cupcake."

"Kathy, are you thinking what I'm thinking about these cupcakes?" asked Romaine's aunt.

"Yes, I think I am. They are *so* delicious!" said Romaine's mom.

Turning to me, Romaine's aunt said, "Could we hire your cupcake club to bake some cupcakes for our bridal shower? I'm Romaine's aunt, Maureen Shipley, and I'm the hostess for the event. These would be lovely for the dessert."

Oh my gosh! Could this day get any better? Somehow I found my voice.

"Absolutely. Showers are our specialty! I'll give you my card when I go back to the fitting room," I promised. I silently thanked Alexis for insisting we each have our own business cards made.

In the fitting room, I carefully changed back into my now pathetic-looking everyday clothes. I grabbed a business card from my bag and went to say good-bye.

Romaine saw me in the doorway and jumped up. "Oh, Emma, honey, you were the best! Thank you so much for your hard work today and last week. It was such a treat to have you here, and you are just gorgeous. Adorable. Right, Mom?"

Romaine's aunt said, "Honey, let's get a photo, so we can all remember the fun we've had together." She pulled out her camera and had Patricia snap a few shots, including one of just me and Romaine together. Then she double-checked she had my e-mail address and promised to send me the photos.

I was sad to leave—I don't think any of us wanted it to be over—but I knew Mona was eager to open the store, so I said my good-byes and headed out of the Bridal Suite. Before I reached the front of the store, Mona caught up with me. She slipped a white business envelope into my hand.

"Emma, a little something for all your hard work."

"Oh no, Mona, I couldn't. Thank you. It was so much fun and such an incredible experience."

"I insist! From one businesswoman to another.

Please take it. Fun or not, it was hard work, and you were divine! Just divine!"

It's hard to argue against a force of nature like Mona, so I laughed and thanked her for the opportunity to model.

Outside, who should I run into walking by but Kira and her oldest sister!

"Hi, Kira!" I said, still flying high after my fun morning.

"Hi, Emma! Oh, Leslie, this is my friend Emma who I was telling you about, who got to meet Romaine Ford! Emma, this is my sister Leslie. She's taking me to get a new bathing suit. What are you doing here?"

I felt funny telling them what I'd been doing. But as it turned out, I didn't need to. Because who should come strolling out of The Special Day but Romaine and her group.

"Oh, look who's still here! Bye, honey!" said Romaine's mom.

I waved, smiling.

"Bye, Emma! Thanks again!" called Romaine with a smile.

"Oh my gosh!" said Kira, her jaw dropping open. "That's her! And she knows your name! Oh my gosh! I think I'm hyperventilating! Oh my gosh!"

She started fanning herself, and tears welled up in her eyes. "I can't believe it's really her."

Romaine and her mom, aunt, and sister were all standing outside The Special Day, as if deciding where they should head to next. Impulsively, I grabbed Kira's arm and quickly dragged her over to Romaine's side.

"Romaine, I'm sorry to interrupt," I said. "But this is my friend Kira. She thinks you are so great, and I wanted you to meet her." I kind of shoved Kira toward Romaine. Kira was in shock, her mouth still wide open and speechless.

Romaine was very friendly. "Hi, Kira! It's nice to meet you! Any friend of Emma's is a friend of mine! Are you in the same class at school?" she asked politely.

Kira couldn't talk. She just shook her head no and continued to stare, wide-eyed at Romaine.

Romaine looked at me and giggled, then looked back to Kira. "How do you two know each other?" she asked.

"Oh, camp. We go to day camp together," I said, since it was clear that Kira wouldn't be able to answer. "Right, Kira?" I prompted.

Kira closed her mouth, and gulped. "Uh-huh. Camp."

"What camp is it?" asked Romaine.

"Spring Lake Day Camp," I said. Kira nodded.

"Oh my gosh! I went there in sixth grade!" cried Romaine. "Mom! Emma and her friend go to Spring Lake Day Camp!"

Romaine's mom smiled. "Oh, what fun! You loved that place!" she said.

"I really did. Well, have a great time there. I have to get going now, but it was nice to meet you, Kira, and thanks again, Emma!" She gave me another hug and then walked away. Kira was still rooted to the spot, speechless.

Leslie came up and showed us a photo she'd snapped on her iPhone of Kira and Romaine chatting.

"Oh wow!" said Kira, coming back to life, as if she'd been in a trance. "I can't believe it! I just met Romaine Ford! Oh, Emma!" She wheeled around to face me. "You're the best. I feel like I dreamed the whole thing."

Leslie was laughing at her now. "Come on, dreamy. Let's go find you a swimsuit. Bye, Emma!"

"Okay, bye! Nice to meet you, Leslie!'

They called their good-byes and strolled off, Kira staring intently at Leslie's iPhone.

I was so glad I'd done what I did. It wasn't the

smoothest thing in the world, but it had obviously meant a lot to Kira, who in general needed a boost. I was just happy to have provided it.

I texted my mom for a ride and sat down to wait. What a great summer this was turning out to be!

fun!

CHAPTER 9

Hotcakes and Cupcakes

Camp was out-of-control fun. For starters, because it was separated into boys' and girls' campuses, there wasn't a lot of worrying what boys would think or even, for me, dealing with boys' gross-out behaviors like I did at home. It was a complete break from burping and stinky socks and football. I was in all-girl heaven!

We sang all the time, whatever we were doing. Show tunes, Top 40 songs, camp songs—anything. We braided one another's hair during free time, and one day Georgia brought in a manicure set and gave us all wild, decorative manicures, with tiny flower and star decals and stuff. We also made friendship bracelets like maniacs, taping the embroidery thread to any available surface and twisting, braiding, and tying it into rainbows to wear or give away. We had Tie-Dye Day, when we brought in anything from home that we wanted to tie-dye and made incredible designs with bright colors, like a kaleidoscope. (I brought white drawstring pj pants, plus, the camp gave us each a white cotton T-shirt.)

We had also started to seriously train for the Camp Olympics. There would be events in archery, swimming, diving, track and field, canoeing, not to mention soccer and softball games, four square, tetherball, and relay races (some of them funny, like potato-sack and egg-on-a-spoon races). Not everyone had to participate in every event; you just needed enough people from your team to do it. So Maryanne and Raoul were working on how to divide up everyone and play to their strengths.

Every morning we'd gather at our rally zone and chat about what had happened in the fifteen or so hours since we'd last been together (covering TV shows, celebrity gossip, family news—anything, really). Kira was always there first, her wet hair pulled back into a neat ponytail. Leslie dropped her off way early on her way to work. Alexis was a pretty early arrival too, and Georgia and Charlotte, so they'd all be up to speed by the time I arrived with the the rest of the bus crew.

I was not wild about canoeing or softball, so I didn't plan to participate in those events, but Maryanne and Raoul felt they would have a pretty good team for softball even without me. I volunteered to be the water girl for that game. I was psyched for the running events, because I am fast, and I was feeling really good about the swimming and diving, which I knew I'd ace (not that I'd ever say it out loud). The only bummer was that the swim events required six-person teams, so we could only really field one team from the Hotcakes, with Kira being a noncompeter in that category. We were all really careful not to make her feel responsible, because we didn't want her to feel bad. Alexis and Elle both said early on that they didn't want to do the swim competition (I think they planned it for Kira's sake, because they are both great swimmers), and a few other people said they didn't care either way, so I was on the team that would compete.

The Hotcakes were pretty good athletes, if I do say so myself. Plus, we were training hard. We did warm-ups, calisthenics, drills, and had little mini-competitions within our team. We cheered on everyone's progress all the time. It felt great to be part of a group like this, where everyone was fun and they had your back. Kind of like the Cupcake Club, but all new.

Meanwhile, Sydney was being a nightmare. She was so determined that the Angels would win the whole competition that she was tormenting her teammates to train harder and harder. It would have been funny if she wasn't so awful. Sometimes we Hotcakes just stopped and stared while she lit into one of her teammates. It would only last a moment, until one of her counselors rushed over to put an end to it, but it was still just unbelievable.

One day, after track-and-field training, we were all hot and sweaty, and we jumped in the pool with our clothes on. Maryanne and Raoul were kind of annoyed at us at first, but then they saw how much fun we were having and they jumped in with their clothes on too! It was hilarious. Afterward, we hauled ourselves out and stretched out on the grass, drying off in the sun and talking about our summer plans.

That was when Elle announced that her birthday was coming up, and her plan was to have a party with all the Hotcakes, at her house! It sounded like a blast. She would have us over, we'd eat pizza, and the night she planned to do it, there was an outdoor movie showing in a park downtown, so we'd all go with blankets and watch the outdoor movie and eat treats. Then we'd go back to her house and sleep over. Everyone said they wanted to go. But when she told me the date, my heart sank. It was for a Friday night—the night before the Camp Finale Talent Show, actually—and that was, of course, the Cupcake Club's special baking night for Mona.

Alexis and I looked at each other, knowing what the other person was thinking. It was not going to be easy to tell Mia and Katie that we couldn't make it on a Friday night because we were doing something without them. And we'd pinkie promised not to sell Mona two-day-old cupcakes again.

We tried to discuss it later on the bus home, but Jake was in one of his moods.

"Stop talking, Emmy! I'm trying to sleep!" He moaned, his head against my upper arm.

Alexis and I tried to whisper. "What do we say? Do we tell them the truth?" I asked.

Alexis shot me a look. "Lying didn't do us any good the last time."

I sighed.

"Stop breathing hard, Emmy! It's making my head bounce!" wailed Jake.

Alexis shot me a sympathetic look. I tried to remain calm, but all I wanted to do was chuck him out the window.

That night, while I was practicing my flute piece (I hadn't decided yet whether I'd perform, but I was at least taking care of the talent part by getting a piece in order), my mom tapped on my door. As the only girl in a mostly boy house, I have a strict knocking policy and a big KEEP OUT sign on my door.

"Come in!" I called.

"Oh, honey, I love to hear you play. You're so talented," said my mom. She always says that when she comes in while I'm playing. "Just play a little bit more for me."

She settled into my armchair, which is big and cushy and covered in the prettiest white fabric with sprigs of pink flowers on it. She put her head back, closed her eyes, and smiled.

I played the piece through from beginning to end, and she said, "Again," without lifting her head or opening her eyes. I shook my head and laughed, but I played it again.

My mom's eyes opened and she sat up. "You play the flute beautifully," she said. "I'm so proud of you."

"It's pretty fun," I said, shrugging. "I'm thinking about playing that piece in the camp talent show."

"Oh, you have to!" said my mom. "It would be lovely!"

"I don't know, though. I'd hate to have all those people watch me. And . . . well . . ." I didn't have the dress excuse anymore, or the talent excuse, because the piece was sounding pretty darn good. But how do you tell your own mother that you have no charm and expect her to leave it at that?

She tilted her head to the side. "So?"

"Well, I might play. That's all."

"I suggest you go for it. What do you have to lose? Everyone will be impressed. Is it a competition or just a showcase?"

"Well, there are prizes, so I guess it's a competition."

"What kinds of prizes? Like first, second, third place?"

I shook my head. "No, like categories: talent, presentation, charm, and all-around winner."

My mom put her hand up for a high five. "You could definitely win!"

I high-fived her weakly. "Which category?"

"Any of them! All of them! If I was the judge, you'd take home all the prizes."

We laughed. "Thanks," I said.

"It seems like you're really enjoying camp," said my mom.

"Yeah." I smiled. "I love it. And I've made so many good, new friends. . . ." I bit my lip.

"Wait, why do you suddenly look so sad?" my mom asked with a laugh. "It's like someone just flipped a switch! I thought you were happy!"

"I am. It's just . . ." I proceeded to fill her in on the conflict for Elle's party and the Cupcakers, as well as the incident a couple of weeks ago when Alexis and I had to bake for our camp friends.

"Cupcakes, Hotcakes . . . How do you keep all these people straight?" My mom was smiling. "Seriously, though, I agree with Alexis. Look, the sleepover is a onetime thing. These are new friends; they might not be lifelong friends. Or they might be, who knows? You just need to let Katie and Mia know that they come first, but on this one special occasion, you want to go to this special event. And just make a plan to do something fun with them on a different night. I think it will be fine. Old friends are very important, but you have to have room in your life for new friends, too, right?"

I sighed. "Yeah. I just wish they could all be friends together," I said.

My mom thought for a minute. "Then maybe you should figure out how to make that happen!"

Hmm. Maybe she had a point! I thought about it for a second.

"Wait, maybe I should have them all over—like not *all* the Hotcakes, but maybe just Elle and Kira? Along with the Cupcakers? That could be fun!"

My mom smiled and lifted her hands in the air, palms up. "Why not?" she said enthusiastically.

I reached across and gave her a hug. "Thanks, Mom. Great thinking."

"Oooh! Those words are music to my ears!"

CHAPTER 10

Friendship, Favors, and Flute Practice

A week had passed before I got the e-mail from Mrs. Shipley, Romaine's aunt, but it was a doozy, in good ways and in bad! The good parts were, it had three great photos from The Special Day attached—one group shot and two of me and Romaine that were amazing! (I instantly made it my desktop background!) And it had an order for ten dozen mini cupcakes!

The bad part was that the shower was going to be on a Saturday morning—the morning after Elle's Friday night party *and* the same day as our camp's talent show. Now, it's one thing to bake a day in advance for Mona, a regular customer. But I did not want Romaine Ford's cupcakes to be anything less than fresh and perfect. For starters, it was such a big job, and it might lead to other big jobs. Our cupcakes had to be at their very best that day!

I forwarded the e-mail to Alexis and then called her.

"Hi, Emma," she answered. She also has caller ID, so she knew it was me.

"Hey. Did you see my e-mail?"

"Just opening it. Wow, great photos! Oh, the order! Goody! Oh. Not goody. Hmm."

"I know."

We sat there in silence, thinking.

"Well, we could get up early and bake Saturday morning?" she suggested.

"I guess," I said. "It's cutting it a little close. I mean, ten dozen cupcakes! We'd have to leave Elle's at, like, six in the morning."

"Hmm," said Alexis.

"It's too bad we couldn't have Mia and Katie bake the cupcakes Friday night, then we get together at, like, eight o'clock Saturday morning and do the frosting and delivery."

"That would be kind of mean. Like, 'Hey, we're taking the night off, but why don't you two do this big job for us, and we'll catch up with you later?'" said Alexis in an annoyed voice.

I had to giggle. "But maybe we could ask them.

Maybe we'll just offer them something in return—
a night off, or whatever. And we *are* helping Katie
for her cooking class's bake-off, remember?"

Alexis sighed. "I guess."

"Honesty is the best policy, remember?"

"I'll call a meeting," said Alexis.

The next afternoon, we had an emergency
Cupcake meeting at Mia's house. Alexis hadn't told
Mia and Katie exactly why we needed to meet (she
just said we had major scheduling issues), so they
were a little in the dark.

Alexis wasted no time in calling the meeting
to order. "First topic on today's list, Jake's birthday
party. Emma, please confirm the details."

"Well . . . Jake loved the dirt with worms cupcakes! He said they were his 'most favoritest ever.'"

I rolled my eyes while Mia and Katie said,
"Awww . . ."

I continued, "His party is next Saturday afternoon, so we can bake Friday night and then
assemble Saturday morning. They have fourteen
boys coming—my worst nightmare—so they'll
need four dozen cupcakes, accounting for Matt and
Sam and various babysitters and parents."

Alexis interrupted me. "Now, if you'd like,
Emma and I can handle the baking on Friday and

give you girls the night off. We'll do Mona and Jake all in one marathon session, and you two can, like, go out or something." She tried to look really casual as she said this, but I could see she was nervous.

Mia and Katie were confused. "Where would we go without you guys?" asked Katie, her eyebrows knit together, like she didn't understand.

"Yeah, why wouldn't we want to do the baking for the Jakester?" asked Mia.

"Well, I was just saying. I mean, maybe we don't all need to be there . . . ," said Alexis, shrugging.

Honesty is the best policy, I reminded myself. I took a deep breath and plunged in. "Guys. The weekend after that, Alexis and I were invited to a sleepover on Friday night by our friend Elle from camp. Our whole team is going. But, drumroll, please, Romaine Ford's wedding shower is the next day, and they ordered ten dozen cupcakes!"

Mia and Katie squealed and jumped in the air. They hugged each other, then me, then Alexis, who received them awkwardly. She was still nervous.

"Oh, Emma, that is so awesome! I can't wait to meet Romaine Ford!" said Mia.

"I know." I smiled.

"It's just a bummer that you have to miss your sleepover," said Katie.

Gulp.

"Um . . . well . . ." I looked helplessly at Alexis. She wouldn't meet my eye. "We were actually thinking, maybe . . ."

"Oh! Wait! I get it!" said Mia, who is usually much quicker on the uptake. "You'll give us the Friday before off, so we'll work while you're at the slumber party."

I nodded, feeling like a jerk.

"Wow," said Katie. "Um . . ."

"The other thing is, I'm having a sleepover at my house the night before Jake's party. It's for the Cupcake Club and two of my friends from camp, Elle and Kira. It's going to be really fun, and I won't do it unless you two will come," I said impulsively.

Alexis's head whipped to the side and she stared at me with a question in her eyes.

There was a pause in the room that seemed to drag on forever. Then Mia said, "You know what? We'll do it. Right, Katie? That's what friends are for."

I looked at Katie. She still had kind of a hurt, skeptical look on her face. I knew this would be hardest on her, because of the Callie/Sydney history.

"Katie, we're not going to dump you for our

camp friends. I promise," I said quietly. "They're fun, you'll see, but they're not like the Cupcake Club. It's not at the same level, and it never will be." I knew in my heart that that was true. Once school started again and the Cupcake Club was together every day, I knew I'd drift a little apart from Elle and Kira.

Katie took a deep breath in and then sighed. "Okay. I understand. New friends are great, really. I'm just so cautious ever since Callie."

Mia hugged her. "We know. Don't worry. You'll always have us hanging around, right, Cupcakers?"

"Right!" Alexis and I yelled, then we piled in for a group hug.

It was settled. Now I just had to break the news to my mom about the sleepover.

Okay, that last part didn't go so well.

"Wait, the night before Jake's party you want to have a sleepover for six friends? Are you joking?" said my mother in exasperation.

"Well, actually, it's five friends, plus me. So that's not so—"

She interrupted me. "I'm sorry. I don't care how many friends it's for. There is not going to be a sleepover the night before we're having fifteen six-year-olds running all over this house for the day. You'll have the whole house up all night, you'll have the place a mess, and Jake will be overtired for his party, not to mention me!"

I was starting to fume. The worst part was, I could kind of see what she meant.

"You're the one who had the brilliant idea to get all my friends together from camp and school!"

"Not for a sleepover on that particular night I didn't!" she said firmly.

I knew I wouldn't win this one, but I couldn't face undoing the plan. I'd be so embarrassed. After all, Kira and Elle barely knew me when it came right down to it. They might think I was nuts or that my mom was a mean psycho.

"How am I going to tell everyone they're uninvited, then?" I said. I knew I was being bratty, but I didn't care.

"Just like that. You're uninvited!" said my mom with a toss of her head. "Think of a new plan," she said, and she stormed into her bathroom to take a shower.

I left her room and went into mine, slamming the door behind me. When my anger had cleared, I sat and thought about all the things that were coming up and needed attention.

There was the Camp Olympics, which our team was pretty well set for. There was another superjocky team of girls, the Wolverines, who would probably give us a run for our money, but it wouldn't kill me to lose to them, in that they were so athletic and talented. I just wanted to make sure we beat Sydney's team.

Next, there was Jake's party to bake for and survive. It was going to be hard work.

Then there was Elle's slumber party, my non-slumber party, and Romaine's shower—they were all tied up into one big snarl that needed untangling.

And finally, there was the Camp Finale. Was I in or not? And if I was in, where was I going to find some charm? Time was running out.

CHAPTER 11

Cupcakes, Meet the Hotcakes

Raoul passed around an official sign-up sheet the next morning at camp.

"Okay, girls! Everyone needs to sign up and give a description of their act. They're printing the programs this week, so this is final. If you're in, you're in, and if you're out, you're out, but don't make the mistake of being out!" He laughed. "We've got a lot of talent in this group, and I know my Hotcakes are going to bring home the gold!" He pumped his fist in the air, and everyone cheered.

When the clipboard reached me, I stared down at it, unsure and paralyzed. Suddenly, Alexis reached across, grabbed the clipboard, and quickly wrote down my name. Then she wrote "Flute Performance" and passed the pen and clipboard to the next person. She folded her arms across her chest and smiled at me smugly.

I just shook my head slowly from side to side. Finally I said, "But what about charm?"

"Leave it to me," said Alexis, but she didn't look too confident.

I had already e-mailed Alexis, Mia, and Katie the bad news about Friday's sleepover. We'd just have a regular baking session instead, so that was okay. But all morning I had been dreading uninviting Elle and Kira. I had a pit in my stomach and could think of nothing else. Finally, at lunch, Kira said, "I can't wait for Friday night! Should I bring an air mattress?" Alexis and I looked at each other, and sighed.

"Guys, I have bad news. My mom said no sleepover on Friday," I admitted, wincing at the mom reference. (I had been avoiding any mention of mine when I was around Kira.)

"Oh, don't worry about it!" said Elle with a wave of her hand. "No problem." She took a bite out of her sandwich, unfazed. Elle was a trooper, and I loved her for it. She didn't even need an explanation. "You're still coming to mine though, right?" she asked, through a mouthful of turkey.

"Yes," I said. "The problem with my sleepover

plan is, it's my little brother's birthday party at our house the next day, and, well, my mom said we'd all be exhausted if I had a sleepover the night before. I could do it another time, though."

"Bummer," said Kira. I could see that she'd been looking forward to it.

"I know." I wondered if she understood, not having a mom and all that.

"But maybe we could still do something?" Alexis suggested brightly. "Like maybe the girls want to come bake Jake's cupcakes with us!" she said with a smile.

"I'm not sure how much fun that would be, with all that work?" I said, glaring at her. What was she thinking? It would be boring for Elle and Kira, and what would Katie and Mia think about us inviting non-Cupcakers to join us at work? But before I could say anything, in jumped Kira and Elle.

"We'd love to!" said Kira enthusiastically. "That would be so fun!"

"I'm in," said Elle with a grin.

"Ookaaay . . . Great, then!" I said, faking confidence. "You guys can just come home on the bus with me from camp." I'd let Alexis do the explaining to Mia and Katie since it was her idea.

✿

Just as I suspected, Katie was not thrilled. I guess she felt threatened by our new friends and kind of resentful of them and the time they got to spend with us all day while she was with a bunch of strangers down at the Y. I totally understood, but at the same time it couldn't always just be the four of us, could it?

When Friday rolled around and we all showed up in my kitchen, things were a little awkward to say the least, even though everyone had been prepared in advance for the new plan.

Mia was nice, if not all that chatty at first. But Katie was downright cold. I saw Elle and Kira exchange a look of confusion after Katie basically said hi and turned her back on them, but Alexis, bless her heart, kept on chattering away to make up for it. I had brought Jake home from camp and settled him in front of the TV, and my other two brothers would be home soon to look after him.

We set out the ingredients and told the new girls what we were doing. Alexis designated Kira as the Oreo smasher and Elle as the cupcake-liner person, meaning she'd set the papers into the baking tins. Alexis had found awesome camouflage patterned cupcake liners in green, so that's what we were using for the Jake Cakes, as we were calling them.

Katie busied herself at the mixer, and Mia and I were working on the frosting. Alexis was setting out the necessities for Mona's minis, which also needed to be made. It was a regular assembly line!

Elle started telling funny stories about camp, and that kind of broke the ice. Mia offered up some stories from the fashion world, and Kira was really interested in that. But the more they chatted, the more withdrawn Katie became. I knew she was insecure, but it was really annoying me, and rude. Finally, I stood up to talk to her in private, but right then my older brothers came crashing through the door in their usual noisy style.

"Hey, Cupcakers! What's up!" called Sam. Did I mention that Sam is gorgeous? All my friends basically pass out whenever he is around, which makes me feel kind of proud and kind of annoyed. He's a lot older than us (seventeen) and not around that much, but he's tall with blond, wavy hair and bright blue eyes like my dad. Plus, he's superathletic, so he's in really good shape. He also likes to joke around.

"Ooh! Batter!" he said, spying Katie at the mixer.

"Not so fast, mister!" said Katie, covering the mixer with her arms.

Elle and Kira were just watching, speechless. Neither of them had brothers, of course, so these guys were like aliens to them.

Meanwhile, Matt, who, I guess, is also pretty good-looking (according to Alexis, with her on-again off-again crush on him), was talking to Alexis and Mia, teasing them about camp and cupcakes and everything, trying to get them to give him gummy worms and promise him the first cupcakes out of the oven.

It was kind of total boy chaos, but Sam and Matt were making my old friends laugh and making a big deal out of them. I interrupted to introduce Elle and Kira, and although my brothers were polite, they went right back to teasing the Cupcakers.

Finally, I shooed them out, and they went in to take over the TV from Jake. The room was very, very quiet after they left. Katie was standing at the mixer, smiling to herself, Kira and Elle were wide-eyed, and Alexis and Mia were still laughing.

"Phew!" I said. "Those two are a nightmare!" I was kind of embarrassed by all the commotion.

"No, they're not!" whispered Elle, her eyebrows raised up high on her forehead. "They're gorgeous!"

"And they're in love with all the Cupcake girls!" Kira sighed, genuinely wistful. "You're so lucky!"

"Aw, no, they're not," protested Mia and Alexis, but they were pleased.

Katie looked up, unsure if Kira was for real, but when she saw that Kira was serious, she allowed herself to smile at her. My anger at Katie melted a little bit then.

"Seriously," said Elle.

Then Jake came running into the room, crying about how the big boys had taken over the TV and changed *SpongeBob* to *SportsCenter*. He ran straight to Mia, buried his head in her legs, and wailed.

Mia scooped him up and began to soothe him, but he whined that he wanted Katie, too, and wouldn't settle down until the two of them were fawning over him, feeding him gummy worms and setting him up with a little workstation of his own.

I was apologetic and mortified, but Elle and Kira were just bowled over by my brothers and how much the boys loved my Cupcake friends.

"You girls are so lucky," Kira said admiringly. "Especially you, Emma, to have all these boys around all the time."

"Ha! As if!" I laughed.

But I could see Katie smiling out of the corner of my eyes.

Against all odds, my annoying brothers had broken the ice. Hotcakes and Cupcakers united as the afternoon wore on, and by the time my parents got home at six and ordered pizza for everyone, we were well ahead of schedule on both baking jobs. All us girls were sitting around the kitchen table, laughing and talking, as the boys periodically wandered in and out and caused silences and then outbursts of giggles. It was so fun!

At the end of the night, Kira pulled out her phone to call her sister for a ride. I could see Katie looking at her with curiosity. Just as I realized what Katie was thinking, it was too late.

"Why does your sister pick you up instead of your parents?" she asked.

I winced and looked down at my hands. I didn't know what to say.

Kira bit her lip. "Well, my mom died last year, and my dad travels for work all the time. I mean, he has to. That's his job. So, I have three older sisters, and they take turns taking care of me."

"Oh, I'm so sorry. I didn't know," said Katie. And to her credit, she was visibly upset.

"That's okay," said Kira graciously. "Thanks."

"I'd love to have three older sisters!" I said, to change the subject.

Kira groaned. "No, you wouldn't! They are so bossy!"

"It's true!" agreed Alexis. "Older sisters are the worst!"

And just like that, things were back to normal. We chatted as we put the finishing touches on the cupcakes. Too soon, Kira's sister was at the door, and we all hugged good-bye, with Mia and Katie even hugging Elle and Kira!

After they left, it was just the Cupcakers in the kitchen, waiting for Mia's stepdad to come pick them up.

"Wow, those girls are really nice!" said Mia. "I'm proud of you two for going out in the world and finding such nice new friends for us all," she joked.

Katie agreed. "Yeah, and I'm sorry I wasn't very friendly at first. I was just shy, and I felt like, you know, you were kind of replacing us with those two."

"It's okay," I said, putting my arm around her shoulders. "And don't worry. You're irreplaceable!"

That night my mom came to tuck me in.

"Good job, lovebug," she said. "It was really nice

to see all those girls getting along and having such fun. You're a great judge of character, and I love your friends. I'm sorry about the sleepover, but I'm glad you worked something out."

I snuggled under my pink duvet. "I know, Mama," I said, using my baby name for her. "It was really nice. Thanks for the pizza!" I yawned.

"See? Wasn't I right? Aren't you glad you're not lying on the TV room floor in a sleeping bag for the next three hours, giggling?" She gave me a kiss on the forehead.

"Yes. I actually am," I said.

And I was.

CHAPTER 12

Happy Birthday, Jake!

*T*ake fifteen six-year-old boys, add fifteen water guns, two hundred water balloons, mud, tears, and lots of junk food, and what do you get? Total chaos. That was Jake's party.

I had invited Mia, Alexis, and Katie to help with the party. My mom was actually paying us to help wrangle the kids, keep the refreshments going, and stay on top of the garbage and cleanup. We also had to guard the doors, so the kids didn't end up inside watching TV or trashing Jake's room or anything.

For me, the best part was that Mia, Alexis, and Katie got to sample what my life is really all about. There was no time to be squeamish when one kid gashed his foot open. There was nowhere to run when Jake's friend Ben picked up a toad and brought it right up to us to see. Replenishing the snacks and drinks was an endless task. The minute a bowl of Cheetos had been filled, the bowl of chips was empty and needed to be refilled, and so on.

As the party wore on (only two hours had passed!), Mia, Katie, and Alexis began to look more and more bedraggled and overwhelmed. When Jake and another kid got into a fight over whose water gun was whose, my friends were horrified.

"But they're friends!" said Katie, observing the chaos with a hand to her mouth. "Why do they fight like that? Look, that guy is punching Jake!"

"I know," I said. "That's what boys do. They just work it out on the spot and move on. Hey! Guys! No hitting! Use words!" I called, to no real effect. I shrugged.

"Wow, Emma. I had no idea," said Mia.

"Yeah, how cute do you think Jake is now?" I asked.

We all looked at him. He was covered in mud, his hair was soaked and sticking up all over, and he had a scratch on his arm from a tree branch (it was bleeding). He had orange Cheetos dust all over his face and had on ratty clothes. Well, they were ratty now. They didn't start out that way. And he and his buddy Justin were saying horrible things to each other as they yanked a water gun back and forth.

Suddenly, Jake realized we were looking at him. He let go of the water gun, leaving Justin to collapse in a heap, and came over with a big, sweet smile on his face. "Where are my cupcakes, girls?" he asked.

"Awww . . . ," said Mia and Katie, melting all over again.

I rolled my eyes and then looked at my watch. "Five more minutes," I said. "Go back and play, and be a good host! Let your guest have the water gun he wants!" I watched to make sure he did, then I turned to the girls. "Shall we?" I asked.

We went inside to get the cupcakes, candles, and camera, as well as the party plates and napkins. Outside, the boys saw us coming and swarmed us. "Down, boys! We'll call you in just one minute. We're not ready yet!"

"Oh wow!" said Mia, laughing with shock as she held the cupcake platter high above the boys' heads. "They really are savages!"

"See?" I said. "Okay, guys. We have to light the candles and then sing." The boys were busy forming themselves into a straggly line, insisting who was first and second to get cupcakes. I started a rousing rendition of the birthday song, and everyone joined in. Jake looked cute as everyone sang, then he blew out his candle and the crowd surged.

Suddenly, Jake yelled, "STOP!" at the top of his lungs, and miraculously, everyone stopped. Jake smiled, then said, "Let's give a cheer for my big sister, Emma, who is the best! She and her friends all made these cupcakes for us and they are going to be awesome! Yay, Cupcake girls!"

All the little boys cheered and applauded, and there was nothing for us girls to do but take a bow. I turned to smile at Alexis, and I saw she had a funny look on her face, the one she gets when she has an idea. I couldn't begin to imagine what she'd be thinking of now, but I was just glad to see she, Mia, and Katie were happy and Jake was having a ball. All in all, a great party!

It took forever to get the backyard and kitchen back in order. But the Cupcakers were great. They'd stayed late to help clean up, then flopped on the couch to watch TV afterward. We were pooped. They said it gave them new respect for me, living with all those boys.

"See?" I'd said. "I told you so!"

The week after Jake's party, no one at camp could talk about anything but the Camp Olympics and the talent show. We trained for our sporting events like we were in boot camp, and at home I practiced my piece and took out my bridesmaid dress for my mom to press. I was nervous about the charm portion, but Alexis was assuring me she had it all figured out. That kind of scared me, but since I didn't have any better ideas, I had to just let it go.

Sydney was like a slave driver to her team, totally dissatisfied with their performances as the time of the talent show drew near. We watched in horror as she yelled at one girl after another for what she considered their bad performances, and we discussed in whispers the rumor we'd heard that Sydney would not be permitted back at camp for the second session.

Finally, it was Friday!

The Hotcakes got to camp early and warmed up, stretching and dancing to great music. We were pumped. Raoul and Maryanne had brought us granola bars and yogurts to keep up our energy.

The games got off to a great start, with an awesome, three-inning softball game, which we won! Tricia hit an amazing home run, and Louise knocked a double that brought in two runners. I kept the water coming, and before we knew it, the game was over and we were at the track for relays and sprints. This was my moment.

I lined up alongside the other girls my age in the first heat of the first race: a five-hundred-yard sprint. Elle was running too, and so was Charlotte. To my left was Sydney. Nothing could make me run faster than that.

The camp director blew the whistle, and we were off! I didn't look to the left or the right. I just pumped my arms hard and lifted my legs high, and I ran like Sydney Whitman was chasing me. Which she was. After I crossed the finish line (first! Yay!), I looked back, and Sydney was still about twenty yards back. I had beaten her handily and so had one of her teammates, a girl she'd repeatedly yelled at for being slow.

"Nice race, girls!" said the camp director as three of us were given medals for first, second, and third place. Sydney crossed the finish line and then pouted, tossing her hair. I heard her saying to someone that there had been a "false start," and she hadn't been ready, so that race didn't really count. I had to just shake my head.

Our team did well through the track-and-field events, and we had a lead heading into the swimming. We trooped over to the pool as the boys' teams exited, and I saw Sydney trying to chat up a bunch of boys who were clearly having a hard time figuring out what to do or say. Their heads were in the game, but they were interested in her. They just didn't know whether to stay and talk or keep on walking. I almost felt sorry for them.

At the pool, the Hotcakes huddled for a pep talk and a strategy meeting, and Raoul, with a huge smile on his face, asked for our attention.

"Chicas, I have some very exciting news. We will be fielding two swim squads today, after all." He grinned.

Everyone looked around in confusion and chattered while he called for silence.

"One of your teammates has made an extra effort so that everyone would be able to participate in these events. Kira has been coming to camp early all month to work with Mr. Collins, and she is ready to bust out her new moves in the pool today and show you all what she can do!"

I looked at Kira in shock. She was smiling shyly as everyone congratulated her. I thought back to her early morning drop-offs and the wet hair, and was annoyed at myself for not figuring it out sooner.

"Oh, Kira! I am so proud of you!" I cried, and I threw my arms around her in a hug.

We assembled for the relay: two squads, with three swimmers from each at either end of the pool. I noticed Kira was swimming from the deep end, which would be easier for her. If she started to fail, she'd be in the shallow end. But I needn't have worried.

When Mr. Collins blew his whistle, the swimmers dove in and took turns swimming the length of the pool. Kira was in the final heat of the relay, and because her team was a little rusty, she wound up swimming alone, dead last. But she dove into the pool and glided, and the Hotcakes were silent until she surfaced. Then we went wild, screaming and cheering until we were hoarse. We walked the length of the pool with Kira as she swam, encouraging her all the way. Her stroke wasn't perfect and she wasn't that fast, and her team obviously did not win, but it was, for us Hotcakes, the sweetest victory we could ever have imagined. We mobbed her when she got out of the pool, and Maryanne was there with a towel. Kira was crying, and it was the best, best moment of my whole camp experience. It was right then that we all felt we'd won the Camp Olympics, no matter what.

I saw Sydney on the sidelines, looking perplexed, and I was glad she had no idea what was going on. We'd kept this issue private, and we'd celebrate Kira's triumph among ourselves, just the Hotcakes. That was the way it should be. I couldn't have been happier if our team had won every race. Friends were more important than medals, and I was so proud of my new friend Kira. I'd always heard the expression "It's not whether you win or lose; it's how you play the game." But now I finally understood it—and it's true.

CHAPTER 13

Hotcakes to the Rescue!

Well, we didn't win the Camp Olympics overall. The Wolverines did, but that was to be expected. The Angels came in dead last. They were so far behind the rest of us that I had to wonder if Sydney's team mutinied against her and decided to lose on purpose. I would have if I were on the Angels. Still, the Hotcakes came in second, and that was good enough for us. The celebration of Kira's victory continued into Elle's sleepover, and we all toasted her with ginger ale at the movie and again back at Elle's house, when we had a snack before bedtime.

Elle's party was a blast, and for me and Alexis, it cemented our friendships with the summer gang. Even though most of us didn't live in the same part of town—some of us didn't even live in the same town—we knew we'd get together throughout the rest of the year and stay friends forever.

On Saturday morning, Alexis and I were up and packed by seven a.m. Her mom had promised to bring us to Katie's so we could finish frosting the cupcakes. My mom would pick us up from there, after dropping Matt off at soccer, and take the Cupcakers first to Mona's, then to Romaine's aunt's house. *Then* we'd head home to change for the big talent show! I couldn't even think about that last part—I was so nervous. Plus, we had so much to get through before it came time for that.

While we waited for Mrs. Becker, I checked my e-mail on Elle's family computer in her kitchen.

"Oh no!" I said. I couldn't believe the e-mail I'd just received.

"What?" said Alexis, hearing the alarm in my voice.

"Mrs. Shipley e-mailed yesterday, but obviously I didn't get it in time. She wanted to know if we could put daisies on the cupcakes 'cause it's a daisy-themed shower!" I looked at Alexis with horror. "How will we ever have time?"

"Time for what?" Kira yawned, straggling into the room. She was dressed but looked sleepy.

Alexis and I looked at each other in a panic, trying to think. "We need help," she said finally.

"I'll help you!" offered Kira.

"I'll help you with whatever it is too," said Georgia, who'd just come into the kitchen.

Pretty soon we had all of the Hotcakes offering to help us.

"Assembly line?" said Alexis with a smile.

"Totally," I agreed.

With a quick call to Katie and to Mrs. Becker, we rearranged the plan so that Mrs. Becker would pick up Katie, Mia, and all the supplies, and bring them to Elle's, where ten helpers awaited their tasks.

It wasn't an hour before everyone had a spot in Elle's kitchen and dining room, and we were frosting cupcakes and piping flowers onto them, chatting and working hard. Everyone was ecstatic to be working on cupcakes Romaine Ford might eat, so they were taking extra care that things looked perfect.

Mia and Katie were very gracious about the whole change of plan, and Elle even apologized to them, saying, "I'm so sorry I didn't think to invite you two to sleep over, since you're honorary Hotcakes. Next time, you two are at the top of my guest list!" I was so happy to see my friends becoming friends.

Finally, everything was ready and packed to go. My mom was outside in the minivan waiting for us, and the Cupcake Club said our good-byes and thank-yous to everyone. Kira was looking at us so wistfully, and all I could think of was how excited she'd been to meet Romaine at the mall. I whispered a quick question to the Cupcakers, and everyone nodded enthusiastically in reply. So I said, "Hey, Kira, want to come, and we'll drop you off afterward?"

It only took her a nanosecond to process what I meant, but then she cried, "Do I?" and ran to get her things. After all of Kira's hard work for the team, she deserved a special treat like this.

After running Mona's cupcakes to her, we immediately took off for the far side of town and reached Mrs. Shipley's right on time. There was a catering van parked in her driveway, and a few other cars—one of them looked really fancy, like the kind a movie star might drive—so I hoped that meant that Romaine was there.

Nervously, the five of us carried the cupcake bins to the back door. I rang the bell, and Mrs. Shipley herself came to the door.

"Oh, Emma, hello! And this must be the Cupcake Club! Come in, come in!"

I held my breath, waiting for someone to point out that it was the Cupcake Club plus one, but to everyone's credit, they didn't say anything.

"Here we are! Daisy cupcakes!" I said.

"Fabulous! I'm so sorry that was such a last-minute idea, but ooh goody! Let's see!"

We lifted the lid from the cupcake carrier and showed her our work. The cupcakes did look adorable.

"Oooh! Wow! Kathy! Come see!" she called.

Mrs. Ford appeared in the kitchen doorway, decorating supplies in hand. "Hi, girls! I'm Kathy! Hi, Emma, honey, how are you?"

I knew my friends were impressed that these ladies all knew me, and I did feel a little proud, I have to say. But the main thing we were all wondering was, would we get to see Romaine?

And then, "Mom?" I heard her voice!

"In here, honey! Emma's here!"

Mia and Katie nudged me with excitement, their eyes sparkling. I had to smile.

"Emma! And cupcakes! Yay!" Romaine was in the doorway and came over to give me a big hug. I was grinning from ear to ear, and I knew I was blushing. I felt kind of like a dork, but I was proud.

"Hi, girls! Is this the rest of the Cupcake Club?" asked Romaine, superfriendly. "Hi. I've met you before! At the mall, right?" she said to Kira. Kira just about died of happiness.

She nodded.

"That's Kira," I said, taking charge of the introductions. "And this is Mia, Katie, and Alexis."

Everyone said shy hellos, and Alexis congratulated Romaine on her wedding, remembering to mention Liam Carey's name, which I thought was a nice touch.

Then Romaine looked at the cupcakes, and squealed, "I love them! Oh my gosh! They are so pretty!" Then she looked at me with a sneaky expression. "Can I try one?" she asked.

"Go ahead! They're all yours!" I said.

"Mmm! Oh, delicious!" said Romaine through a mouthful of crumbs.

"Speaking of which . . ." Mrs. Shipley handed me a white envelope that said CUPCAKE CLUB on it. "Here's your payment."

I was almost inclined to refuse it, for the honor of baking for Romaine, but Alexis reached out and took the envelope. "Thank you," she said graciously.

"She's our CFO," I said, laughing.

"Good for her! She's doing her job!" said Mrs. Shipley with a smile.

Mrs. Ford suggested a group photo with Romaine, and we all posed with ginormous grins on our faces, Romaine holding up a cupcake like she was about to take a bite.

"Well, we've got to be leaving now," I said.

"Can't you stay a little while longer? Could we get you something to drink?" asked Mrs. Shipley, so gracious.

"Actually, it's our Camp Finale tonight. Our talent show . . . so, we need to get going. . . ."

"Oh, the Camp Finale! I remember that! I did a tap dance for mine!" said Romaine. "Mom, do you remember? That was one of the best nights of my life!"

Mrs. Ford winced and then laughed. "How could I forget?" She put her head in her hands. "Oh, the practicing! I thought I'd never recover!"

We laughed.

"That is so fun. So who's doing what?" Romaine asked.

Alexis and I told Romaine the details, and she asked us what time it was, and what I'd wear and play, and what Kira was singing. Alexis let on that she had a special surprise planned, and while I groaned in dread, Romaine told us how excited she was for us.

Finally, we really did have to go. My mom was waiting in the car, and we knew Mrs. Shipley needed to get back to organizing her party.

With a long good-bye and lots of hugs, we left and tumbled back into the minivan.

We could not stop chattering. "That was so amazing!" and "She's so nice!" and "I can't believe she remembered me!" and on and on. My mom laughed, asking questions as she drove around dropping everyone off. Finally, it was just me and Alexis, who would help me get dressed for the event.

"So what's your surprise?" I asked. "You can tell me now."

"Not yet," said Alexis with a mischievous grin. "Not yet."

CHAPTER 14

Talent and Charm

The butterflies in my stomach had turned into birds by the time we got back to camp. There were so many people milling around—siblings, parents, even grandparents. I could not believe how big a crowd it was.

I had my dress in a garment bag, and I checked in backstage. The camp director handed me a program and told me when I'd go on. Raoul was in charge of props and costumes, and he whisked my flute and dress away for safekeeping while we joined the growing audience.

"Wow. This is major," I said to Alexis, looking around. Because she wasn't performing, her parents hadn't come. She was sitting with me and my parents and brothers. But I noticed she kept

looking around, like she was waiting for someone else.

Finally I said, "Who are you looking for?"

"Oh, just—There they are!" she cried, and I
turned to see Mia and Katie heading right toward
us. Mia had a garment bag too, and I wondered
why until she handed it to Alexis.

"Here's Jake's costume," Mia said. "Hi, Jakey!
Hi, Mr. and Mrs. Taylor." She settled in next to
Alexis and started joking around with Matt and
Sam. Katie smiled.

"You guys are going to be great!" she said.

"Guys?" I looked at Alexis. "Now you have to
tell me."

Alexis sighed and looked at Mia and Katie in
annoyance. They were so busy flirting it up with
my older brothers that they missed the look. "I
guess since *some* people don't know how to keep
a secret," Alexis began loudly, "I will tell you our
plan."

I looked at her expectantly. "This better be
good, or I'm not going up there," I said.

"Oh, you're going! You and Jake, who will introduce you and carry out your chair for you to sit in.
He's the charm."

"Wait, you're having that . . . unpredictable little

slob be the charm in my act?" I said. I couldn't believe this was happening.

"Yes," said Alexis definitely. "And he will not be unpredictable because he has been bribed with a whole dozen Jake Cakes, just for him. And he will not be a slob because"—she unzipped Mia's garment bag—"he will be wearing this!" She pulled out a mini tuxedo and a collapsible top hat.

I began to laugh. "Oh my gosh," I said. "Where did you get that?"

Alexis shrugged and glanced at Mia. "It helps to have connections in the fashion world."

Then everyone started to shush the crowd, and the first act began. It was a bunch of boys who were break dancing, and they were actually pretty good. I had a hard time enjoying it, though, because I was so worried about my own act to come.

Next up was a group of Wolverines who did a rap song about camp that was really funny. Some of it was unintentionally funny because they kept forgetting the words, but in the end they got a lot of applause. Elle and Tricia danced around using Hula-Hoops and were awesome, but it wasn't that much of an act. Just them twirling stuff to music. Caroline sang beautifully, and Charlotte and Georgia did their gymnastics routine, which was pretty impressive.

And then it was Sydney's turn.

The music started up, and she strode out in a cowgirl getup that was waaay too sophisticated for her. She had on piles of makeup—if I could see it from the twentieth row, you had to know it was a lot—and she kind of shimmied in time to the music as she came out. Romaine Ford would have died.

I had to give Sydney a little credit for being brave enough to come out by herself and sing. But then I thought she probably just couldn't find anyone else she thought was good enough to join her.

Until she opened her mouth. Then I realized that probably no one joined her because no one thought she was good enough.

Sydney Whitman can't sing.

At first, it was awkward. People felt bad for her, you could tell. They tipped their heads to the side, as if they were really trying to give her a good listen. But then she started doing these really hammy country dance moves, and people started to giggle. Sydney must've been pleased, seeing all the smiles in the audience. With her ego, she surely thought people were just in awe of how good she was. She began to work the audience, encouraging people to clap along with the song, which they did. And then she sang louder—she was getting progressively worse—and danced more enthusiastically, and people just started to laugh their heads off.

The funny thing was, Sydney was so blindly into herself that she never noticed. When her song ended, she gave a triumphant bow and punched the air with her first, like, "I really nailed that one!" and she skipped off stage.

Alexis, Katie, Mia, and I looked at one another in shock.

"She really doesn't get it, does she?" said Alexis, shaking her head in disbelief.

Katie was smug. "I told you she couldn't sing!"

We didn't have long to marvel over what we'd just witnessed because Alexis was suddenly hustling me backstage. Mia grabbed Jake by the hand (she and Katie were going to be in charge of him), and Alexis led me to my changing area.

"Deep breaths. You are very, very talented," said Alexis as she turned her back to allow me to change privately.

"Ready," I said, even though inside I wasn't. Alexis came to zip me up and help with my hair.

I mentally went through Mona's checklist for modeling, which made me feel more in control. "Chin up, shoulders back, smile, sparkle, and just breathe. . . ."

Mia appeared with Jake all dressed, and I had to admit, he looked absolutely adorable. Alexis hustled me to the curtain and gave last-minute directions as we stood there.

"Jake, you'll carry out the chair, put it down in the center of the stage like you practiced with your mom at home. Then you'll bow and say 'Now presenting, my sister, Emma, who will play . . .'" She looked at Jake.

He nodded and said, "Beethoven's 'Ode to Joy.'"

"Right. Then you turn and hold out your hand, and Emma comes out. Then, Emma, do a little bow, and sit and play. When you're done, stand up, bow, and Jake will come back out to collect the chair, okay? Got it?"

"Got it!" we said.

And then suddenly they were calling my name, and it was all a blur. I remember the crowd clapping for Jake and saying "Awww . . ." when he came out.

I remember sitting to play my piece and that I was amazed that that many people could be so quiet. I caught Sam's eye out in the audience at one point, and he was smiling proudly and nodding, but I had to look away.

Then it was over, and Jake was back out, and this time the crowd roared its approval as we left the stage. I was shaking so hard and smiling and so, so relieved. And most of all, I was so glad Alexis had made me do it! I felt great, like how Kira must've felt when she swam.

Backstage, Alexis grabbed me in a huge hug (so unlike her!), and so did Mia and Katie, and then I was quickly out of my dress and Jake was out of his tux. We were back in the crowd to watch the end of the show with my family. Now I could really relax and enjoy it.

I got to see Kira sing, and she had an amazing voice. I spied what must've been her dad and her sisters in the audience. At the end, her dad gave her a standing ovation and was mopping his eyes with a handkerchief. I was glad he was there for her, and he seemed really proud of her.

And finally, there was a pause at the end while the judge tallied up their results. The crowd chatted quietly among themselves as we waited.

"Cupcakers, thanks for coming," I said to the girls. "And thanks for a great summer so far."

"Don't thank us, thank the Hotcakes!" said Katie really nicely.

"It's been really fun," agreed Mia.

We talked about some of our plans for the rest of the summer and then the camp director was back onstage with the microphone.

"Ladies and gentlemen, we had a wonderful program tonight. All these kids are so talented and worked so hard. All the participants will receive a small silver camp whistle to honor their participation. Now, the winners for tonight are in each of three categories: charm, talent, and presentation. Then we do have one overall winner who nailed all three. But before we announce the winners' names, I would like to introduce a special Spring Lake Day Camp alumna who will be our presenter tonight. Ladies and gentlemen, it gives me great pleasure to introduce to you . . . Romaine Ford!"

There was a shocked silence and then the crowd erupted as Romaine came out, smiling and waving. She was in a pretty white sundress with daisies on it, and the Cupcakers and I exchanged knowing looks. It was the dress she must've worn to the shower. I craned my neck to catch Kira's eye across the crowd, and we smiled at each other and made gestures of surprise.

"Hello, folks, thank you for the warm greeting," began Romaine. "I loved my time here at Spring Lake Day Camp so when my friend Emma Taylor and her Cupcake Club told me that tonight was the Camp Finale, I just couldn't miss it!"

My friends and I all cheered and grabbed one another in excitement that she'd mentioned us. I couldn't believe it! I saw Sydney look around the crowd until she spotted us and scowled in disgust.

"Now there were some really wonderful acts I saw when I got here, and I am impressed by all of your hard work, so congratulations to all of you who performed, and to all the backstage crew who helped the performers. And here we go . . . !" She looked down at a sheet of paper and began reading out the awards.

I was ecstatic when Kira won for talent. She had a lovely voice, and she was thrilled to receive the award from Romaine, who gave her a big hug and a kiss on each cheek. The magic show boys won for presentation—they'd been really organized, with lots of props and stuff—and then Sydney won for charm! I was in shock.

Romaine shook her hand graciously, and maybe I was imagining it, but she didn't seem that friendly toward Sydney. Sydney couldn't tell, though, because she was in heaven. I guess a part of me had to admit that her act *had* had a certain weird, funny charm. And at least this way she did win something, even if she was banned from attending the camp next year.

And finally Romaine said, "The all-around winner is . . . my good friend Emma Taylor!"

I couldn't believe it! It was like I was dreaming. I was up on my feet and on the stage, with Romaine hugging me so hard and rocking me back and forth. I just couldn't believe it! She handed me a big trophy and smiled for a photo Raoul took of us. She called "Good night and good luck!" to the crowd, and we walked offstage together.

Romaine was mobbed afterward, but she managed to sneak over to my family before she left. I introduced her to my parents and my brothers, and she said hi to all the Cupcakers, remembering everyone's name!

"You should be really proud of your sister, boys," she said to Matt, Sam, and Jake. "She's a very talented young woman—in the kitchen, on the runway, and onstage! Watch out, world!"

I never wanted this night to end, but it all went so fast in the end. We dropped off all the Cupcakers and headed home, just the six of us, where we sat and ate some of the dozen Jake Cakes (baked today and dropped off by Mia and Katie) at the kitchen table. (Even though the Cupcakers told Jake all twelve cupcakes were for him, he said we could share them with him.)

"Great job, honey," said my dad. "As usual."

"Yeah, honey, great job introducing us to the hot celeb!" said Sam through a mouthful of cupcake.

I rolled my eyes as the crumbs spilled out of his mouth and onto the table.

"We're proud of you, lovebug," said my mom.

"So am I!" said Jake, with a big Oreo-covered smile.

"Thanks, guys," I said. "You're the best."

I looked at my family and then thought about the Cupcakers and the Hotcakes, and meeting Romaine and all the wonderful things that happened over the summer. I had worried about fitting everyone and everything into my plans, but like a great cupcake recipe, the more things I added to the mix, the more delicious and fun everything became.

Sam, Matt, and Jake were gobbling up all the cupcakes.

"Boys!" Mom cried. "We can make more! Slow down."

And then I realized that sometimes cupcakes are like friends . . . you can always make more!

Alexis

cool

as a

cupcake

PROFITS

CHAPTER 1

Partners? What Partners?

$\mathcal{B}$usiness first. That's one of my mottoes.

When my best friends and I get together to discuss our cupcake company, the Cupcake Club, I am all about business. My name is Alexis Becker, and I am the business planner of the group. This means I kind of take care of everything—pricing, scheduling, and ingredient inventory—the nuts and bolts of it all. So when we actually go to make the cupcakes and sell them, we're all set.

Mia Vélaz-Cruz is our fashion-forward, stylish person, who is great at presentation and coming up with really good ideas, and Katie Brown and Emma Taylor are real bakers, so they have lots of ideas on ingredients and how things should taste. Together we make a great team.

But today, when we were having our weekly meeting at Mia's house, they would not let me do my job. It was so frustrating!

I had out the leather-bound accounts ledger that Mia's mom gave me, and I was going through all our costs and all the money that's owed to us, when Mia interrupted.

"Ooh! I forgot to tell you I had an idea for your costume for the pep rally parade, Katie!" said Mia enthusiastically, as if I wasn't in the middle of reading out columns of numbers for the past two jobs we've had. The high school in our town holds a huge parade and pep rally right before school starts. It's a pretty big deal. One year some kids decided to dress up in costumes for the parade, and now everybody dresses up. The local newspaper sends reporters, and there are usually pictures of it on the first page of the paper the very next day.

"Oh good, what is it?" asked Katie, as if she was thrilled for the interruption.

"Ahem," I said. "Are we conducting business here or having a coffee klatch?" That's what our favorite science teacher, Ms. Biddle, said when we whispered in class. Apparently, a coffee klatch is something gossipy old ladies do: drink coffee and chatter mindlessly.

"Yeah, c'mon, guys. Let's get through this," said Emma. I know she was trying to be supportive of me, but "get through this"? As if they just had to listen to me before they got to the fun stuff? That was kind of insulting!

"I'm not reading this stuff for my own health, you know," I said. I knew I sounded really huffy, but I didn't care. I do way more behind-the-scenes work than anyone else in this club, and I don't think they have any idea how much time and effort it takes. Now, I *do* love it, but everyone has a limit, and I have almost reached mine.

"Sorry, Alexis! I just was spacing out and it crossed my mind," admitted Mia. It was kind of a lame apology, since she was admitting she was spacing out during my presentation.

"Whatever," I said. "Do you want to listen or should I just forget about it?"

"No, no, we're listening!" protested Katie. "Go on!" But I caught her winking and nodding at Mia as Mia nodded and gestured to her.

I shut the ledger. "Anyway, that's all," I said.

Mia and Katie were so engrossed in their sign language that they didn't even realize I'd cut it short. Emma seemed relieved and didn't protest.

So that's how it's going to be, I thought. *Then*

fine! I'd just do the books and buy the supplies and do all the scheduling and keep it to myself. No need to involve the whole club, anyway. I folded my arms across my chest and waited for someone to speak. But of course, it wasn't about business.

"Well?" asked Katie.

"Okay, I was thinking, what about a genie? And you can get George Martinez to be an astronaut. Then you can wear something really dreamy and floaty and magical, like on that old TV show *I Dream of Jeannie* that's on Boomerang?" Mia was smiling with pride at her idea.

"Ooooh! I love that idea!" squealed Katie. "But how do I get George to be an astronaut?" She propped her chin on her hand and frowned.

"Wait!" interrupted Emma. "Why would George Martinez need to be an astronaut?"

Mia looked at her like she was crazy. "Because a *boy* has to be your partner for the parade. You know that!"

Emma flushed a deep red. "No, I did not know that. Who told you that?"

I felt a pit growing in my stomach. Even though I was mad and trying to stay out of this annoying conversation, the news stunned me too, and I couldn't remain silent. "Yeah, who told you that?" I repeated.

Mia and Katie shrugged and looked at each other, then back at us.

"Um, I don't know," said Katie. "It's just common knowledge?"

I found this annoying since it was our first real pep rally and this was major news. "No, it is *not* common knowledge." I glared at Mia.

"Sorry," said Mia sheepishly.

I pressed my lips together. Then I said, "Well? Who are *you* going with?"

Mia looked away. "I haven't really made up my mind," she said.

"Do you have lots of choices?" I asked. I was half annoyed and half jealous. Mia is really pretty and stylish and not that nervous around boys.

She laughed a little. "Not exactly. But Katie does!"

Emma and I looked at each other, like, *How could we have been so clueless?*

"Stop!" Katie laughed, turning beet red again.

"Well, 'fess up! Who are they?" I asked.

Katie rolled her eyes. "Oh, I don't know."

Mia began ticking off names on her fingers. "George Martinez always teases her when he sees her, which we all know means he likes her. He even mentioned something about the parade and asked Katie what her costume was going to be, right?"

Katie nodded.

Mia continued, "And then there's Joe Fraser. Another possibility."

"Stop!" protested Katie. "That's all. This is too mortifying! Let's change the subject to something boring, like Cupcake revenue!"

"Thanks a lot!" I said. I was hurt that she said it because I don't find Cupcake revenue boring. I find it fascinating. I love to think of new ways to make money.

How do my best friends and I have such different interests? I wondered.

"Sorry, but you know what I mean," said Katie. "It stresses me out to talk about who likes whom."

Still.

"Well, no one likes me!" said Emma.

"That's not true. I'm sure people like you," said Mia. But I noticed she didn't try to list anyone.

"What do we do if we don't have a boy to go with?" I asked.

"Well, girls could go with their girl friends, but no one really does that. I think it's just kind of dorky. . . ."

I felt a flash of annoyance. Since when was Mia such a know-it-all about the pep rally and what was done and what wasn't and what was dorky and what wasn't?

"I guess I could go with Matt . . . ," said Emma, kind of thinking out loud.

"What?!" I couldn't contain my surprise. Emma knows I have a crush on her older brother, and in the back of my mind, throughout this whole conversation, I'd been trying to think if I'd have the nerve to ask him. Not that I'd ever ask if he'd do matchy-matchy costumes with me, but just to walk in the parade together. After all, he *had* asked me to dance at my sister's sweet sixteen party.

Emma looked at me. "What?"

I didn't want to admit I'd been thinking that *I'd* ask him, so I said the next thing I could think of. "You'd go with your brother? Isn't *that* kind of dorky?" I felt mean saying it, but I was annoyed.

Emma winced, and I felt a little bad.

But Mia shook her head. "No, not if your brother is older and is cool, like Matt; it's not dorky."

Oh great. Now she'd just given Emma free rein to ask Matt and I had no one! "You know what? I'm going to check with Dylan on all this," I said.

My older sister would certainly know all the details of how this should be done. And she was definitely not dorky.

There was an uncomfortable silence. Finally, I said, "Look, we don't have to worry about all this right now, so let's just get back to business, okay?" And at last they were eager to discuss my favorite subject, if only because the other topics had turned out to be so stressful for us.

I cleared my throat and read from my notebook. "We have Jake's best friend Max's party, and Max's mom wants something like what we did for Jake. . . ." We'd made Jake Cakes—dirt with worms cupcakes made out of crushed Oreos and gummy worms for Emma's little brother's party, and they were a huge hit.

"Right," said Emma, nodding. "I was thinking maybe we could do Mud Pies?"

"Excellent. Let's think about what we need for the ingredients. There's—"

"Sorry to interrupt, but . . ."

We all looked at Katie.

"Just one more tiny question? Do you think Joe Fraser is a little bit cooler than George Martinez?"

I stared at her coldly. "What does that have to do with Mud Pies?"

"Sorry," said Katie, shrugging. "I was just wondering."

"Anyway, Mud Pie ingredients are . . ."

We brainstormed, uninterrupted, for another five minutes and got a list of things kind of organized for a Mud Pie proposal and sample baking session. Then we turned to our next big job, baking cupcakes for a regional swim meet fund-raiser.

Mia had been absentmindedly sketching in her notebook, and now she looked up. "I have a great idea for what we could do for the cupcakes for the swim meet!"

"Oh, let's see!" I said, assuming she'd sketched it out. I peeked over her shoulder, expecting to see a cupcake drawing, and instead there was a drawing of a glamorous witch costume, like something out of *Wicked*.

"Oh," I said. Here I'd been thinking we were all engaged in the cupcake topic, and it turned out Mia had been still thinking about the pep rally parade all along.

"Sorry," she said. "But I was *thinking* about cupcakes."

"Whatever," I said. I tossed my pen down on the table and closed my notebook. "This meeting is adjourned."

"Come on, Alexis," said Mia. "It's not that big a deal."

"Yeah, all work and no play makes for a bad day, boss lady!" added Katie.

"I am *not* the boss lady!" I said. I was mad and hurt. "I don't want to be the boss lady. In fact, I am not any kind of boss. Not anymore! You guys can figure this all out on your own."

I stood up and quickly gathered my things into my bag.

"Hey, Alexis, please! We aren't trying to be mean, we're just distracted!" said Mia.

"You guys think this is all a joke! If I didn't hustle everything along and keep track, nothing would get done!" I said, swinging my bag up over my shoulder. "I feel like I do all the work, and then you guys don't even care!"

"Look, it's true you do all the work," agreed Emma. "But we thought you enjoyed it. If you're tired of it, we can divvy it up, right, girls?" she said, looking at Mia and Katie.

"Sure! Why not?" said Mia, flinging her hair behind her shoulders in the way she does when she's getting down to work.

"Fine," I said.

"I'll do the swim team project, okay?" said Mia.

"And I'll do the Mud Pies," said Emma.

"And I'll do whatever the next big project is," said Katie.

I looked at them all. "What about invoicing, purchasing, and inventory?"

The girls each claimed one of the areas, and even though I was torn about giving up my responsibilities, I was glad to see them shouldering some of the work for a change. We agreed that they would e-mail or call me with questions when they needed my help.

"Great," I said. "Now I'm leaving." And I walked home from Mia's quickly, so fast I was almost jogging. My pace was fueled by anger about the Cupcake Club *and* the desire to get home to my sister, Dylan, as quickly as possible, so I could start asking questions about the pep rally parade and all that it would entail.

CHAPTER 2

The Quest for Cool Begins

*Y*es, it is dorky to go with a friend," said Dylan. "I mean, not totally dorky, like if you go in a group with some guys, too, but just you and another girl? Dor-ky!" she singsonged.

I had made it home from Mia's in record time and rushed up to Dylan's room. She and I get along pretty well, since it's just the two of us sisters and we're both pretty type A, according to my mom. This means we're both hard workers who never stop or compromise until a job is done perfectly. Anyway, it turned out Mia and Katie *were* right about everything. I couldn't decide who I was more annoyed at: them for knowing first about going with a boy to the parade, or Dylan for never mentioning it to me.

I flopped onto her bed, and then I rolled over and groaned. "So who am I going to go with?" I wailed.

Dylan was filing her nails. "Well," she began, pausing to blow at some imaginary piece of dust on her ring finger, "why not Matt?"

Dylan knows I like Matt Taylor because she helped me make myself over to win his attention a little while back. She also knew I wanted to dance with him at her sweet sixteen, which, as I mentioned earlier, I actually did.

"He'll never ask me," I whimpered.

"So? Ask *him*!" said Dylan.

Me? Ask *him* to march with *me* in the parade? Impossible! That was the same as asking him on a date, and there was just no way I'd ever do that!

"Yeah, as if!" I said.

"Why? You're best friends with his sister. You practically live at his house. You've worked on stuff together before. Look, don't forget boys are just as nervous about all this stuff as girls are, and he'd probably be grateful to not have to ask someone."

Ugh. The very idea gave me full-body shivers. "But I'm sure I'm *not* the someone he'd like to go with," I said.

"Why not?" she said, now slicking on clear nail

polish with an authoritative swipe. Dylan is nothing if not confident.

"Because I'm not . . . cool," I admitted.

Dylan narrowed her eyes and looked at me. "Well, I can help you with that," she said. "You know I love a challenge."

"Oh no," I said.

"Let me think about it, and I will get back to you with a plan of action tomorrow afternoon, okay?"

"Okay . . . ," I said hesitantly.

But she'd already turned to her computer and begun to type furiously. I guess I am quite the inspiring makeover candidate if she's always willing to take me on.

Double oh no!

That night I sent mini-overview e-mails of the Cupcake Club procedures to Mia, Katie, and Emma, explaining inventory, scheduling, purchasing, and invoicing, along with what we had coming up. I kept feeling like I'd forgotten something, but it was really just that I kept searching for Cupcake Club responsibilities and tasks and finding none. There were no columns of costs to doodle in my journal and no long-range schedules to sketch out. I hadn't realized quite how much time and energy—even my thoughts—the Cupcake Club consumed.

The next day I met up with the rest of the Cupcake Club at the school cafeteria. School hadn't started yet, but Mia had volunteered us to be on the decoration committee for the pep rally, much to my annoyance. (If she was going to volunteer us for something why not the refreshments committee, where we could at least promote our cupcakes?) But I held my tongue. I knew Mia loved anything having to do with design, so this was right up her alley.

On my way to the cafeteria, I met the math department head, Mr. Donnelly, in the hallway. He asked me if I had a few minutes to speak to him. I have an A+ average, so I figured he was just asking me to tutor some kid in the coming school year. Now that I had all this free time, I could say yes. But that wasn't it at all!

"Alexis, I have a great opportunity for you," he said. "I think you should join the Future Business Leaders of America, and I'd be happy to nominate you." He smiled at me happily.

Wow! That was not what I'd been expecting at all! "Oh, Mr. Donnelly! That's . . . that's just sooo great! Thank you! I can't believe I'd be eligible."

My stomach flipped over in excitement, and I got goose bumps up and down my arms.

The Future Business Leaders of America is part of a national organization, and we have a small chapter here at Park Street Middle School. The kids who are in it are by far the smartest kids in the school—the ones who are straight A+ students, honor roll all the way (well, like me, I guess). It's hard to get nominated. You can't ask anyone to nominate you—you have to be chosen, and it's a huge honor. They only choose four kids a year from each grade. And the best part is, the kids meet all the time with the faculty supervisor, who teaches them cool business stuff, like marketing and accounting theories, and then at the end of the year they go to a big convention in the city and meet with all kinds of famous businesspeople. It's supposed to be amazing!

Mr. Donnelly could tell I was thrilled. "I've heard so much about your wonderful Cupcake Club, and of course I sampled the goods at the school fund-raiser last year, and I think you've got a terrific business going. Your hands-on experience running it would bring a lot to the group."

"Well, my friends and I all run it together," I said modestly. But that really wasn't true. Except now, maybe it was. I kind of felt unsure of my role and didn't know what to say. I wondered if I'd be joining the FBLA under false pretenses if Mr. Donnelly thought I ran the whole Cupcake Club by myself.

"You'd be an asset either way. What do you think?"

I mentally scanned my other commitments and my time schedule. "Can I think about it for a day and discuss it with my parents? I have so much on my plate right now," I said. I was so flattered, I wanted to say yes immediately, but it's never good to agree to new responsibilities in a spontaneous fashion.

Mr. Donnelly smiled at me. "Spoken like a true professional," he said. "And absolutely. Let me know. The deadline is in about two weeks, so you have a little time to think about it, but it does look better if you submit early." He winked. "The early bird catches the worm."

"I know it!" I agreed. "Thanks, Mr. Donnelly!"

"Anytime. Just keep me posted!" he said as I sailed off to the cafeteria.

I could hardly wait to tell the others, but when I spotted them across the lunchroom, all sitting together and chatting excitedly, I knew they were not discussing Cupcake business but instead the pep rally parade and what they'd wear and who they'd walk with and all that. I felt myself deflate a little. I couldn't tell them about the FBLA. They wouldn't get it. And, anyway, there was something a tiny bit underhanded about only me getting nominated. After all, it's supposed to be all four of us in business together.

I trudged over to sit with them, dreading the discussion and wishing I could share my real news. It would just have to wait until I got home. My parents and Dylan would be ecstatic for me, I realized. Just picturing their reactions cheered me up a little and gave me the patience to listen to the pep rally chatter.

Dylan wasn't ready for my undorking when I got home, so I went to my room to start reading one more book before summer was over. I had decided to save my news for dinner.

At exactly seven o'clock, I skipped down the stairs to the kitchen table. My parents had come up to say hi when they'd gotten home from work a little earlier, but I'd restrained myself, even though I felt like I was going to burst. I wanted to see everyone's faces at the same time when I told them.

I sat down and waited until everyone had settled and we'd passed around the platter of stir-fried shrimp and veggies, and then I said, "Mom, Dad, Dylly, I have major news. Major *good* news!"

I looked with pleasure at the expectant faces of my family: Mom, Dad, and Dylan.

"Matt asked you to be his parade partner?" said Dylan excitedly.

My parents looked back at me with big smiles on their faces. I was irritated.

"No. Nothing to do with that." Now I wasn't sure how to make the transition. "It's about school," I said.

"Oh! I know! You're going to run for class president!" my dad said, grinning.

This was getting more and more irritating. "No. I am not running for class president," I said through gritted teeth. "This is not a guessing game. I am going to tell you."

"Oh! Sorry, dear," said my mother, blotting her mouth with a napkin. "Because I was going to guess that they put you on varsity tennis."

"Noooo! No more guesses!" I huffed. "Now my news isn't so great. I think I'm going to just keep it to myself," I said. Jeez, the nerve of these people.

"No, we're sorry, sweetheart. What is it? We'll

be thrilled for you no matter what, because if you're happy, we're happy!" said my mom, beaming.

I rolled my eyes.

My mom scolded me. "No pouting, now," she said. "Turn that frown upside down!"

Ugh. I hate when she uses her parenting-class voice on me. It's so humiliating.

"Fine. Mr. Donnelly asked me to join the Future Business Leaders of America. It's a really big deal. Only four kids from each grade are picked—"

"Oh, that's wonderful!" said my mom. "What an honor!"

But Dylan did not have the reaction I was expecting.

"No," she said. "Absolutely not." She folded her arms and leaned on the table, in direct defiance of my mom's strict mealtime-manners code, and she looked me in the eye. "You. Will. Not. Do. It. Do I make myself clear?"

"Wait, what?" I asked. I was confused.

"You have to say no. It's one thing to feel like a dork. It's another to take out a billboard announcing it. The FBLA is for *total* dorks. Complete, unredeemable, dorkorama! You cannot do it. Period." Dylan sat back in her chair and patted her mouth with a napkin. Having said her piece, she was confident I would obey.

"Dylan! That was absolutely inappropriate!" said my mom, in shock.

"Don't listen to your sister, sweetheart. Maybe she's just feeling a little . . . tiny, tiny bit envious," said my dad.

"Ha!" Dylan guffawed. If she'd been drinking her milk at the time, it would have come out of her nose. "That is one thing I am *not*."

I was stunned. Dylan was an overachiever, just like me. How could she not think this was a big, exciting deal?

"Dylan, you need to apologize to your sister. I'm counting to three. One, two . . ."

"Mom!" protested Dylan. "Stop! Alexis has hired me to help her undork herself in time to get a date for the pep rally. She has empowered me to advise her. And this is my first piece of advice: The FBLA is sudden social death. Do not join. If you take even one piece of advice from me, let it be that. I shall say no more on the topic." And she picked up her fork and began eating again.

I, on the other hand, had lost my appetite.

CHAPTER 3

The Commandments of Cool

My parents banned the topics of dorkiness and the FBLA for the rest of dinner, but it didn't leave us much to talk about since that was all that was on my mind, anyway.

Afterward, I retreated to my room to continue reading my book while they cleaned the kitchen, and then I took a shower. A few moments after I closed my door, someone knocked.

"Come in," I said warily.

Dylan came in holding a file folder and sat on my bed, all serious. "Listen, you're the one who always says 'knowledge is power,'" she began.

I nodded and then shrugged.

"And you *asked* me to give you help and to share my wisdom."

Annoying but true. I nodded again.

"I've put together a report on the state of dorki-ness and how to convert it to coolness in six easy steps. It's all in here." She fanned the folder at me.

I rolled my eyes. I didn't want to play into her hands, but I really did have an urge to grab the folder and devour its contents. Instead, I waited.

"It's up to you which path you take, but I have illuminated the way to coolness for you, and I hope you will make the right choice. And just to reit-erate, the FBLA is *not* the right choice. Nothing personal."

Dylan moved to hand me the folder and I let it hang in the air for an extra second, then I took it from her and tossed it on my desk supercasually, like I didn't really care what it said.

"Thanks," I said finally, good manners winning out over my annoyance with her and her directives.

"Good luck" was all she said as she closed the door behind her.

I stared at the folder, knowing that once I opened it, my life would be forever changed, whether I acted on her advice or not. Maybe I didn't care if I was a dork. Maybe being cool would take up too much time and keep me from doing the things I really wanted to do, like joining the FBLA.

But knowledge is power; it's true that I always say that. And nothing tempts me like a well-done research project sitting inside a folder.

I sighed and picked it up, and then I began to read.

The report was long and involved. Dylan had really done her homework, as usual. There was a long list of "Don'ts" in the Dork section, as well as a list of individuals we both knew who were cited for their dorkiness (including my parents!). There was a filmography part, referencing movies I should see that would help to illuminate the differences between dorks and cool people, and there was a recommended reading list of magazines and blogs that would "cool me up," according to Dylan. It all looked like a lot of work.

But the main body of the report came down to the Six Commandments of Cool, as Dylan called them. They were:

(1)   Do well in school, but never mention it. Even deny it at times. (See Section A for examples of when and how to deny.)

(2)   Smile and be friendly, but not too friendly. (Do *not* encourage dorks by acting like they are your equals.)

(3)   In public, pretend that you do not care about the following: what you wear, how you look, who likes you. (But in private, DO pay close attention to these things.)

(4)   Do not be too accessible, either via e-mail, online social sites, IM, phone, etc. (and often say you have plans, even if you do not).

(5)   Go with the flow and just let things roll. (It's dorky to make a fuss.)

(6)   Always have a good guy friend. (See Section B for reasons why.)

I slumped in my desk chair and thought about all the advice.

This would be a lot of work. And some of it went against my better instincts. Like, why would I deny getting good grades? That was preposterous to me. And how could I not be friendly to people who were dorks? According to Dylan's list of dorks, many of them were my friends! Maybe not people I'd invite to sleep over, but certainly people I'd pick first as a lab partner in science class. I was suddenly supposed to not be too friendly to them? That would be impossible. And worse, I'd get stuck with a dumb lab partner and get a bad grade!

But the Cool Commandment that was the

hardest for me was number six. I really didn't have any guy friends, and I wasn't even sure who'd be a good candidate.

Section B said guy friends were good for stand-ins when you need a date but don't have one (Hellooo, pep rally parade!), and they can introduce you to other guys, one of whom might be boyfriend material. Guy friends also signal to other guys that a girl is okay. Like, if a girl is cool enough to be friends with this guy, then go ahead and like her because she's preapproved or something. Guy friends also give you a good perspective on what boys like in a girl and what's important to them. Also, talking with boys who you are not romantically interested in gives you practice for talking to the ones you *do* like. And so on and so on.

Section B wiped me out. I closed the folder, set it back on my desk, and then just sat there, stunned. I had an urge to do the only thing that would make me feel better: work on the Cupcake Club. But having resigned my duties, there was nothing for me to do.

There was another knock on the door, and this time it was my dad.

"Hi, sweetheart," he said from my doorway. "Can I come in?"

"Hi, Dad," I said. I was happy to see him, but I knew the lecture that was coming. I could have recited it myself.

He came in and sat on the corner of my bed so recently vacated by Dylan. "Alexis, your mom and I and all your friends and all your teachers think you are wonderful just as you are. You are talented, smart, ambitious, organized—"

I interrupted. "Thanks, Dad. But I'm okay. I don't need a pep talk. I really did ask Dylan for her help."

My dad pressed his lips together into a thin line and looked up at the ceiling while he gathered his thoughts. "I guess what your mom and I want you to know is . . . cool is temporary. It's a barometer kids use for a few years, when they are too unsure of themselves to be individuals. So they create this system that evaluates people based on criteria that literally have no bearing on the rest of your life. Trust me, once you are out of middle school and high school, there's no such thing as who's cool and who's not. So we suggest you forget about all that temporary stuff and just follow your passions. Those are what make a person great and attractive to others—being energized and excited about life! Not being boxed in by some rules or regulations . . ."

163

Boy, would his eyes pop out at Section A, I thought. I tried not to smile. It was just that his advice was such a contrast to Dylan's. I knew he was right when I really thought about it, but the truth was, I *did* have to get through these next few years worrying about the cool factor. That was just a fact of life. Following your passions, if they were dorky, did not exactly get you a partner for the pep rally parade.

"I know, Dad. You guys tell me this all the time," I said, trying to be kind but also wanting him to stop.

"We do?" My dad's face brightened. "Oh good! Then you're actually listening! That's great news!"

I smiled.

"Listen, honey, I just came up here to tell you that your mom and I think you should go for it with the Future Business Leaders of America. And don't listen to anything Dylan the Drama Queen tells you. Even if you did ask for her help. Okay?"

I nodded. "Thanks," I said, though I had every intention of doing the opposite of what he'd just told me.

He stood up and then planted a kiss on my head. "Get some sleep, now. It's late." And he walked out the door.

"Good night, Dad," I said.

I heard my dad enter Dylan's room and start lecturing her. I smiled with happiness, pushing aside the twinge of guilt I felt for bringing this all on Dylan. She really was just trying to help me, after all.

I picked up a pen and chewed on the cap, which is what I always do when I'm thinking. I was at a loss. I kept feeling anxious, like there was something I had to do. Then I'd realize it was the Cupcake Club and that, in fact, there *wasn't* anything for me to do now. I was so stressed about the other girls getting it all done, but at the same time I refused to chase them down with IMs and e-mails to make sure they were. It was just that one or two botched jobs could ruin our business for months, if not for good. When you run a business on word of mouth and good recommendations, your reputation is all you have. I chewed the pen harder.

Finally, I snapped. I decided to send an e-mail to the club to ask them for a Cupcake meeting at lunch tomorrow after our decorations committee discussion. With so many loose ends assigned to other people, we needed a meeting to catch up and to see how things were going, just for the good of the business. I vowed to myself that I would not take over or do any of the other girls' assignments. I just needed to put my mind at ease that the others were doing their jobs.

I hopped onto my e-mail account and sent the group the lunch meeting request. There was an e-mail in my in-box requesting that we do cup-cakes for a book club meeting of a friend of Katie's mom. I forwarded it to Katie, since she was doing the scheduling now.

After pressing send, I packed my ledger and CC notebook in my backpack and then went to brush my teeth, wash my face, and get into my pj's. With my retainer in, I called downstairs to my mom that I was ready for her to come up to say good night.

While I waited I climbed into bed and grabbed the Cool folder from my desk. I just couldn't help myself. I flipped it open and then began to read it again.

CHAPTER 4

Go with the Flow

There were lots of kids at school the next day for various pep rally committees: the refreshments committee, the entertainment committee, and, of course, the decorations committee. I strained to hear if anyone was talking about who they'd march with, but I didn't hear any of the other girls mention boys' names. I hated to ask them directly; it would be rude. But I was dying to know if they were marching with boys.

I ran into Mr. Donnelly on the way to the cafeteria, and he immediately wanted to chat about the FBLA.

"Alexis! I haven't heard back from you about the Future Business Leaders of America! Are you interested? Did you discuss it with your parents?" He smiled expectantly at me.

I was a little taken aback. He had just asked me about it the day before! "Um. Oh, Mr. Donnelly. I'm so sorry to be slow on this. It's . . . uh . . . a big decision, and I just need a little more time to assess my workload. I'm sorry. I've just been so swamped with the Cupcake Club," I lied, crossing my toes inside my shoes and feeling guilty. I knew that if it were up to Dylan, I'd say that my parents and I had discussed it and I wasn't going to be able to fit it in for this year and thank you so much. But I still really wanted to do it. The battle raged inside my heart as I struggled not to let on one way or the other.

"Wonderful! Lots of big jobs coming up? All organized?" he asked enthusiastically.

"Uh-huh. You bet!" I said with false confidence. Little did he know, I had absolutely no idea whether things were under control or not, but I couldn't exactly explain that! I'm sure being cool and going with the flow are not quite part of the FBLA agenda.

"All righty then. Just let me know soon, because I don't want to wait until the last minute to propose you. And if you can't do it, I need a little time to find someone else, okay?" he said.

"Absolutely. I'm so sorry for the delay," I agreed. We said good-bye, and I practically ran away.

Being all cool and relaxed sure is stressful.

I met the Cupcakers at our usual table at lunch, my ledger and notebook secured in my bag. I wouldn't take them out unless I absolutely had to. I just couldn't imagine having a meeting without them, but we'd see.

Naturally, the conversation was about the parade as soon as we sat down.

"Mia! I think someone likes you!" said Katie mischievously as I put my tray onto the table.

Mia's face turned pink. "Who?" she asked.

Katie grinned. "Chris Howard! I saw him staring at you on the bus this morning, with his head propped on his hand, all dreamylike!"

Mia's face grew even redder. "Stop! No way, you're just imagining things!" she protested, but she had a little smile, like she was pleased by the idea.

"He'd be great to go with!" said Emma, a little wistfully, I thought. "He's cute and nice, and he's pretty tall!"

Mia nodded, but she seemed like she didn't want to commit.

Katie shrugged. "Anyway, I'm just saying . . ."

"We've still got some time to figure it all out," said Emma.

Mia nodded, happy, it seemed, to change the subject. "Yes. We should at the very least be working on our costumes. There's not that much time. I should organize a schedule, maybe."

"Yes! Please do!" said Katie.

Emma nodded vigorously. "That would be so helpful!" she agreed.

Have these people lost their minds? I wondered.

"Ahem," I said. "A schedule? For costume making?" I looked at each of them, but they didn't understand what I meant. "Hello? How about a schedule for cupcake baking?"

"Oh, Alexis! We're getting to that!" said Katie breezily. "Just let us have our fun first, before you start being a slave driver."

"I thought the *Cupcake Club* was supposed to be fun!" I said. I couldn't help myself.

Emma looked at me, all sympathetic. "It is fun, Alexis. Just . . . not as fun as pep rallies and parades! Come on. Be reasonable. You know that," she said.

"Hmph!" I said. I decided to just eat my lunch while they chattered on, talking about anything but our slowly shriveling business. My mind drifted back to Dylan's directives. *Go with the flow,* I told myself. *Stay cool.*

Fine.

After nearly an hour of costume and decorations chatter, the others finally decided to address the Cupcake Club agenda. I felt like I was about to burst from going with the flow!

"Sorry, Alexis." At least Emma had the decency to remember. "I know you wanted this to also be a Cupcake meeting," she said.

I shrugged, flowing (outwardly at least!).

"So when's the Mud Pie sample baking?" asked Emma.

"Let's do it this Friday at my house," offered Mia. I knew she was trying to make up for her previous lack of interest in the topic, but I wasn't going to be fooled.

"Okay. Have you finalized the order amount for the swim meet?" I asked her. I couldn't help myself. It had been keeping me up at night, worrying about it.

"No, not yet," said Mia casually. "But I will."

"When?" I asked.

Mia narrowed her eyes at me. "Later today. Is that okay, boss?"

I shrugged. "Whatever you want," I said.

"I'm just here to advise, not to boss." As much as I wanted to just let go and be cool, I couldn't. Instead I asked, "Do you know how much they'll be charging for the cupcakes at the fund-raiser?" That was the other thing that had been keeping me up at night.

"Why does that matter to us?" asked Mia, confused.

"Because that is a factor in where we set our wholesale price," I said. How could people not know something so obvious?

"Why?" asked Mia.

I sighed. *Stay cool, just stay cool,* I told myself. "Because if they are only going to charge a dollar and fifty cents for their cupcakes, we can't charge them a dollar and twenty-five cents wholesale. Then the margin is too small for them."

"What's a margin?" asked Katie.

"It's the difference between the buying and selling prices. The profit." I gritted my teeth, but I really wanted to scream. *Really, people? After all this time, you don't even know what a* margin *is?*

"Well, I don't know. But I do have a really cool idea for how to decorate them!" said Mia.

I sighed again. "How's the invoicing coming along?" I asked, turning to Emma. I didn't like to hear myself being such a taskmaster, but with all these loose ends that were driving me crazy, I had to carpe diem! (Seize the day! It's another one of my mottoes.)

Emma sat up straight in her chair. "Oh. Well, I started last night but . . . I felt really tired and went to sleep instead. I'll finish it tonight." She looked uncomfortable.

I was dying to ask if she'd even read my e-mail describing how to do it, but I restrained myself, thinking of Dylan's advice again.

Katie piped up. "I did do the ingredient inventory, though! We need to stock up on everything: eggs, flour, sugar—you name it. And I got your e-mail about the book club event. We're all set for that," she said, obviously proud of herself for being the only one who had actually done some work.

This made me relish bursting her bubble, cool or not.

"But, Katie, we have the swim meet to bake for that day, remember? And for inventory, I'm the one who has all the new stuff from BJ's. I have the new twenty-pound bags of flour and of sugar from last week. Remember? I said it in my e-mail."

Katie seemed to sink in her chair. "Oh."

I had to wonder if they ever read any of the

e-mail updates I sent out. It was starting to seem like they'd gotten in the habit of just ignoring them, knowing I'd take care of everything.

I didn't want my friends to hate me, but I was so incredibly frustrated. I knew it wasn't cool to care so much, but I couldn't help it. The three of them sat there, looking dejected and kind of lost.

"Well . . . anyone else heading home now?" I asked. But no one spoke up. "Then bye! See you later."

I was sure they'd be talking about me behind my back once I left, and I didn't feel so cool with that. Up ahead I spied Janelle Bernstein, my admittedly nerdy friend from science last year, who was also walking in the same direction. I was about to call out to her to wait up, but suddenly Dylan's words echoed in my mind. *Be friendly but not too friendly,* she had said. So I didn't call out. I walked out of the school alone, about twenty-five paces behind Janelle, and very, very lonely.

I decided I didn't want to walk home like I normally do, so I took the bus. Unfortunately, the dreaded girls of the PGC, the Popular Girls Club, decided that they were taking the bus that afternoon too. These girls are cool, and they sure didn't need a research report to tell them how to be that way. They're also mean. Or at least their leader, Sydney Whitman, is. The rest of them are just followers, I guess. Not too bad if you meet up with them somewhere random, one on one, but they're very intimidating in a group.

Anyway, they were, of course, discussing the parade, and everyone else on the bus was all ears. The PGC girls knew they were, and it seemed like they were kind of onstage, hamming it up for the less cool girls who were hanging on their every word.

"I'm going to get fitted for my fairy costume this week!" announced Sydney, as if it was the most solemn and important news of the year. "My mom is taking me into the city to a costume designer she knows, who works on all the big Broadway shows. They're going to hand make the costume—masses of shimmery green tulle and floaty layers. It's going to be breathtaking!"

The PGC girls sighed with envy, all starry-eyed. It was annoying. *Go with the flow, go with the flow,* I reminded myself. Was I uncool for thinking Sydney was taking this all waaay too seriously? If I were cool, would I be more organized and psyched for it myself?

"Have you asked you know who?" Callie

Wilson asked Sydney. My ears perked up. I might learn something since the boy aspect was, of course, the most interesting and stressful part of the parade for me.

You could have heard a pin drop on the bus as everyone awaited Sydney's answer. And we didn't even know who "you know who" was! I was tempted to ask the boy behind me for the time, just to show I didn't care. Except that I did care. So I stayed quiet.

I glanced up to see Sydney grinning, faking modesty. "You'll never believe it, but *he* asked *me!*"

I looked away quickly.

As if Sydney would ever have to ask a boy out, not with her long, white-blond hair and fashion-forward clothes and chic little posse of friends. Not to mention her steamroller attitude. If the boy she wanted hadn't asked her, then I'm sure she would have engineered a way to march with him in the parade. Even if it meant poisoning his date.

I was dying to know who it was.

"How about you? Did lover boy call yet?" Sydney asked Callie.

Oh no! I felt a surge of adrenaline. Sydney must mean Matt Taylor!

Callie also has a crush on Matt Taylor, and she and Sydney have engineered lots of "coincidental" (not!) meetings between the two of them, sometimes when I'm actually there. I think it's mostly Sydney, really. It's like she's Callie's agent, the way she pushes Callie at Matt. Emma doesn't think Matt likes Callie, but it's not like it's exactly bad news if you're a guy and one of the coolest and prettiest girls in the school is after you.

"No," Callie said, all quiet.

WHEW! I wanted to yell. But I didn't (staying very cool!), and I had no excuse to stick around since the bus had arrived at my stop. I stood up to get off.

Sydney had a shocked look on her face. "Then *you'll* just have to ask *him!*" she said to Callie.

"Me? Call Matt? And ask him myself?"

Aha! So it was Matt. The idea sickened me. I started to walk down the bus aisle to leave.

I was happy to see that Callie clearly didn't like Sydney's idea.

"If you don't, I will. And that will look worse!" said Sydney.

I glanced at Callie one last time as I left the bus. She looked stricken, like Sydney had slapped her. Which I guess she kind of had.

Sydney is really just a bully who likes to push people around, I thought for the millionth time. Well, she wasn't going to push me around too. I needed to do something to get Matt to agree to be my date. But what?

CHAPTER 5

Half Cool

$\mathscr{F}$riday afternoon, after finishing up some more pep rally decorations at school, we went to Mia's house for a baking session. I was feeling really disconnected from the other girls because I hadn't been sending them Cupcake e-mails and, I noticed, none of them had been e-mailing me about anything. I was starting to wonder if we'd still be friends if we didn't have the Cupcake Club. I also wondered if we'd still have the Cupcake Club if I wasn't running it. These were both nerve-wracking thoughts.

As we walked to Mia's, Callie caught up with us on the sidewalk and walked a few blocks with us. I noticed her looking over her shoulder, as if to make sure Sydney didn't see her. Sometimes Callie is friends with us because she and Katie were best friends growing up, and their moms are still best friends. It's hard for them. It's like they're friends when they're alone together but not in public.

I tried to act cool, which meant basically not talking. I hoped some other kids like Janelle would see me walking with Callie and assume I was cool, maybe even in the PGC too. I looked around, but no one seemed to notice or care.

Anyway, as we walked, the others were discussing our eighth grade math placement test, which had been really hard. Even Emma, who usually gets really good grades, had thought she bombed it. I, on the other hand, was pretty sure I had aced it. We hadn't gotten our schedules yet, so we didn't know who made it into math honors.

"How do you think you did, Alexis?" asked Callie, trying to gauge how well she did.

I don't like to brag about grades, but I'm usually honest with my friends. Except this was Callie, who was not my friend. "Oh, I . . ." I was about to say I was sure I'd be scheduled for Mr. Donnelly's math honors class when I remembered Dylan's advice: Get good grades, but never mention it. So I clammed up. "I did okay," I said, and shrugged. It felt so weird to give the impression that I was less prepared or less smart than I really am. It felt like I was wearing a shirt that was three sizes too small.

Callie nodded, probably assuming I'd be in regular math like the rest of them. If one of the other girls had pressed me, I might have told the truth. But I didn't want Callie to think I was a dork, so I just left it like that.

Naturally, the conversation next turned to Topic Number One: the pep rally and the costume parade.

"Sydney's got us all organized," said Callie. "She says we each have to have a date and a particular kind of costume." She laughed it off, but her eyes weren't smiling along with her mouth. "What are you guys doing?"

Katie and Mia took the lead, discussing their costume plans and Katie's potential date with either Joe or George. Katie announced that Chris had asked Mia to go with him, but that she hadn't accepted yet because she was waiting to hear if a guy she liked in the city might come.

I was mortified. This was all news to me! I looked at Emma to see if she'd known any of this stuff, and it was clear that she was totally up-to-date. I was the only one in the dark! I wasn't about to look clueless in front of Callie by asking all sorts of questions, but as we walked on, I started to get really, really mad. After all, I work my butt off to include everyone in the Cupcake Club on every decision and every plan. And now they go making all sorts of plans without me!

Then the worst part came.

"What about you two?" Callie asked me and Emma.

"Oh, um . . ." I had nothing to say. No costume plan, no marching partner who was a boy. Should I have just announced that I'm a hopeless loser and got it over with? Put myself out of my misery?

But then Emma said, "I'm marching with my brother. We're going to be wizards together."

My stomach dropped and my heart lurched. *Really?* I looked quickly at Callie's face to see if it showed any emotion, but she must've been really good at "going with the flow" because she just nodded and looked away, saying, "Cool. Well, I'm heading off here." We all said good-bye to her and kept on walking to Mia's.

Now I was getting madder than I already was. I dropped back behind the others and brooded. Emma had known I was dying to go with Matt, and now she'd asked him and planned a matching costume with him. Talk about an opportunist!

Maybe I just wouldn't go after all!

I walked in silence while Mia and Katie chattered away. After about half a block, Emma dropped back and fell into step beside me. Then she turned to me and said, "You know I was just saying that so she wouldn't ask him, right?"

"What?" I was still blazing with anger, so I couldn't quite process what Emma had said.

"I'm not marching with Matt. I just didn't want Callie to!" said Emma.

The truth dawned on me, and I could feel my whole mood turn around, all my gripes forgotten. "What? *Really?*" I yelled, totally elated now. "Emma, you're the best!" I grabbed her in a big hug, even though I'm not much of a hugger, and Katie and Mia turned to look at us in confusion as I swung Emma around like a rag doll.

"Stop! Enough! Put me down!" yelled Emma, and finally, I did.

"What's all this about?" asked Mia.

"Emma is not marching with Matt."

"But you'd better ask him before someone else tries to," said Emma, wagging her finger at me.

"Do you think Callie would do that? Even though she knows you're marching with him? Or thinks you are?" I asked.

Emma shrugged. "Maybe not. But Sydney would."

"Hmm. Good point," I said. I guess I wasn't out of the woods yet. Plus, Emma had said I'd need to ask him.

Gulp. I had to figure this out fast!

Mia hadn't requested any ingredients from me, and I hadn't brought any, so we had to kind of scrounge around her house for our ingredients. Luckily, her mom had bought supplies for some cookies she was baking for her clients, so there was enough flour and sugar and butter to go around.

I was irritated, though. I almost wished Mia hadn't had the supplies, just so everyone could see the importance of planning ahead and being organized. Instead, Mia managed to slide by without doing any of the usual prep work that I had to coordinate for our baking sessions.

We had three batches going: one of Mud Pie samples, one of swim meet samples, and one for the book club Katie had double booked for us.

We usually have to bake mini cupcakes for Mona's bridal shop every Friday, but thank goodness Mona was on vacation and her shop was closed. I don't think we could have handled another order.

While we baked, we played one of our favorite games. It was easier than having a real conversation. Less stressful.

"Okay . . . orange cream cheese frosting, cinnamon pumpkin cake, a few candy corns on top, and orange wrappers . . . ," said Mia.

"Jack-o'-lanterns, of course!" said Katie. "That's too easy."

"Or you could call them Halloweenies!" said Emma with a laugh.

I wanted to be lighthearted and go with the flow, but I was stressing about the other girls' lack of plans for our upcoming events. I searched for a conversational opening in order to bring it up. Finally, when Katie had stumped the others with a request to name "marble cake, marble frosting, marbleized cupcake wrappers," I jumped in.

"Hey, um, I'm just wondering, speaking of marbles . . . Um, maybe I'm losing mine . . . but, Mia, what did you say the plan is for the swim meet cupcakes?"

Mia was making the Mud Pie frosting with cocoa powder, sugar, and butter. It was hard work to mix it, and she was almost panting with the effort. "Well . . . ," she huffed. "I was thinking we'd do white cake, with silver wrappers, and"—*huff,*

185

puff—"swimming-pool blue frosting!" She paused to blow a lock of hair upward and out of her face. "And we'll lay them all out in the shape of a wave!" She smiled triumphantly at us.

"Cute!" said Emma.

I nodded. But Mia hadn't understood my question. I had to ask again.

"So, like, what are we charging them wholesale and how many cupcakes do we need and what's our unit cost? What's our timetable that day, now that we also have a book club to bake for?" I pressed, studiously avoiding looking at Katie, who was responsible for the double booking.

Mia stared up at the ceiling, like she was thinking. "Oh, I don't know. I'll confirm the cupcake count with them. For the wholesale price we can just kind of wing it, right?"

"Wing it?" I said. I felt like she wasn't speaking English. I just wasn't comprehending. I shook my head, as if I was clearing it.

"You know what I mean!" protested Mia. "They tell us the quantity and their retail price and then we can just back it out from there."

I shrugged. "I guess. That's not how we usually do it."

"But it will work, right?" said Mia.

Flow. Go with it. "Sure."

By the end of our baking session, we had reached a temporary truce, and I was feeling a little more included and up-to-date on everyone. We discussed Chris Howard. (Apparently Mia likes him but had been holding out to see if she could get a boy from her old school to come out for the pep rally. In the end she gave up because the travel logistics were too much.) So Mia said yes to Chris, and we joked that they could go as Angelina Jolie and Brad Pitt. We laughed really hard just thinking about it.

Katie told us she had decided to go with George because he had asked her first, and he was willing to dress up as an astronaut while she was a genie. They were just going as friends, even though "he'd like it to be more," according to Katie. We all whooped and hollered at that.

Emma and I looked at each other. "We'd better get cracking on this," she said quietly.

"I know. I guess I need Dylan's help," I said.

Emma knows Dylan almost as well as I do. "Oh no, it's come to that?" she joked.

"Unfortunately, yes," I said, and we laughed.

The first thing I did when I got home was attack Dylan and beg her to go to the Chamber Street

Mall with me the next day to work on my costume. I was surprised, but she readily agreed. It did make me wonder why she was so willing to help me. Was it because it looked bad for her to have a sister who was a dork? Was it because it was a fun hobby for her, making people over? Worst of all, was I such a dork that she felt sorry for me?

In any case, I was glad to have her help. I only hoped she wouldn't tire of the project and give up, leaving me only half cool. That was always a possibility.

Anyway, I decided to not ask too many questions but instead to just . . . you guessed it! Go with the flow!

But that night in bed, I tossed and turned, thinking about the pep rally parade and Matt, my costume, and the Cupcake Club jobs. At about one a.m., I decided that above all, I had to take charge of one thing: the costume. That way, even if I ended up marching with my grandma, at least I'd look good. Right?

CHAPTER 6

I Survived Shopping at Icon

The Chamber Street Mall is pretty big and pretty good. You have to have an idea of what you want before you go or you can waste lots of time going upstairs and down, back and forth.

Dylan had brainstormed a list of costume ideas, printed out a map of the mall at home, and made a plan of attack for all the shops we'd need to hit. My mom offered to take us, though I wasn't exactly psyched about that. First of all, it's not very cool to shop with your mom; even *I* know that. And second of all, whenever she and Dylan shop together, it turns into a war zone. They always fight about price, what's appropriate, how long it's taking to make a decision, and so on. The bottom line is: My mom hates to shop and Dylan loves it.

In the car, I looked over the list.

"Dylan, some of this is just . . . I mean, are you kidding me? Marilyn Monroe?"

"Oh, Dylly! No!" said my mom in alarm.

Dylan fumed. "Look, I was just brainstorming and trying to think of things that were kind of pretty and not too dorky."

"I'm all for dorky!" my mom said.

Dylan rolled her eyes at me from the front seat. (She always gets the front seat; it's not even a question.) "We know, Mom," she said.

"We'd better hear the rest of it," said my mom, skillfully piloting the car into the mall's parking lot.

"So . . . 'Marilyn Monroe, hippie chick, Pippi Longstocking'?" I read out. "Even *I* know that's dorky!"

"Oooh, I love that idea!" cried my mom "Braids and knee socks! With your red hair, it will be adorable!"

"Yuck!" I continued to read as we parked. "'Night sky' . . . What's that?"

"All black—leggings, long-sleeved T-shirt, socks, and shoes, and then silver or glow-in-the-dark star stickers all over," said Dylan.

"Hmm. That's kind of cool," I said. "'Cow girl, Gypsy, angel, cat'—kind of babyish, Dyl—'fairy . . .'

No can do," I said, thinking of Sydney.

"Fairy! That's it! That would be the best one!" said my mom enthusiastically. "Great idea, Dylly!" We all climbed out of the car, and my mom and Dylan collected their purses and my mom locked the car.

"I know," agreed Dylan. "Once I hit on that one, I almost just scrapped the rest of the list. It's pretty, it's current, and it has a lot of possible variations. . . ."

"And it is not happening," I said vehemently. "Sorry to burst your bubble."

They looked at me in shock. They'd been so engrossed in agreeing about this idea that they hadn't realized I wasn't on board.

"Why ever not?" asked my mom.

"Because," I said. It was too hard to explain, and also kind of humiliating.

"Don't write it off so quickly," said my mom. "We can look around at the other ideas, but keep this one in your back pocket. I'm sure we'll come back to it in the end."

Store number one was the costume store, and it was very picked over. There were a handful of interesting costumes left, but they'd obviously been tried on and shoved back into their plastic bags, so they looked kind of dirty and used. Plus, most of those store-bought costumes were kind of junky and uncomfortable. I wanted to make a bigger statement than just a little polyester and some funny glasses. My reputation might be riding on it.

We went to Big Blue, which is my favorite store. Dylan thought maybe we'd find some bell-bottom jeans and flowing tie-dyed shirts for a hippie look, but those styles were over, and everything was preppy.

"Ooh! How about a nerd?" said my mom, lifting up a plaid sweater vest.

Dylan and I looked at each other and then burst out laughing. "I don't need a *costume* for that, Mom!" I said.

"Don't be ridiculous, sweetheart," said my mom. But I knew from Dylan's silence that she agreed with me. She was just being polite because Mom was there.

We looked in the fabric store and in Claire's, just to get a feel for what they had. And finally we were at Icon, which is Dylan's favorite store in the world and my least favorite. The music is too loud, the aroma too strong, and the lighting too dark. It totally overloads my senses. Luckily, my mom feels the same way.

"Dylan, I think I'll just wait outside if you don't mind," said my mom.

Lucky!

"But, Mom!" Dylan pouted. I think she was hoping she'd hook my mom into buying her something, too, if she came in. I felt bad for Dylan, but I could totally relate to my mom.

"Why don't we do a preview scan, and then I'll get Mom to come look at our choices," I said. I always end up being the diplomat with these two.

They agreed, and in Dylan and I went.

Boom, boom went the music, and *blink, blink* went my eyes, and *GAG* went my throat, which was filled with tea-rose perfume and some other smoky scent I did not like.

"Isn't this great?" yelled Dylan. "Come over here where they keep the new stuff!"

Dylan and I turned a corner and almost crashed into Sydney and the rest of the PGC. Ugh.

I grabbed Dylan and tried to steer her down another aisle, but she was having none of it.

"Aren't those girls from your class?" she asked, rooted to the spot, refusing to budge.

I tried to drag her away. "Yes, but they're not my—"

"Hey, Alexis!" Callie called over the music.

"Hey," I said, suddenly feeling like a total dork to be shopping with my sister.

I saw Sydney shoot Callie a glare for saying hi to me, but then do a double take when she saw Dylan.

"Who have we here?" said Dylan, pouring on the charm all of a sudden. "Are you girls from Lexi's class?"

Oh gosh, why did she have to call me by my private family nickname in front of these girls?

Sydney narrowed her eyes and sized up Dylan. I could literally see her ticking things off a mental checklist. Cool outfit? Check. Pretty? Check. Good figure? Check. Only then did she put out her hand to introduce herself.

"Sydney Whitman," she said, tossing her blond hair in kind of a snotty, confident way.

Not to be outdone, Dylan took Sydney's hand and shook it, tossing her own hair. "Dylan Becker. You're the one who crashed my sweet sixteen," she said, regaining the upper hand. I saw Sydney cringe a little. *Yahoo! Score one for Dylan,* I thought. Maybe this wouldn't be all bad.

The other girls drew near, sensing their leader had respect for this new alpha female in their midst. I stuck close to Dylan's side, hoping some of the halo of her coolness would cast its protective light over me too.

Dylan and Sydney began a weird competitive shopping thing, where they'd each pull something out and show it to their little team (me and the PGC, respectively). They'd make comments about how you could accessorize it to make a total look. This was all well and good, but none of it was helping me find a costume.

"So, what are you girls dressing up as for the parade?" asked Dylan.

"Fairies," said Sydney breezily.

Dylan looked at me like *Gotcha!* "That's so funny! So is Lexi!"

But I shook my head emphatically. "No, actually. I'm not."

Sydney was staring at me like she'd just noticed me. She tilted her head to the side. "So what *are* you going as?" she asked. Everyone waited.

"Uhhhh . . . maybe . . . Marilyn Monroe?" I said.

"Cool!" said Callie. But Sydney shot her a look, and she shut up.

"But you have red hair!" said Sydney.

Suddenly there was someone standing beside me, saying, "Haven't you ever heard of a blond wig?" It was Mia!

I'd never been so happy to see someone in all my life, even if she did stink at scheduling and pricing. "Mia!" I cried, and I hugged her. Thank goodness she didn't act surprised by the hug, but instead hugged me back. I looked over her shoulder and saw her mom. "And Mrs. Valdes!" I cried. Another lifeline.

Mrs. Valdes said, "Alexis, *mi amor*," and double kissed my cheeks, European-style.

I turned to introduce Dylan and saw her and all of the PGC staring wide-eyed at Mrs. Valdes, who is gorgeous and probably the most chic person you'll ever meet in real life. She is a fashion stylist and always has on the latest styles, tweaked just so. Today she looked amazing in a riding outfit: black leggings, knee-high brown-and-black boots, and a longish fitted blazer with slanted pockets and a velvet collar. Her hair was in a bun, and she had on big gold knots for earrings.

"What are you up to?" I asked.

"Costumes, of course! I'm here to find a base for my witch dress that my mom can have Hector sew things onto," said Mia. Hector is Mrs. Valdes's kind of sewing wizard. He makes samples and stuff for her.

"Cool!" I said, remembering Mia's sketch from the Cupcake meeting.

"Do you need help too, *mi amor*?" asked Mrs. Valdes. "You know I love to dress gorgeous red-heads!" She always makes a big deal about loving my hair, even though I don't see at all why.

Dylan nudged me, looking at Mrs. Valdes

"Oh, duh! Sorry! Mrs. Valdes, this my sister, Dylan." I said.

"Of course, darling. Dylan, Mia just adores you, and I remember seeing photos from your fabulous party," she said, shaking Dylan's hand. "I love your outfit!"

Dylan actually blushed and smiled. "I've heard a lot about you, Mrs. Valdes. Alexis loved being in your wedding!"

I glanced at the PGC and saw they were hanging on their every word.

"Let's go look at the dresses in the back!" said Mia. She linked her arm through mine and pulled me away.

It looked like Mrs. Valdes thought we might introduce her to the PGC, but through unspoken agreement, Mia and I knew we would not.

"Bye!" we said, and we wiggled our fingers at them as we walked away. Dylan was now in an animated conversation with Mia's mom about hemlines and trends.

It wasn't long before Mrs. Valdes and Dylan had pulled a bunch of dresses for me and Mia to try. Mrs. Valdes was enthusiastic about one of them in particular for me. It was long and white and flowy in a fabric called jersey. I don't know if she was thinking Marilyn Monroe too or what she had in mind, but I wasn't about to second-guess a professional. Mia and I squeezed into the tiny, dark dressing room together and tried on the things.

Once I had on the white dress, I stepped outside. It was hard to see because it was so dark. I walked to the end of the hall and stood in front of a mirror under a lone spotlight.

"Oooh! *Yes!*" Mrs. Valdes clapped her hands and strode over to my side. Dylan followed.

Dylan was sizing me up. "It is very flattering," she agreed. "But not exactly Marilyn Monroe. Not at that length. Are you thinking we would shorten it?"

Meanwhile, the PGC had walked up and were waiting on a newly formed line for a fitting room. They too were sizing me up and whispering. I cringed. Then I thought of Commandment Three (since I've memorized them all): *In public, pretend that you do not care about the following: what you wear, how you look, who likes you. (But in private, DO pay close attention to these things.)* I tossed my hair and stood stock-still while Mrs. Valdes and Dylan brainstormed.

"I'm thinking maybe snow princess!" said Dylan.

"Love it!" said Mrs. Valdes She tapped her chin with her finger. "Or . . ." She gathered the fabric at my left and right shoulders and bunched it together, so it looked like thick straps. "Hector can gather and sew these, and we can pin on some vintage brooches and make her a Greek goddess!"

"Yes!" yelled Dylan.

I could tell the PGC was straining to hear what we were saying. I smiled smugly at them, like a real snow princess, or an ice princess for that matter, and let them wonder what we were discussing.

Then Mia came out, and I relinquished my spot and watched her get the Dylan-and–Mrs. Valdes treatment. By now the line had gotten shorter, and the PGC was within earshot.

"Hop back up, honey," Mrs. Valdes said to me, "and let's get another look, so Dylan and I can figure out the accessories." She began list-ing: strappy tie-up Roman sandals, a garland of greens for my hair, a gold lamé belt . . .

"Won't all that turn Matt's head!" said Dylan enthusiastically.

Wait, what?

"Matt who?" said Sydney while I was still stand-ing there in shock.

Dylan turned to her. "Matt Taylor, of course! Lexi's marching with him in the parade!"

I turned every shade of red at that moment. I sneaked a peek at Callie, and she was red too.

"Wait, *the* Matt Taylor?" said Sydney, mad all of a sudden.

"The one and only!" singsonged Dylan. "You know he and Alexis have always been close."

I was speechless. *Oh gosh, Dylan. What have you done?* I thought. *Play it cool. Go with the flow.* But the flow had turned into a tidal wave!

Sydney turned to Callie and whispered furi-ously into Callie's ear.

"But I never had a chance!" protested Callie. And Sydney whispered again.

The only part I caught was "a dork like her!" I knew she meant me.

Callie eyed me guiltily.

"Tonight!" commanded Sydney, and Callie jumped.

Then their number was called, and they hustled into their fitting room, all four of them, like sardines in a can. I was left with my bubble totally burst, feeling like the least powerful goddess on Mount Olympus.

CHAPTER 7

Style Versus Substance

The rest of the Icon expedition was a blur. I hurried out of my costume and ran outside to tell Mom we found something. I wanted to go wait in the car, but Dylan said that would be rude to Mrs. Valdes, who was going to help us find the rest of the accessories, and my mom said it was dangerous for kids to stay in parking lots alone.

So I hid behind a planter.

I heard the PGC come out of the store, and I flattened myself, hoping they weren't coming my way. I was furious at Dylan! How could she have blurted out a lie like that about me and Matt? But worst of all was hearing Sydney call me a dork.

I mean, I know it's kind of true. Look, I like

school and don't mind homework. And I really don't care that much about things like school dances and pep rallies. It's just hard to hear it said out loud like that, plain as day. Especially from someone like Sydney. Especially when it's said with anger. I really wanted to cry. I wondered if Dylan heard Sydney say it. If she did, she ignored it.

Thank goodness the PGC went in the other direction, and then my mom and Mia and Dylan and Mrs. Valdes were soon upon me. Dylan and Mrs. Valdes were chattering happily and my mom and Mia were commiserating about Icon and how overwhelming it is.

I wanted to get Mia alone and ask her what I should do. I knew she would know. The truth about Mia is, she actually had a chance to be in the PGC. But she chose us, the Cupcake Club, instead. I always appreciated that about her, but it also gave her a social standing that was a little above the rest of us, which I sometimes liked and sometimes hated. On the plus side, it made her kind of our senior advisor when it came to social stuff. She was just good at it and a little more savvy. It's probably because she grew up in the city before she lived here.

In the shoe store, while Dylan scouted the sale

area for appropriate goddess sandals, Mia pulled me aside.

"Listen, I heard what happened in there. It's not your problem. You weren't the one who said it. No one could hold you to it."

I wondered if she'd heard Sydney call me a dork too. I could feel my eyes welling up with tears, but I didn't want to cry here. It was unprofessional. What if a client saw me? I sniffed and took a deep breath, then I touched my cuff to each eye to blot the tears.

Mia put her hands on my shoulders and looked at me carefully. "There is one radical thing you could do to make this all better," she said.

"What?" I croaked.

"Ask Matt to march with you."

"Oh, for goodness sake!" That wasn't the answer I wanted to hear.

"I'm serious, though. I know he'd say yes. He likes you, Alexis," she said.

No way. I shook my head. "I could never," I said. "What if he said no?"

"Even if he said no, which I doubt he would, I think he's smart enough and nice enough not to just say no, you know? He'd say something like, 'Oh man, I told Joe I'd march with him and be Tweedledee and Tweedledum' or something. . . ."

I had to laugh at that image and at Mia's imitation of him talking. Mia laughed too. "At the very least he's a good guy. He wouldn't embarrass you," she said. "And no one would have to know."

I thought about it. Would Matt tell Emma? Would he tell Callie? I pictured him saying, *Oh sure, Callie. You'll save me from going with that dork Alexis.*

"Alexis!" Mia said. "Come on! Just think about it. Anyway, you know you'll be looking great!"

With that we rejoined the shopping party and put together the rest of the things Mia and I needed for our costumes.

That night at the dinner table, Dylan could not stop raving about Mrs. Valdes and how cool she was.

"Would you like to trade moms?" asked my mom. "Because I'm going to start getting a complex!"

"But she's so chic! Imagine having someone so stylish living in your very own house! Imagine having access to her closet! I can't believe Mia doesn't just go hog wild every day!" said Dylan.

My mom and I rolled our eyes at each other, and my dad slurped his soup, oblivious.

"Mia is very cool too," said Dylan. "Not quite as cool as Sydney and her gang, but cool. Alexis, why don't you try to hang out more with those girls? They know what cool is."

"I *have* friends. And, anyway, the PGC are not nice. In fact, they're horrible, and they treat people badly. You know that," I said. Then I added, "Plus, I'd be friends with Mia even if she wasn't cool."

"That's your problem right there," said Dylan. "You have no standards. Don't sell yourself short. You and Mia could be friends with those girls. I don't know about Emma and Katie. You'd probably have to ditch them. They're kind of just luggage, but you two should go for it."

I winced. How could she say that about Emma and Katie?

My dad stopped slurping. "Dylan, you've got to be kidding me. Are we talking about Alexis's dearest friends as if they were slabs of beef?"

Dylan looked indignant. "I'm just trying to help," she said.

"You're not helping," said my dad. "Case closed."

"Whatever," said Dylan. And she finished her dinner in silence.

That night I heard my dad trudge up the stairs and give Dylan his old style-versus-substance lecture. We'd all heard it a few times, and it was about how to value the important things in life and how not to follow trends or overvalue superficial things. When he said it, it always made sense, but as soon as he walked away, you could feel yourself weakening and slipping back into bad habits almost immediately.

In my room, I sat there stressing, wondering whether Callie had called Matt yet to ask him out. Or if, in fact, she would. I couldn't stop thinking about it. Only one thing would distract me from all this, and I wasn't supposed to do it. But my fingers itched to get on the keyboard and organize. Finally, I couldn't resist doing a little research for the swim meet job. After all, Mia and her mom had been so nice and helpful to me today, the least I could do was repay the favor, right?

First, I went online to see if I could get a sense of how many people showed up for these regional swim meets. After some searching and doodling of numbers, I figured out an average of about one hundred and twenty attendees. That would mean about ten dozen cupcakes. We'd have to get up really early next Saturday to get that going, and we'd probably have to bake at Emma's because they have two ovens. I'd have to bring over the flour, sugar, eggs, and butter when I went, but it was worth it because baking at Emma's could mean a Matt sighting! My stomach clenched at the idea of him. Was Callie calling him right now? Would he find out what Dylan had told the PGC about us marching together? I decided I'd better warn Emma, in case it did get back to him, so she could defend my honor. I picked up the phone and dialed the Taylors', absentmindedly clicking through the regional swim meet photos on my computer.

Suddenly something occurred to me as I looked at all those photos of people in their bathing suits and the steamy windows in the big indoor pool rooms. It was going to be hot in there! And one thing that doesn't do well in the heat is buttercream frosting!

"Darn it!" I said out loud, just as someone picked up at the Taylors'.

"Uh, hello?"

It was Matt!

Oh no . . . I wanted to hang up! But caller ID! He would know it was me! What should I do?

"Hello? Alexis?"

Oh NO! He *did* know it was me!

"Uh, oh, hi. Matt?"

"Yup. What were you saying when I picked up?" he asked, sounding confused.

"Oh, nothing. Just . . . I just realized something bad on my computer right then, so . . ."

This was so awkward. My adrenaline surged. Should I just ask him? Right now? Should I do it? YES.

"Um, anyway, I was wondering—"

"Hello? Alexis?" It was Emma. She'd picked up on another phone!

"Oh, hey! Hi! There you are!" I said with relief. I felt like I was climbing down from the high dive, legs all shaky.

"Well, bye," said Matt.

"Oh, okay. Bye, Matt," I said.

"What's up?" asked Emma.

And then I started to laugh like a maniac, and I couldn't stop. It was giddy laughter, which was better than crying. I realized I couldn't tell Emma the story now—not over the phone. Not when there was a chance Matt might pick up and hear his name and stay on to listen. That's what I'd do, anyway, if it were me, whether or not it's cool.

"Okaaay . . . ," said Emma. "So why did you call, exactly?"

I didn't want to tell her about the cupcakes that would melt at the swim meet, and I didn't want to tell her about being called a dork at the mall, and I didn't want to tell her how much I loved her brother and hated my sister, even though I *did* want to tell her all of that. So I just decided to go with the flow. I said, "No reason. Just called to say hi."

"Okay. Hi," she said. And then we both started laughing really hard. Emma really is my best friend.

Luggage. Hmph!

CHAPTER 8

A Flirting Failure

At our pep rally committee meeting on Monday, Mia and I filled the Cupcake Club in on what had happened at the mall. I apologized profusely to Emma for putting her and/or Matt in an awkward position, but she waved it off.

"Anyway, he'd probably think it was funny, girls fighting over him at Icon. Hard to imagine old Stink Foot generating that kind of adoration," she said with a laugh.

"So did, uh . . . did Callie call him?" I ventured.

"Nope. Not as far as I know. I can scroll through caller ID when I get home and find out for sure."

"Thanks," I gushed. I was relieved, but not totally relieved. I wouldn't be until I knew for sure. Now I had to think about whether I was going to ask him myself. And if so, how and when?

Just then Chris Howard walked by with his friends, and he and Mia waved and smiled at each other.

"I'm so jealous of your love life," said Emma sadly.

"Don't be. It's not love. It's just a little bit of like," said Mia, all cool.

"On your part," said Katie knowledgeably.

"Well, whatever."

"At least you have someone to march with. Alexis and I are going to be stuck marching together," said Emma.

"Well . . ." I actually wasn't planning on marching with Emma if I couldn't find anyone. I had promised myself that if it came to that, I just wouldn't go. Better to be thought a fool than to show up and prove it. That's another one of my mottoes.

"Wait, you *are* going to march with me, right? I mean, if these girls have dates, who else would I go with?" she asked, gesturing at Katie and Mia.

I decided to turn it into a joke. "It depends on your costume," I said.

"I'm being a hippie," said Emma.

I tapped my chin and acted like I was evaluating

her idea. She swatted me and said, "Shut up! You know we're marching together, so just stop!"

Not if I can help it, I thought, but I didn't say it aloud. Cool Commandment Four rolled through my mind: *Do not be too accessible . . . say you have plans, even if you do not.*

It was time to change the subject.

"Hey, so, um, getting back to my favorite topic . . ."

"Matt or the Cupcake Club?" said Mia wryly, and the others laughed.

I tossed my head and then sat up straight. "The club, of course. Jeez. Anyway, I know it's not my project or anything, but it's going to be pretty hot at the swim meet, you know? So I was wondering, is butter cream the best option?"

The others looked at me blankly.

"Because, you know, it will probably melt and then slide off," I added.

"Oh," said Mia. "Well. I already agreed on the recipe and the price with them."

"What price?" I asked. I couldn't help myself. She should have checked with me before she agreed to anything.

"One dollar a unit?" Mia didn't sound confident.

"One dollar a unit? But we never make

cupcakes for that price! It's always at least a dollar and twenty-five cents! We'd be losing money at one dollar a unit! This isn't a volunteer organization! What are they selling them for?" I tried not to lose my cool, but I felt like my head was going to pop off.

"Three dollars each?" said Mia sheepishly.

"So they make two dollars a cupcake and we lose money? That is a nightmare. We should be splitting the profit, which is standard in almost any industry, or at the very least taking twenty-five percent." I put my head in my hands. I knew something like this was going to happen!

I looked up, and the other three Cupcakers were glancing nervously at one another.

"Can you fix it?" Mia asked finally.

"Look. I'll figure something out. Just . . . next time, make sure you check first. Or, sorry—you should be making the decisions on your own, but at least consult the e-mails I sent you with the overview of how everything runs, okay?"

Mia nodded. "Sorry," she said.

"I liked it better when you were in charge, I think," said Emma.

"Yeah, well . . ." I wanted to say, *So did I.* But I didn't. It wouldn't have been cool.

The rest of the week was a blur of doing but not doing Cupcake Club work, avoiding the FBLA decision and Mr. Donnelly, dodging the PGC, reading the articles Dylan clipped for me from magazines (if *Teen Magazine* tells me to "be a free spirit," which I'm totally not, but also to "always be true to yourself," then which is it?), and relentlessly checking in with Emma to make sure Callie hadn't called Matt. It was stressful, to say the least.

By the end of the week, all I wanted was to curl up in my room with a good Cupcake Club work-sheet in front of me and relax. But it was not to be.

On Friday afternoon we went to Emma's to bake for the book club job Katie had taken on. We decided we'd wake up early on Saturday to bake for the swim meet. Matt wasn't going to be home, according to Emma, so I felt a little more relaxed when we got there, but also a little less psyched than normal.

The book club order wasn't that big of a job, and they'd requested one of our old standbys, caramel cupcakes with bacon frosting, so it would be easy for us to make. The only problem was that Katie had forgotten to do the preshopping for the ingredients, and there was no bacon at the Taylors'.

"Okay, well . . . I guess a quick bike ride to the Quickie Mart to buy some bacon is in order," I said. I wasn't going to volunteer. It wasn't me who had forgotten.

"I'll go. It's my fault," said Katie. "Could I have some Cupcake Club money, please?"

I looked at Emma. "Our account is empty. But Emma must have received the payments on those invoices she sent, right?"

Emma looked sheepish. "Um. I haven't had a chance to send them yet. Honestly, Alexis! I don't know how you do it! Between flute practice and baking and dog walking . . . there just isn't time!"

I shrugged. "You have to make time," I said.

Everyone sat there looking morose.

Finally, I sighed. I wanted to teach these people a lesson, but I also didn't want to run the Cupcake Club into the ground.

"Fine. Look, I always keep a cushion of cash for the business. It's called capital. You aren't supposed to use it except maybe, maybe in an emergency. I guess this is a small emergency." I reached into my book bag and pulled out a portfolio-style wallet.

Inside I had bank envelopes filled with bills of different denominations.

"Wow, Alexis, how much is in there?" asked Katie.

"We've saved a hundred dollars. I think we probably only need to take out ten right now, for the bacon, unless there's anything else you think we might need. What about tomorrow, Mia?" I asked. I didn't want to be the taskmaster, but this was getting ridiculous.

Mia bit her lip and looked at the ceiling, as if mentally reviewing her list. "Actually, we could use some silver foil cupcake papers," she said.

I sighed, then took another ten out of an envelope. I closed the wallet and then put it away. "Who's got a safe place to put this for the bike ride?" I asked.

Just then we heard the Taylors' back door open. My heart leaped! Matt! But it wasn't. It was Emma's oldest (and some say cutest, but not me) brother, Sam.

"Hey, Cupcakers," he said, throwing his backpack into his locker in the mudroom. (Yes, the Taylors have lockers, just like at school.) He took off his baseball cap, running his fingers through his wavy blond hair.

"Hi, Sam!" said Mia and Katie in unison, all perky. They love him. Mia batted her eyelashes at him, and Katie grinned a megawatt smile.

Emma's eyes narrowed with a plan. "Sammy? Could you take us to the Quickie Mart to get some bacon? Please, please, please? It would save us so much time!"

Sam was pulling food out of the fridge to make a salad or a huge hero or something. All the Taylor boys do is eat, I swear! He looked down at his ingredients, then he said, "I guess so. I could probably use some more mayo. Will you save me some cupcakes as payment?" he asked, his bright blue eyes twinkling.

Katie and Mia couldn't promise him fast enough.

"Then let's go!" he said.

Being annoyed with everyone and having just arrived, I really didn't feel like going. Emma had to go, because it was her brother taking them. And Mia and Katie would not miss an opportunity to be seen driving anywhere with Sam Taylor, even if it was only on a bacon errand.

"I'll just stay here and start the batter," I said.

"Okay. Be right back!" called Emma.

I know the Taylors' kitchen as well as I know my own. I could reasonably show up and prepare a three-course meal there without anyone batting an eye, so I felt totally comfortable being left there by myself, especially knowing no one else was due back for a while. I turned on the TV to watch a rerun of my favorite dancing show, *Celebrity Ballroom*, and I quickly whipped up the batter in Emma's pride and joy: her pink KitchenAid stand mixer. I then ladled the batter into the cupcake liners that Emma had on hand. We were only making four dozen cupcakes today, so it was pretty fast and easy. When I'd finished, I put them in the oven and then began to wash the dishes, turning up the TV volume to hear over the water.

Between the hiss of the water from the faucet and the dance music blaring out of the TV, I didn't hear anyone come in. So when I heard someone call my name right beside me, I screamed and jumped about ten feet in the air.

"Sorry!" said Matt, hands in the air, backing away. "I didn't mean to scare you!"

I turned off the water and stood there shaking, my wet hands over my heart, which was pounding.

"TV's a little loud too, don't you think?" he asked, laughing as he turned down the volume.

"You scared me to death!" I said. I hate being scared. It always makes me feel cranky afterward. Somehow, today my annoyance negated my usual nervousness around Matt. I only felt mad.

"Smells good in here," said Matt, sniffing appreciatively.

I nodded. "Book club job," I said. "Caramel and bacon."

"Oh, those are one of my favorites! I love that bacon-caramel combo! Are you going to have any extras?" he asked hopefully.

Between the disorganized club members (not me) and the terrifying scare I'd just had, I was not in a nice mood. "Well, we already have to give some to Sam for driving to the Quickie Mart to buy bacon. I don't know how many they promised him, but we can't just keep giving away our profits like this . . . ," I said without thinking.

"Oh, hey, no problem. Sorry. I wouldn't want to eat up all your profits . . . ," said Matt, and he turned to leave the room.

Oh no. I suddenly realized I'd just been really mean. After all, there I was, taking over his kitchen, without his sister even being there, baking with his family's supplies, saying his brother could have some cupcakes but he couldn't. And worst of all, I was not being cool. I was caring way too much and being uptight and definitely not being a free spirit.

"Wait! Sorry! I'm sorry, Matt. That was really rude. I just . . . of course you can have some cupcakes. I love that you love them!" Ugh. Did I really just say that? Uncool!

"No, I get it. I totally understand. You guys are trying to run a business, so . . . that's chill. I'm just going to finish a design I've been working on. Later!" And he left the room.

I sat down heavily in a chair. *Why am I such a dork?* I thought, staring into space. *Why can I not know the right things to say or do at the right times?* Callie would have immediately turned that whole thing into a major flirt session. She would have said, *For you, Matt, anything! I'll save you the best ones, with extra bacon!* Then she would have flipped her hair and smiled a big sparkly smile at him. I, on the other hand, squashed all of Matt's friendliness and enthusiasm, turned him down, and barked at him in his own home.

I wanted to die.

CHAPTER 9

The CEO in the FBLA

$\mathcal{M}$att didn't come downstairs again before I left that Friday. I told the others sort of vaguely what had happened, and I set aside three cupcakes on a plate for Matt, kicking in three of my own dollars to make up for it. I felt awful.

The next morning, as I headed to Emma's to bake for the swim meet, I half hoped I'd see him and half feared it. Luckily, he was at cross-country practice when we arrived, and I was quickly swept up in all the work that needed to be done.

After thinking over the options on unit price, I'd decided we just needed to make the cupcakes a little smaller than usual. Instead of filling each wrapper three-quarters of the way with batter, we'd just fill them halfway, leaving us with cakes that were level with the tops of the wrappers once they were baked, rather than puffing into big, muffinlike crowns.

Mia was willing to agree to anything to redeem herself, and Emma and Katie were fine with the somewhat skimpy cupcakes.

"Never again, though!" I said as we filled the cupcake wrappers.

"Never!" promised the others.

Then Katie spoke up: "Alexis, um, we've been talking about it and . . . we think the Cupcake Club runs a lot better when you're in charge."

I looked up in surprise. Emma and Mia were nodding.

"We know it's a lot of work for you . . . ," Emma added.

"Actually, I don't know how you fit it all in!" said Mia.

"But we'd like to ask you to officially be our CEO," Katie finished.

"The boss!" said Emma, laughing.

"We really can't do it unless you run it," said Mia.

Of course I was thrilled to receive such acknowledgment. But I wasn't willing to accept so easily.

"Thanks," I said. "That's really nice. I do love it.

For me, it's as fun as . . . fashion design is for Mia! It's just, it does take a lot of time. And I hate always being the bad guy, the taskmaster."

The other girls were quiet while we filled cupcake wrappers and mixed frosting and thought about it.

"Maybe we need some flow charts or something. Like a company structure, where each of us has the same job all the time and we know how it needs to be done and when, and on a regular basis," suggested Mia.

"Yeah. It's too bad we can't send you to business school, Alexis!" Katie joked.

"I wish!" I said. But then suddenly, I thought of the FBLA. "Actually . . . Mr. Donnelly invited me to join the Future Business Leaders of America at school," I said. I felt like I was bragging by telling them. I was also nervous they'd think I was taking all the credit for the club or, worse, that it was too dorky to even consider doing. I regretted my words as soon as they left my mouth.

But I wasn't expecting the reactions I got!

Mia was so impressed. She said a high school girl who interned for her mom last summer had been a member of the FBLA in middle school, and that was where the girl learned everything she knew about business—and she knew a lot. Emma thought it was an honor to be asked. And Katie said, "I think I'm speaking for all of us when I say, first of all, congratulations. And second of all, it would be an honor to have you represent the Cupcake Club! You deserve it!"

We hadn't heard Matt come in (that guy sure is quiet). But suddenly he was there, saying, "Who's being congratulated? And who's representing the Cupcake Club in what?"

He sat at the kitchen table and began to pull off his sneakers, his light hair sweaty and matted, his dimples appearing in his cheeks as he grimaced. He looked gorgeous and strong and fit.

"Ew! Get out of here, Stinky!" said Emma.

"No, Emma, it's fine!" I said, quick to defend Matt.

"We were just congratulating Alexis," said Mia. "She's—"

"It's nothing," I interrupted. Dylan's words about social death floated through my mind. Could I join the FBLA and keep it a secret?

But Katie wouldn't be hushed. "Alexis was asked by Mr. Donnelly to join the Future Business Leaders of America at school! Isn't that great?"

I wanted to die. There was no flow to go with,

no way to act cool. Matt now knew for sure that I was a dork. It was curtains for me. I couldn't even look up.

"Wait, is that the thing where you get to go to the conference in the city at the end of the year?" asked Matt.

I looked at him and nodded miserably, bracing myself for a snide comment.

But instead Matt said, "Wow! That is so cool! Will you tell me if you learn anything I can use for my graphic design business?" Matt designs things on the computer for people (including the Cupcake Club), like flyers, signs, campaign posters—stuff like that.

At first I thought he might be teasing me, but he wasn't even smiling. He was dead serious. "Sure," I said.

"It's gonna be so interesting. You're lucky!" Matt got up and then walked into the mudroom. He flipped his sneakers into his locker, then went to wash his hands.

"And thanks for the cupcakes last night, Alexis. You didn't need to do that," he said, his back to me as he stood at the sink. I couldn't see his face.

I quickly looked at Emma. She shrugged and smiled. So she must've told him they were from me.

"Oh, no problem. I just . . . I know you like them so . . ." I tried to channel Callie and the other PGCs. It didn't feel right, but I went for it. "I made those especially for you, with extra bacon. I hope they were okay!" I blushed. I couldn't believe I'd been so flirty.

Matt turned around with a big smile on his face. "Thanks. Any more today?"

"No!" interrupted Mia. "Alexis is being very stern about our unit price and our markup. If we give any of the swim team's cupcakes away, the boss lady is going to dock our pay," she teased.

But I was mortified. "Oh, come on. Surely we could spare a couple of cupcakes for Matt!"

"Uh-uh. You said so!" said Katie. "Sorry, pal!"

But luckily Matt was laughing. "How much profit would I be eating if I had one?"

Everyone looked at me expectantly. I couldn't help myself. I quickly did the calculations in my head. "One dollar's worth. Or about three percent. It's fine, though," I insisted. "I'll cover it for the swim team."

"Nope! Every penny counts! Especially for future business leaders! Hey, maybe you should go as Donald Trump for the costume parade!" Matt cackled.

I froze. Matt had mentioned the parade. Here was my big opening! But could I really ask him on a date in front of all these people, including his own sister, my best friend? I thought of Dylan and all her advice. *Don't be too accessible* and *Have a good guy friend* were kind of canceling each other out right here. I knew she'd want me to march with Matt. But would it be cool if *I* asked *him*? Not so much.

While I stood there thinking, Emma piped up, "What are you doing for the parade, Matty?"

"Ah, you know I hate that stuff, I'm not going," he said, turning away to grab a bag by the door.

What?!

Luckily, Emma wasn't going to let him get away with that. "You can't hate it! It's a rite of passage! You've got to go!"

"Nah," he said. "Not for me. See ya!" And he left the room to go upstairs.

I looked at Emma after he left. I was aghast. "What do we do now?" I asked.

"I was waiting for you to ask him!" she said.

"Why should I ask him? You should have asked him! He's your brother!"

"Exactly! And if I do the asking, he'll say no. It's got to be you!"

"Why is this so hard?" I wailed, and covered my face.

Just then the timer went off for the first batches of cupcakes, and we had to get the next ones in. Time was ticking away. I snapped into action. Anything to distract myself from yet another missed opportunity. We flipped the cupcakes out onto the cooling racks and began filling the cupcake pans with new liners, being careful not to burn ourselves on the metal trays. It wasn't until I started ladling in the batter that something occurred to me.

"Emma," I said quietly. "If Matt isn't going to the pep rally parade, then Callie doesn't have a chance. Even if she does ask."

Emma looked at me like I was an idiot. "First of all, that doesn't solve any of our problems. We still have no one to march with. Second of all, don't you know he's just saying that? He's either too shy or too lazy to ask someone himself. But you can bet if someone asks him, he'll say yes."

Huh. "I guess you really do know boys," I said.

"Occupational hazard," Emma said with a shrug. "But I had another idea. I think you should ask him if he and Joe Fraser want to walk with you and me. Then it's like a group thing and not so date-y, which I know bothers you."

"It doesn't bother me. I just . . . I'm nervous, that's all."

"Well, the next time you see him, you have to ask him, okay?" she said. "It's only a week away, and I know for sure he doesn't have a costume of any sort. We can't let that become an excuse for him to not go. Okay? Pinkie promise?"

Ugh. I hate to pinkie promise, because then it means I have to do whatever dreaded thing I've promised to do. "Fine," I said, irritated. "Now let's focus on this swim team thing!"

CHAPTER 10

Take a Dive

It felt good to be back in business, especially in the driver's seat. I ran the rest of our morning like a drill sergeant, but a nice drill sergeant. I tried not to be bossy, and the others tried not to mind when I was.

We got the bacon cupcakes assembled and delivered to the book club. Then we rushed back to the Taylors' to frost and pack the swim team cupcakes. At the last minute I grabbed the extra frosting and a bunch of plastic knives, and stuck them in my insulated tote bag. You never know.

Mia's stepbrother, Dan, picked us up in her mom's Mini Cooper, to give us a ride to the town's pool, where the meet was being held. It was pretty tricky fitting all us girls and all those cupcakes into the car. Suddenly (with visions of cupcakes splattered on the pavement) I called my dad and asked him to come in the Suburban. I sent the other three ahead with the first load and took three cupcake carriers and waited for my dad on the Taylors' driveway.

My dad pulled up quickly, and we loaded the Suburban and safely stowed the cupcakes, then headed out to the town's pool.

"Any extras?" my dad asked hopefully. My mom keeps us on a major health-food diet, so my dad is always looking for any little crumb of junk food he can get his hands on.

"Sorry, Dad, not today," I said. "It would be bad business. Our margins are too tight as it is. I'll make another batch soon, though, and save you some," I said, thinking of Matt.

"Hey, I meant to ask you, what did you ever decide to do about that business club at school?" he said, taking his eyes off the road to glance sideways at me.

I looked away, staring out the window. "Oh, I don't know. I'm not sure it's for me . . . ," I said. But I thought of Matt's reaction as I said it.

"Listen, sweetheart, I think you should go for

it. Don't listen to Dylan. It would be a wonderful experience for you," he said.

"It would officially make me a dork," I said. "With no hope of ever being considered cool."

"That's ridiculous. Being cool is a state of mind. As long as you're cool with who you are, you'll be fine," he said.

"Easy for you to say," I said.

"Well, you're right. But it's much more important to follow your passions and to be true to yourself. I mean look at all the people who didn't follow convention and who went on to do great things. Innovators, like Steve Jobs, Bill Gates, Jim Henson . . ."

"I know, I know," I said.

"The list of leaders is endless. And it's cool to lead. It's not cool to follow, to do what other people tell you to, or what you think other people think you should do. Does that make sense?"

"I guess. But Dylan . . ."

"Look at Dylan! A perfect example," said my dad. "Do you see her following anyone?"

I shook my head. "No. I guess not."

"So, there you go. Why should you follow her? Or anyone? Just follow your heart, follow your passions. Go for what excites you!" he said.

We pulled into the parking lot and then jumped out to get the cupcakes.

"Thanks for saving the day, Dad," I said, and I gave him a big hug.

"Anytime!" he said, kissing the top of my head.

Inside, it was hot and humid, just as I'd suspected. I reached the table where the other girls had been directed to set up the cupcakes, and I found them in a panic.

"Alexis! Thank goodness you're here! Look!" cried Mia.

She had arranged the cupcakes in a wave design, just as she'd planned. The pale blue frosting was pretty, and it did look kind of like a wave. Except for one thing. All the icing was sliding off the cupcakes from the heat.

"Oh," I said. "Okay. Well . . . let me think."

Emma stood there wringing her hands while Katie bit her lip and Mia hyperventilated. I looked around the room. It was starting to fill up. We didn't have time to go home and rethink this. I watched a kid dive off a diving board into the water, his hands slicing the surface, but his body leaving not a ripple on the water. Pretty amazing, those divers, headfirst . . .

"I've got it!" I said suddenly, snapping my fingers as it came to me. I began calling out orders.

"Emma, we have to get Matt to do a quick poster for us, in bright blues and greens. Just type. It needs to say, 'Take a Dive with the Swim Team's Cupcakes!' Okay? Can you call him and ask him to do that for us? He can put a credit and contact info for his company at the bottom of the sign. Tell him. He just needs to get it over here in the next . . . oh . . . half hour. Okay?"

Emma nodded, flipping open her phone.

"Mia and Katie, you're not going to like this, but bear with me . . ." I explained my plan.

Matt arrived, breathless, twenty-five minutes later, with three copies of an awesome poster for us to hang around the table. It said what we'd asked, but he'd figured out a way for the words to be splashing into water, with little droplets flinging off the letters, all green and blue.

"Oh, Matt, it's amazing! You're a genius!" I said. And I wasn't even hamming it up or flirting like Callie would have. I meant it! He actually blushed.

"No prob," he said.

He hung up the posters while I instructed the swim team cocaptains who were manning the table on what they'd do to sell the cupcakes.

"Okay, you're going to take the money—three dollars each—and put it into the cash box. Then you're going to pick up a cupcake . . ." We'd arranged them top down on the table, so they were resting on their frosted tops, with their bottoms in the air, still in Mia's original wave design. "Then you grab a knife and scrape the frosting off the platter, then get a little extra frosting from the bowl, and slather it all on top and hand it over. Okay?"

"Awesome!" one of them said.

"This is so cool! How did you ever think of this? It's so clever!" the other one asked.

"It was Mia's idea," I said, gesturing at her.

"No way. It was our boss, Alexis. She thought up the whole thing," protested Mia.

"Well, Matt Taylor did the signs!" I said. "You know what? It was a team effort!"

"A team effort for a team effort!" said Katie, and we all laughed.

"Let me be the first to buy a couple!" I said. I handed over six dollars and then gave the finished cupcakes to Matt.

"Thanks!" he said, surprised. "You didn't need to do that!"

"It's the least I could do after you saved the day like that for us."

"It sounds like you're the one who saved the day, actually. Here, I can't eat them both right now. Why don't you have one?"

I shrugged and took the cupcake from his hand. "Thanks."

"Cheers," he said, and he tapped his cupcake against mine.

"Cheers," I said back. I took a deep breath and decided to go for it. "Matt . . ."

I swear I was about to ask him to march with me right then when who should be walking up to us but Sydney, Callie, and Bella from the PGC. I didn't know Sydney and Callie were on the swim team, but they must've been. They were wearing bikini tops and short shorts with flip-flops, and Sydney was carrying pom-poms.

"Hey, Matt!" they singsonged as they walked up to him.

"Hey," he said, licking off frosting from his lip.

"Wow! Look at those cupcakes!" said Callie eagerly.

"Yeah, talk about fattening," said Sydney as I smushed my final, slightly too-large bite into my mouth. Whoops.

237

"Look at these cool posters," said Bella. "The letters are all drippy. It would be cool to do it in red, like vampire blood."

Sydney rolled her eyes. "Not everything in life comes back to vampires, Bella," she said.

I had finished chewing and was just standing there like an idiot, but I wasn't about to walk away from Matt and leave him to the wolves. I turned to Callie.

"I didn't know you guys are on the swim team," I said.

Callie looked at me, confused. "What?"

I gestured to her bathing suit and Sydney's. "I didn't realize you two were on the swim team."

Callie looked embarrassed. "Oh, we're not. We just . . . got dressed up to support the team, right, Sydney?" She kind of tried to laugh it off.

Sydney gave her a haughty look. "Yeah. The girls' swim team is for dorks. But we like coming to see the boys in their bathing suits. And we didn't want them to feel self-conscious, so we decided to turn it into a pool party! Right, girls?" She squealed and waved her pom-poms in the air.

"Buy a cupcake to support the team?" said one of the cocaptains, noting Sydney was a fan.

"Sure!" said Callie, reaching into her shorts pocket.

But Sydney stopped her by grabbing her arm. "No, thanks! Bikinis and cupcakes don't mix!"

Callie looked disappointed, but Sydney said, "We want to make sure we fit into our fairy outfits for the *pep rally parade*." She glared at Callie as she said it.

Callie blushed and then shook her head a tiny bit and looked down at the floor.

Sydney sighed in aggravation. "I have to do everything myself around here," she said.

I knew how she felt, but I wasn't exactly sympathetic. I knew things were about to spiral out of control. My control. I knew I should go with the flow, play it cool, be a free spirit, not be seen to care too much. But how do you get anything you want in life if you act like that? That's what I want to know. I steeled myself for what was coming next, and all the while my brain was racing to see if I could figure out how to get Matt away from the PGC and then invite him to march with me.

"What are you being for the parade, Matty?" asked Sydney, all flirty.

"Oh . . . I'm not . . ."

I knew what he was about to say, and I weighed

the risk of social ruin (the PGC finding out Dylan had lied about my parade plans) against mortification (inviting Matt in front of these girls), and I just blurted out the first thing that came to my mind.

"He's being a Greek god," I said. "He's marching with me." I couldn't even look at him as I said it. I just prayed he'd go along with it.

I could see him turn to me in surprise, and now I needed to cover for that. I looked at him. "You hadn't heard what our final costume plan was. Now I ruined the surprise! Silly me!" I said, and I laughed, all flirty. *Get me out of here, get me out of here,* I thought.

Matt was looking at me in confusion. Sydney looked mad, and Callie still looked embarrassed.

I pressed on. *If you're going to go down, at least go down in flames,* I thought. I said to Matt, "I know, I know, you didn't know what Emma and I had cooked up for you and Joe to wear when you marched with us. But failing to plan is planning to fail! That's one of my mottoes."

Finally, a big grin spread across Matt's face. "Whatever you say, boss," he said, chuckling.

Boss? I fake laughed. "Ha-ha. I'm not anyone's boss."

Luckily, the swim team coach chose that

moment to get on the bullhorn and announce the cupcake sale. The table was stormed, and Matt and I got jostled out of the way and separated from the PGC. As my adrenaline wore off, my knees started to shake when I realized what I'd done. *Oh my goodness!* I thought. I needed to cover my tracks.

I turned to Matt and said weakly, "Hey, so, I'm sorry about that back there. I just . . ."

He was smiling, though. "Thanks. You saved me from looking like a major dork for not having any plans. I appreciate it. That was funny. Greek gods. Quick thinking!"

Wait, did he not realize I had actually just invited him? He thought that was just a joke? Like a bail out? What could I say? What should I do? If I told him I'd been serious, would I look like a major dork? I decided to go with the flow.

"Oh, yeah. Anytime. So . . . I guess . . . I mean, were you planning on going with them and I just messed it all up?" I asked. *Please say no, please say no,* I chanted in my head.

"No. Those girls are too much. I mean, Callie's fine, but Sydney is torture. She's so aggressive and bossy."

Bossy? "Is bossy bad?" I asked, thinking how he'd just called me "boss" and also seeing as how

I was the boss of the Cupcake Club.

"Well, yeah. Who wants to be bossed around?"

"Yeah. No one, I guess," I said. *Callie's fine* was floating in my head. *Is that a good "fine" or just an okay "fine"?* I wanted to ask, but that wouldn't be going with the flow, either.

Mia, Katie, and Emma appeared at our side. "Should we go?" asked Mia.

"I guess," said Emma. Turning to me, she asked, "What do you say, boss?"

"I am not the boss!" I said. It came out a little more forcefully than I had meant it to. Emma jumped and looked surprised.

"Okay! Sorry! I get it!" she said.

I rolled my eyes.

"Let's go," said Katie. "Alexis, is your dad coming back?"

I looked at my watch. "Yup. He should be here by now. He can drive us all. Let's get the cupcake carriers and head out."

"So, I guess you guys aren't staying for the meet . . . ," Matt said.

"Matt, thanks so much for your help," I said, all businesslike.

"No prob. Glad to be of service. Thanks for the cupcake," he said. Then he added, "And . . . for saving me." He hesitated a minute. It looked like he was going to say something else or ask me something. But then it seemed as if he changed his mind. "Anyway . . ."

I looked at him. "Okay, then," I said finally, going with the flow. "Thanks for the awesome posters."

"Bye."

"Bye," I said, and walked away.

CHAPTER 11

Greek Goddesses and Friends

That night, as I sat in my room—working on flow charts for the Cupcake Club, but actually thinking only about Matt and my bungling of the invitation today—there was a knock on my door.

"Come in," I said.

It was Dylan. "Dad says I have to tell you to stop worrying about being cool," she said with absolutely no animation or enthusiasm. Then she continued in a monotone voice as she took a seat on my bed. "I'm supposed to say it doesn't matter, follow your dreams."

I spun around in my desk chair to face her, put my fingertips together, and looked at Dylan. "Wow. You're doing a really convincing job," I said, echoing her monotone.

She smiled, then she sighed and began to speak normally. "Listen, just for the record, you're the one who wanted my help. It's not like I grabbed you and said, 'You're a dork. Let me help' or anything like that. Make sure Dad knows that, because it doesn't seem like he does."

"Okay," I said, nodding at her. "But just explain this to me: How is it that going with the flow makes such a mess of everything? It seems like it should be the opposite."

"I'm not answering any more questions. It only gets me into trouble," said Dylan, examining her nails.

"Come on, Dylly, just this last one!" I protested.

Dylan sighed heavily. "Look, I'm not an expert. I just know what I see. I'm starting to think maybe there are different kinds of cool. There's, like, 'leader cool,' where you do everything a little ahead of everyone else, and then there's, like, 'renegade cool,' where you just march to your own drummer. I guess I should have been a little clearer on that. I'm thinking you probably fall more into the renegade category, since you're not a cookie-cutter type of person."

"Oh great. I'm a weirdo," I said. "I knew it."

"No! Stop. You're not at all. You're just . . . You

have interests that are a little outside the norm for people your age. But that doesn't mean they're bad. It's just, if you're going to take a chance on them, you have to go for it, whole hog. Don't just do it halfway, you know? Like, if you're going to do the Cupcake Club, then go all out: run it, be a serious CEO, join the FBLA, read business books—whatever. Go for what you want. That's what is cool. Not doing it is dorky, and doing something only halfway . . . well, that's not really cool at all. It's just kind of lame. Do you get it?"

"I guess so," I said.

Dylan got mad then. "Don't tell Dad I gave you more advice on coolness, though, okay?"

"Okay! I won't! I already swore I wouldn't!"

Dylan stood up, satisfied with my answer.

First thing Sunday morning, Mia called me, all excited. "Come over! My mom got the costumes back from Hector! We need to try them on! The others are coming with their stuff too, and my mom's going to help us style them. Bring the sandals, okay?"

I had my mom drive me over to Mia's in a flash. Emma was already there, and Katie arrived soon after.

Mrs. Valdes took my dress and Mia's out of black garment bags and laid them out on the sofas in the living room.

"Wow!" Emma exclaimed breathlessly. "That's gorgeous, Alexis."

I leaned in to finger the soft material. Hector had added rectangular jeweled clasps to the shoulders, bunching the material so that it gathered in tiny pleats at the top, then draped down across the front in a graceful arc. I couldn't wait to try it on.

"Okay, *mis amores*, run and get into your costumes and then meet me in my room. We'll go through one by one and accessorize you!" Mrs. Valdes said.

We spent the next hour and a half playing fashion show, with Mrs. Valdes raiding her closet and trying things on us to enhance our outfits. Emma wound up looking amazing in her hippie costume. Mrs. Valdes added a hairpiece called a "fall" to her hair that made it look really long, then she lent Emma a suede fringed vest to go over the bell bottoms and tie-dyed shirt Emma had brought. Mia had a pair of platform boots that fit Emma perfectly, and they dug out a pair of round tinted glasses of Dan's to complete the look.

Next up was Katie, the genie. She had a pair of culottes and a long-sleeved shirt with a scarf to wrap around her head. Mrs. Valdes swapped out her shirt for this flowy, white one with billowy arms, and wrapped a gold lamé scarf around her middle as a belt. Then she took a little pillbox hat and attached Katie's head scarf to it, so it flowed down the back. Finally, she produced a pair of shoes from Tibet that curled up into pointy toes and looked magical. Mia gave Katie an anklet made up of tiny bells, which would jingle as she walked. She looked unbelievable!

I went next, and I was so psyched with how my dress came out. It was soft, it fit perfectly, and it was sooo comfortable, like liquid swirling around me. I strapped on my tie-up gold Roman sandals. Mrs. Valdes put my hair up into this loose bun and then pinned it, sticking little silk leaves all around my head. Then she put a garland of silk leaves around my waist, so it looked like a belt.

"And now for the finishing touch!" she said. I watched as she ran over to her jewelry box on her dressing table and pulled out the gold knot earrings she'd had on that day at Icon. She held them up and crossed back to clip them onto my ears.

"Oh, Mrs. Valdes. I can't wear these! What if I lose one?" I protested.

"I know you, Alexis, and you won't lose one. But even if you did, it's okay. I got them for fifteen dollars at H&M last year. They are temporary by nature. Now turn around, and let's see the full effect."

I spun in place, and everyone cheered. "Oh, I wish Dylan were here to see you!" Mrs. Valdes said as she clapped her hands.

"Me too!" I agreed. "She'll be so jealous when she finds out we raided your closet without her."

Mia went last, and her costume was the simplest but the best of all, just because it took kind of a standard idea (witch—black dress, black hat, black shoes) and made it so glamorous. Her dress had scraps of floaty black tulle sewn on that flitted and flicked as she moved. There were little sequins hidden here and there to catch your eye amid all the black. Her hat was very, very tall and very, very pointy—almost kind of kooky-looking, but chic. And her shoes were superhigh heels with superpointy toes and bursts of tulle pointing off the toes and heels, like a little shoe Mohawk. Mia's mom gave her tons of silvery necklaces and jangly silver bracelets to wear, so she made a tinkly noise as she moved.

"Wow, Mia! You look beautiful!" I said. We all agreed. Her costume was fantastic!

Mrs. Valdes ran to get her camera, since she wasn't sure where we'd all be dressing for the parade next weekend.

"I'm so glad we're not fairies," said Katie.

"I know. Also, I think it's cooler that we're not all matchy, matchy. It's kind of babyish to go in a big group theme," said Emma.

"What are your partners being?" I asked Katie and Mia, thinking of Matt.

"Chris is a warlock," said Mia. "I helped him with the costume." She smiled. "It was fun."

Katie laughed. "I convinced George to be an astronaut like on the TV show, so he's going for it! His dad was going to help him make the costume. He's going to wear a bubble helmet and everything!"

"Fun!" I said. But I was feeling a little wistful. I wish I had had the guts to tell Matt I'd really been serious yesterday. I shouldn't have gone with the flow.

Emma and I avoided eye contact. We hadn't recently discussed going with Matt and Joe. But now that I had this great costume, I really wanted to march with Matt. I didn't want to waste it.

"Going with the flow doesn't get you what you want in life," I said out loud.

The others looked at me strangely.

"Of course not, silly!" said Katie. "Only limp noodles go with the flow!"

I giggled. "That sounds so appetizing. Like something a witch would make!"

Mia cackled. "Heh, heh, heh, my pretties! Who would like some limp noodle pie?"

We all started acting out our costume characters as Mrs. Valdes came back into the room with her camera. We hammed it up in all sorts of shots, and then reluctantly took everything off. It had been fun. And now I knew I had to get up the nerve to ask Matt. No more limp noodle pie for me!

CHAPTER 12

Carpe Diem—Seize the Day!

I knew all the teachers would be back at school Monday, getting everything ready for the new school year. So I called and left Mr. Donnelly a message. He called me back a few minutes later.

"Hi! Mr. Donnelly! Am I too late?" I asked.

"Hello, Alexis. I'm assuming you mean the Future Business Leaders of America? No, you're not too late. I was taking a calculated risk that you wouldn't take so long to think about it and then say no." He laughed. "So shall I write the letter?"

"Yes, please. And is there anything I need to do on my end?"

"You'll need to pull together a résumé. . . . I can e-mail you some samples. And then just write a one-paragraph essay on why you want to join and what your focus will be. Can you have it to me by Wednesday?" he asked.

I nodded. "I can have it to you by tomorrow."

"Even better! Great!"

That night, my mom helped me put together a really good résumé that listed all my business experience (babysitting, Cupcake Club, running bake sales at school, selling Girl Scout cookies when I was younger—stuff like that). I listed my areas of responsibility in the Cupcake Club, including the financial planning I do, along with the marketing ideas I'd had for Emma's dog-walking business, and a few other things.

Then it was time to write my paragraph. I sat at my desk and then cracked my knuckles. I'm better at math than writing, so I always have a hard time getting started. The clock ticked, and I shifted in my seat. Finally, I caved.

"Dad!" I yelled.

For the next fifteen minutes, my dad and I brainstormed, talking about what I enjoyed most in business and where I felt I needed to grow. I took notes and jotted down key words as we talked, and when he left, I felt energized. I knew what I wanted to say, and here's what I wrote:

My name is Alexis Becker. My business experience to date has been customer driven and marketing oriented, mainly in the food service industry, and now I'd like to take it to the next level. If I were accepted into the Future Business Leaders of America, my focus would be on innovations in leadership. I would like to learn how to better lead employees by inspiring them to be creative and by empowering them to work independently. I do not want to be a micromanager. I would also like to learn how to lead in my industry, developing new products before my competitors and finding new ways to reach customers through marketing. I would appreciate the opportunity to harness my enthusiasm and passions and turn them into action—to just go for it, to never hold back, and to learn how to lead by example. Thank you for your consideration of my application.

I thought it was pretty good, and my parents liked it too. Even Dylan, who was passing by as I read it aloud to them, gave me a thumbs-up. I felt great. I printed out the final copy and put it in an envelope to deliver to Mr. Donnelly the next day.

After finishing the letter, I wrapped up some Cupcake business, and it was still kind of early. There was something I needed to do, and it was on my mind. I just wouldn't feel settled until I did it. I thought of my own words from the FBLA paragraph. How I wanted to go for it and to never hold back. How I wanted to lead by example.

I can do this, I can do this, I told myself.

I took a deep breath, and I punched the familiar sequence of numbers into the phone.

"Hello?" asked a familiar voice.

"Emma, it's me, Alexis," I said.

"Oh hi! I was going to call you! When are we getting together to bake for the retirement party this weekend?"

"I just e-mailed everyone about that," I said. "It should be in your in-box. But we'll do it at Katie's first thing on Saturday, so we can get ready for the parade by three o'clock, okay?"

"Perfect. Anything else going on?" She was obviously looking to chat, but I didn't have time. I'd lose momentum.

I cringed. "Actually, I wonder if I could speak to Matt?"

There was a pause, then Emma said, "Oh. Right. Sure. Hang on. I'll get him."

The phone clunked on the table. I could just picture the upstairs hallway and Emma walking to Matt's room. I had kind of an unfair advantage in all this, in that I'd been to Matt's so many times and was so comfortable with his whole family. *Why should I be nervous, anyway?* I thought. *Why don't I just pretend I'm the CEO of a big company making a sales call. CEOs never take no for an answer!*

"Hello?" His scratchy, deepish voice startled me.

"Hey, Matt, it's Alexis." I gulped. I didn't feel so CEO-ish anymore. *Go with the flow,* I started to tell myself. But no! There's no flow anymore. *Carpe diem!* I reminded myself. *Seize the day!* That's better.

"Hey. How's it going?" he asked.

"Good. Listen, I'm just going to cut to the chase. . . ."

I could hear Dylan's advice in my head. *Go for what you want. That's what is cool. Not doing it is dorky.* I thought of making this into a big group invitation thing. I thought of inviting him and Joe to join me and Emma as a foursome. But then I thought about what I really wanted, what my own goal was: I wanted to march with Matt Taylor in the parade, darn it!

"Would you like to come march with me in the parade on Saturday?" I said it in one really quick rush. I guess it came out a little too fast, because Matt didn't catch it.

"What?" he asked.

I took another deep breath, dying that I had to say it all again. "The parade. Would you like to march with me on Saturday?"

There was a pause. I could hear the wheels turning in his mind as he struggled to find an answer, a gentle way to say no, to turn me down. I cringed and closed my eyes.

"Sure. Thanks," he said. "What do I need to wear?"

What?!

YAHOO!

Now I wasn't sure what to say, so I started to ramble a little. "Um, well, I actually am going as a Greek goddess. I wasn't kidding about that. You can wear whatever you want. Or you could be a Greek god and wear a toga. Like a white sheet, you know?"

"Oh yeah. Sam knows how to do that. His friend had a toga party last year. I could do that."

"Really? Oh, that's so great!" I said. I didn't want to sound dorky or overly enthusiastic, but this was turning out fantastically. Success made me generous. "Also, listen, Emma might need someone to walk with too. I don't know if she's talked to you about it or not, but . . ." I was just totally going for it now, covering all my bases.

Matt replied, "Well, I could bring Joe. I don't think he has a plan. We were just going to bail on the parade and go to the pep rally and bonfire, so . . . I'm sure he'd be happy to march. Should he wear a toga too?"

"Um, maybe he should be a hippie," I said. "That's what Emma's dressing up as, and she looks great."

"Cool. Okay. So we'll just meet you . . ."

"There. We'll meet at your house on Saturday, and we can all go over together. How's that?"

"Great. Sounds like a plan! Thanks," he said. I could tell by his voice that he really *was* happy about it. Maybe Emma knew her brother better than I gave her credit for. Maybe he was just too nervous—or too lazy—to ask anyone.

"It'll be fun," I said.

I hung up the phone and sat at my desk, staring at it with a huge, dorky smile on my face. I didn't care if I wasn't cool. I was sure I was the happiest girl in America right then. I'd gone for what I wanted and gotten it! And I'd hooked Emma up at the same time!

I went down the hall to Dylan's room in a trance. "You're fired," I said, walking in without knocking.

"What?" asked Dylan, looking up from her book in confusion.

"Your work is done," I said. "I'm cool."

Dylan rolled her eyes. "You can't fire me. I already quit," she said, and she turned back to her book.

"Either way," I said. "Mission accomplished."

CHAPTER 13

My Perfect Day

Saturday was beautiful: a perfectly warm summer day, but there was a hint of fall in the air too. We were at Katie's bright and early, chatting about the parade route and whether we'd be cold in our costumes since the temperature was supposed to drop that night. Dylan had told me that kids in the past have gone to the stadium in advance to drop off bags with jackets and sweaters and stuff to save seats. I thought that was a pretty cool way to plan ahead, and I suggested we do that. Everyone loved the idea.

"How about the boys?" asked Emma. "Should we call and tell them too?"

"Well . . ." Not if I had to do the calling.

"Come on," said Emma. "It's not fair to them. They'll be freezing, and we'll be warm and toasty."

"Oh! I bet I could get Dan to lend me his jacket that would work great with Chris's costume. I'm going to call him and Chris right now!" said Mia.

"Alexis, you should call Matt," said Emma sternly.

"Fine," I said. And I did it too.

Lucky for me, he wasn't home, so I left a message with Mrs. Taylor. Phew!

We finished our cinnamon bun cupcakes with cream cheese frosting with plenty of time to spare. Katie's mom had Saturday morning hours at her office, but she was going to give us a ride, with our cupcakes, at twelve, so we had some time to kill.

"Hey, want to watch the last episode of *Celebrity Ballroom*? I DVRed it last night!" said Katie.

Emma and Mia were totally up for it, but I had to step in. "Ladies, let's do a quick meeting and then we can watch the show, okay? We just have some loose ends to tie up."

They moaned a little bit, but it was more for show, and I wasn't having any of it anymore. "If you want to stay in the club, pipe down. I'm toning down my management style, so you have to tone down your worker complaints, okay?" That shut them up fast.

I handed out flow charts that detailed the responsibilities of each person, the general time schedule we worked on, and an overview of the upcoming jobs we had for the next month. I also included a profit-and-loss statement that showed how much the cupcakes cost to bake and how much we could charge for them and how much we'd make. It was all organized by cupcake style, based on ingredients and unit cost.

"Wow, Alexis, this is awesome!" said Katie.

"You've been working really hard!" agreed Mia.

"I have. And the reason is so I don't have to be a nag anymore." I walked them through everything, and because it was laid out so cleanly and so simply, they understood it and were into it. It wasn't just some vague meeting with me nattering on about numbers. Mia had some good ideas about where we could innovate (display, supplying party goods) and where we might spend some of our profits (new platters, a new carrier to replace the one with the broken handle), and Emma made three suggestions for new recipes to try. Katie mentioned she'd seen the fancy vanilla extract we like for way cheaper at Williams-Sonoma, and we decided to take a field trip there the following week to stock up. All in all, it was a very productive meeting in which everyone felt heard and like they contributed.

"Okay? So we're all set," I said, closing my ledger and putting it away in my tote bag.

"Wait, that's it?" said Mia. "Usually we go way longer."

"Nope. Not anymore," I said. "Long, boring meetings are a thing of the past. Now let's go watch that show!"

At four o'clock, my mom dropped me off with my costume at the Taylors'. I was so nervous, I actually rang the doorbell. I felt like I wasn't sure who I was really going there to see.

Mrs. Taylor opened the door. "Alexis, honey! I'm so happy to see you! But why are you ringing the doorbell?"

"Um? I don't know. Practicing for Halloween, I guess!"

She laughed. "Come on in. They're upstairs."

"The Cupcakers? Who else is here already?"

"Oh, you're the first, honey. I meant Matt and Emma. Matt! Emma!" she called. "Alexis is here!"

"Okay! Hi, Alexis!" called Matt from upstairs.

I couldn't help it. I grinned from ear to ear.

"Come on up, Alexis!" yelled Emma.

I went upstairs with my bag, nervous and excited. My stomach was doing flip-flops and my palms were actually sweating. "Hello?" I called.

Matt cracked open his door. "We're in here, getting ready. Emma's in her room. We'll see you soon for the big reveal!" And then he shut the door again. I had to laugh.

"Emma?" I rapped on her door with my knuckles and then went in.

Pretty soon all four of us Cupcakers were there, laughing and playing music and getting ready. But I didn't want it to be too much about us four, so I hustled a little bit in order to get downstairs and meet up with Matt and Joe in the kitchen or TV room. I had heard them go down about ten minutes before we were ready.

"Let's go, girls," I said. They were all putting final dollops of makeup on and tweaking their belts and stuff as they looked in the mirror. Mia had done my hair, and I had dressed myself, carefully slipping on the glorious dress and adjusting my accessories. I had to admit, I looked great. I couldn't wait to see what Matt thought.

"You just want to get downstairs and see your date!" whispered Katie.

"So what if I do?" I laughed. I wasn't going to

hide my happiness or to play it cool. This was the best day of my life so far.

Just then there was a knock on the door. It was Mrs. Taylor. "Alexis, honey, your dad's on the phone."

"Okay, weird, but thanks." The Taylors were driving us over to the stadium in their minivan, so we could drop off our bag of sweaters and jackets, and then us to the start of the parade. I wondered why my dad could be calling.

"Hello?" I said, picking up the phone in the upstairs hallway. I smiled to think this was where Matt had been standing when I asked him out!

"Hi, sweetheart! I just couldn't wait to tell you. Mr. Donnelly called to say the head of the Future Business Leaders of America has accepted your application and that they were very excited about your essay and were looking forward to working with you. He said they don't usually call on the weekends, so he knew they were very impressed. Way to go, Lexi, my love!"

"Yahoo!" I squealed. "Thanks, Dad!"

I hung up the phone and went to tell the others. They were very happy for me, and we finally got downstairs, only moments before we were due to leave.

As I walked down the stairs, I thought about Dylan's advice on not being too friendly, acting like you don't care about stuff, playing it cool. I realized that's just no fun! Why hide your excitement?

As we rounded the corner and went into the kitchen, I saw Matt look up, his eyes searching for me. When they landed on me, they lit up. "Wow! Alexis, you look great!" he said.

"Thanks," I said, smiling. "So do you." And he did.

The parade was amazing, and the pep rally—with all our decorations—was even better. We stayed till the very end. The bonfire smoldered just at the end of the field, and the smell of the wood smoke, mixed with the smell of the popcorn and the hot dogs they were selling, created a delicious aroma I will never forget. It smelled like happiness. (I did make a mental note to approach the concession stand manager about selling cupcakes in the school's colors for the upcoming football games. Life's not all fun and games when there's money to be made!) We ate and cheered for our town's high school's fall sports teams. We had so much fun.

And of course we saw the PGC in their fairy costumes at the parade. Callie and Bella marched behind Sydney and her date. The outfits had actually turned out well. The girls looked beautiful, but they were clearly freezing to death. Their costumes were very light and sleeveless, and it was a bit chilly even for a summer night.

"Why do some girls think they need to wear so much makeup?" Matt asked as we walked by.

I shrugged. "I guess they think it makes them look cool," I said.

"It doesn't," said Matt, stating the obvious. Still, I was happy to hear it.

I felt Callie's eyes on us as we walked by, and I felt a little bad. But she did have a chance to invite Matt, after all, and she never went for it. Anyway, a part of me wondered if she really even liked him or if Sydney had just picked him out for her and bossed her into going for him. It was hard to tell. Either way, though, I was thrilled to be there—me, Matt, great costumes, fun night. It all worked out just right.

"Hey, Alexis!" I heard someone call. It was Janelle, who was dressed up as a nerd.

I cringed for a second at the thought of acknowledging her as a friend, right when the PGC was watching me, but then I pulled myself together and stopped to chat with her. After all, I had Matt by my side, so how uncool could I be?

By the end of the night, Chris and Mia were holding hands, and I saw George try to put his arm around Katie, but she swatted him away, laughing. I could feel Matt sneaking sideways glances at me, and it made me feel great. Emma and Joe had fun too, rating people's costumes and throwing popcorn at each other to see if they could catch it in their mouths. They were old friends after all, even though there was no romance there. By the end of the night, when Mr. Taylor came back to pick us up at our assigned meeting place, I didn't want to leave.

We dropped off Mia and then Katie. Chris and George had gotten their own rides home. Joe was sleeping at the Taylors', so he and Emma were still in the car—and Matt, of course—when Mr. Taylor pulled into my driveway.

Matt was sitting in one of the bucket seats next to the sliding door, so he hopped out to let me pass. Or so I thought.

"It's dark, so walk Alexis to the door," said Mr. Taylor.

"I was going to!" Matt said, and he walked me to my back door, which is kind of out of the way, on the other side of the garage.

"That was fun, Alexis. Thanks for inviting me.

I really had never planned on going. I thought it was . . . I don't know. Not such a cool thing to do. But you made it really cool, actually."

I smiled. "Thanks for coming with me. I had a great time too. I'm really glad we all went together too. Next time, I'll bring cupcakes," I said, laughing nervously.

We'd reached the door.

"Well, see you around school. Or, who knows, see you at my house tomorrow probably!" said Matt. And he leaned over and kissed me good-bye, really quickly, on my cheek.

I turned scarlet, but luckily he was already walking really fast down the path back to the car. "Bye!" I called, ecstatically happy. "Thanks!"

I sighed and just enjoyed the moment. Matt Taylor had kind of, sort of kissed me good night. It was absolutely, definitely the coolest thing ever.

Katie
and the
cupcake
war

CHAPTER 1

You Are *Not* Going to Believe This!

Mia! Is it really you? I haven't seen you in a gazillion years!" I cried, hugging my friend.

Mia laughed. "Katie, I was only gone for, like, four days," she said.

"That is four days, ninety-six hours, or five thousand, seven hundred, and sixty minutes," I said. Then I dramatically put my hand over my heart. "I know, because I counted them all."

"I missed you too," Mia said. "But you couldn't have missed me too much. You were trying out new recipes with the techniques you learned at cooking camp, weren't you?"

"Yes," I told her, "but it felt like you were gone forever. I almost didn't recognize you!"

Actually, I was kidding. Mia looked pretty much

the same, with her straight black hair and dark eyes. She might have gotten a little bit tanner from her long weekend at the beach. She was wearing white shorts and a white tank top with a picture of a pink cupcake on it.

"Hey, I just noticed your shirt!" I said. "That's so cool!"

Mia smiled. "I made it at camp. One of the counselors there was totally into fashion, and she showed me how do this computer thing where you can turn your drawing into a T-shirt design."

I was definitely impressed. "You drew that? It's awesome."

"Thanks," Mia said. "I was thinking maybe I could make T-shirts for the Cupcake Club, for when we go on jobs. You know, so we could all dress alike."

Now it was my turn to laugh. We all like to bake cupcakes, but when it comes to fashion, the members of the Cupcake Club don't have much in common. "Well, I know we all wore matching sweatshirts when we won our first baking contest," I said. "But that was a special occasion. I don't know if you could create one T-shirt we would all be happy wearing on a semiregular basis."

Then the doorbell rang. It was Emma and

Alexis, and what they were wearing proved my point. Emma is a real "girlie girl," although I don't mean that in a bad way, it just describes Emma really well. Pink is her favorite color, and I don't blame her, because pink looks really nice on you when you have blond hair and blue eyes like Emma does. She wore a pink sundress with tiny white flowers on it and pink flip-flops to match her dress.

Alexis had her curly red hair pulled back in a scrunchie, and she wore a light blue tennis shirt and jean shorts with white sneakers. And I might as well tell you what I was wearing: a yellow T-shirt from my cooking camp signed by all the kids who went there, ripped jeans with iron-on patches, and bare feet, because I was in my house, after all. Oh, and I painted each of my toenails a different color when I was bored.

"Mia! I missed you!" Emma cried, giving Mia a hug.

"So how was your first vacation with your mom, Eddie, and Dan?" Alexis asked. Eddie and Dan are Mia's stepdad and stepbrother, respectively.

"Pretty good," Mia replied. "The beach house was nice, and we got to play a lot of volleyball. And the boardwalk food was delicious."

"That reminds me," I said. "Follow me to the kitchen, guys."

My cooking camp experience had inspired me to surprise my friends for our Cupcake Club meeting. I had covered the kitchen table with my favorite tablecloth, a yellow one with orange and red flowers with green leaves. (Mom says she needs to wear sunglasses to eat when we use it, but I love the bright colors. Plus, they reminded me of the colors of Mexico, and it matched all the food I had made.)

Laid out on the table was a bowl of bright green guacamole, a platter of enchiladas with red sauce on top, homemade tortilla chips, a pitcher of fresh lemonade, and a plate of tiny cupcakes, each one topped with a dollop of whipped cream and sprinkled with cinnamon.

My friends gasped, and I felt really proud.

"Katie, this looks amazingly fantastic!" Mia said. "Did you make all this yourself?"

I nodded. "We had Mexican day in cooking camp, and I learned how to do all this stuff," I said. I pointed to the mini cupcakes. "Those are *tres leches* cupcakes."

"Three milks," Mia translated. "Those are sweet and delicious. My *abuela* makes a *tres leches* cake when somebody has a birthday."

I nodded. "Emma, I thought they might be good for the bridal shop."

One of the Cupcake Club's biggest clients is the The Special Day bridal shop. We make mini cupcakes that they give to their customers, and the only requirement is that the frosting has to be white. Emma usually helps delivers them. She has even modeled the bridesmaids dresses at the bridal shop too. (I told you she was a girlie girl.)

"They look perfect!" Emma agreed. "So pretty. And I bet they taste as good as they look."

"Then let's start eating so you can find out," I suggested. "I think the enchiladas are getting cold."

Then my mom walked into the kitchen. She has brown hair, like me, but hers is curly, and today it was all messy. She looked tired, but I thought maybe it was because she had patients all morning. She's a dentist and has to work a lot.

"Oh, girls, you're here!" she said. "Alexis, how was your trip to the shore?"

"Actually, Mia's the one who went to beach," Alexis answered politely. "But thanks for asking."

Mom blushed. "Sorry, girls. I'm exhausted. My head feels like it's full of spaghetti today."

"That's okay, Mrs. Brown," Mia said. "I had a good time."

Then the phone rang. "That's probably your grandmother," Mom said to me. "Come find me if you need anything, okay?"

"Shmpf," I replied. Actually, I was saying "sure," but my mouth was full of guacamole.

Alexis took a chip and dipped it in the guacamole.

"Wow, that's really good," she remarked when she was done chewing. (Unlike me, Alexis doesn't ever talk with her mouth full.)

"Thanks," I said. "Guacamole is my new favorite food. I could eat it all day. Guacamole on pancakes, guacamole pizza for dinner . . ."

"Guacamole-and-jelly sandwiches for lunch," Mia said, giggling.

"Gross!" Emma squealed.

"I think I'll stick to guacamole and chips," Alexis said matter-of-factly. Then she wiped her hands on a napkin and opened up her notebook. Alexis loves to get down to business at a Cupcake Club meeting.

"Okay. So, I was looking at our client list," she began. "The only thing on our schedule this fall is our usual gig at The Special Day. We need to drum up some new business. I was thinking that we could send out a postcard to everyone who's ever ordered cupcakes from us. You know, something like 'Summer's Over, and Cupcake Season Has Started.'"

"I like it," I said. Emma and Mia nodded in agreement.

"That reminds me," Mia said, pointing to her shirt. "I designed this. I could make a T-shirt for each of us. I thought we could wear them when we go on jobs."

"Oh, it's so cute!" Emma said. "Could my shirt be pink?"

Mia smiled. "I guess so. We could each have a different color shirt if we want. Unless you want it to be more like a uniform."

"Or we could expand our business and sell the T-shirts, too," Alexis said, sounding excited. "I bet we could find a site online where we could get the shirts made cheaply, and sell them for a profit."

Mia frowned a little bit. "I don't know, Alexis. I was thinking these should just be for us, you know? Special."

"But you want to be a fashion designer, don't you?" Alexis asked. "This could be the start of your business. Mia's Cupcake Clothing!"

Mia looked thoughtful, and I couldn't tell if she liked the idea or not. I decided to change the subject. If Mia decided she was interested, she'd bring up the idea again. Sometimes Alexis can get a little pushy when she wants the club to do something. Which is mostly good, because otherwise we'd never get anything done.

"Wow, I can't believe school is starting so soon." Then I said with a nod to Emma and Alexis, "Though what I really still can't believe is Sydney's singing routine at your day camp's talent show. It's in my nightmares."

When I first started middle school last year, Sydney Whitman made my life miserable. So I didn't feel bad about making fun of her—well, not *too* bad, anyway. My grandma Carole says that two wrongs don't make a right, and she's got a point. But Sydney really made my life miserable.

"Oh my gosh, I can't believe I forgot to tell you!" Emma said. "I have big news. *Huge!* You guys are *not* going to believe this!"

"Tell us what?" I asked.

"It's about Sydney," Emma said. "Sydney's mom returned a bunch of library books and told my mom that they were moving—to California!"

"No WAY!" I cried, jumping out of my chair. "Are you serious?"

Emma nodded. "I'm pretty sure they moved already. Sydney's dad got transferred to some company in San Diego or something. Sydney's mom said they had to move immediately for Sydney to start school there on time."

I started jumping up and down and waving my hands in the air.

"Look out, everyone. Katie's doing her happy dance," Mia said.

"This is awesome! Amazing! Stupendous! Wonderful! Did I say awesome?" I cried. "No more Sydney! No more Popular Girls Club to ruin our lives!"

"Well, actually, I'm sure the PGC will continue," Alexis replied. "They've still got Maggie and Bella and Callie. I bet Callie will become their new leader."

I felt like a balloon that somebody just popped. One of the reasons Sydney made my life miserable last year was because she took my best friend, Callie, away from me. Yes, I know that nobody forced Callie to dump me and become a member of the PGC. But it was always easier to blame Sydney than to get mad at Callie. Callie and I have been friends since we were babies.

Oh, and the Popular Girls Club is just what it sounds like. It's a club Sydney started where they invite popular girls to join. They do everything together. I started to get so mad just thinking about it, then I realized Mia was talking to me.

"So Callie didn't mention any of this to you?" Mia asked.

"No!" I said, feeling a little exasperated. "I mean, I barely talk to her anymore."

I know I shouldn't get so freaked out about Callie. If she hadn't dumped me, I probably never would have become friends with Mia, Emma, and Alexis. There would be no Cupcake Club. But something happened to Callie when she got into middle school. Sometimes she could be not so nice. So it was probably for the best that we weren't friends. We saw each other when our families got together—our moms are best friends, and, yes, that gets really weird—but that was about it.

Anyway, I must admit, there was a little part of me that hoped, now that Sydney was gone, that Callie would be friends with me again. I imagined her showing up at the front door.

Oh, Katie, I have treated you so badly, she would say. *Can I please join your Cupcake Club?*

Of course, I would say, trying to be the better person. *I forgive you, Callie.*

Then again, that would make things pretty confusing, because Mia was my best friend now, and I'm not sure how this would all work. Now *my* head felt like it was full of spaghetti. (Although I would never say that out loud, because that is such a weird mom thing to say.)

"Earth to Katie," Mia said. "You there?"

I snapped myself out of my fantasy. "Sorry. I must be in a guacamole haze," I said, taking my seat. "Okay. Enough about the PGC. Let's get down to business."

Maybe Alexis had the right idea after all.

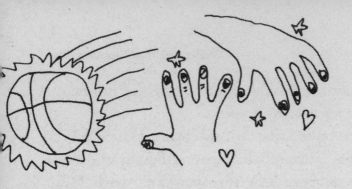

CHAPTER 2

What Was *That* All About?

Once I stopped worrying about what Callie was going to do, I spent the next few days on a Sydney-free cloud of happiness. A world without Sydney was a world filled with rainbows, cotton candy, and sunshine every day. I didn't even get nervous about my first day of school.

Any normal person would have been nervous. Last year, the first day of middle school was one of the worst days of my life. I lost my best friend, got in trouble for using my cell phone, couldn't open my locker, and couldn't find my way around the school and was nearly late getting to every class.

But this year, things started out amazingly great. When I got on the bus, Mia was sitting in our usual seat in the sixth row from the front, saving it for me, just like always.

"Hey, you're wearing your lucky purple shirt," Mia said as I slid into my seat. She always notices what I'm wearing.

"Yeah, I need all the luck I can get," I said. "I do not want this year's first day of school to be like last year's."

Mia made a fake-hurt face. "Hey, you met me on the first day of school last year."

"That was the only good thing, believe me," I said. Then I remembered. "Besides meeting Alexis and Emma, too."

Then Mia noticed my hands. "Cool nails."

I wiggled my fingers. I had painted each fingernail in a different color this time. "For extra luck!"

"You don't need luck, Katie," Mia said. "You know how to do stuff this time. You'll be fine."

"I hope so," I said.

Then a boy with brown hair looked over the seat behind us. It was George Martinez, a kid I've known since elementary school. George always says a lot of funny stuff that makes me laugh. Sometimes he teases me, which is annoying, but he's still kind of funny. He was sitting next to his friend Ken Watanabe, as usual.

"Hi, Katie," he said. "How was the rest of your summer?"

George has never asked me a normal question like that before. For a second I didn't know what to say. I was trying to think of a funny reply, because I can usually make George laugh.

Then Mia nudged me, and I realized I was staring into space like a zombie again.

"Um, good," I finally answered.

"That's good," George said. Then he sat back down.

Mia leaned over to whisper into my ear. "He *so* likes you!"

"*Sshhh!*" I warned her. If George heard her, that would be so embarrassing. Mostly because I think I kind of like George, even though I'm not entirely sure what that's supposed to feel like. And if he liked me back, it might be awesome or it might be very weird.

Then the bus arrived at Park Street Middle School, a big U-shaped school made of bricks the color of sand. Before I climbed up the front steps with Mia, I stopped and got my schedule out of the front pocket of my backpack. I knew my home-room class was in room number 322, but I wanted to make sure.

Just then Emma and Alexis walked up. They both live a few blocks away from the school, so they don't have to take the bus.

"Katie! Hooray! Now we can go to homeroom together," Emma said.

"Oh yeah! I forgot," I admitted. A few nights ago, we had all texted our schedules to one another to see if we were in the same classes together. Last year, I didn't have any friends in my homeroom class. I smiled. "Hey, I'm really lucky that you're in my homeroom. My good luck shirt must be working."

"*And* your good luck nail polish," Mia reminded me.

The front of the school was starting to get crowded, so I said good-bye to Alexis and Mia, and Emma and I headed to homeroom. We got to room 322 without getting lost, because we knew our way around the school already.

Inside the room we were greeted by these words written on the board: WELCOME, STUDENTS! GET READY FOR A MATH ADVENTURE! MR. KAZINSKI. The teacher sitting behind the desk at the front of the room was a tall man with sandy-blond hair and glasses. The walls around the room were decorated with posters that said stuff like "Believe

You Can Achieve," and others had math symbols on them.

Emma and I found seats in the row by the window before the bell rang. Mr. Kazinski stood up and smiled at us.

"Hey, it's good to see everyone today," he said. "I've got some announcements, but first, the news."

Right then Principal LaCosta's voice came over the PA speaker.

"Good morning, everyone, and welcome to the first day of school at Park Street," she said. "I can tell it's going to be a wonderful year. Let's start out by saying the Pledge of Allegiance together."

After the pledge, Mr. Kazinski started talking again. "By now you've guessed that my name is Mr. Kazinski, but you guys can call me Mr. K.," he said. "You'll see me for ten minutes every morning here in homeroom, and if you are taking my math class, you'll see me for forty minutes more."

I glanced at my schedule. I had math next, in this very room, with Mr. K. More good luck! I don't love math, but I already liked Mr. K. My math teacher last year, Mrs. Moore, was okay but she was pretty strict and not very friendly. She was a cloudy day compared to Mr. K.'s sunny day, if you know what I mean.

Another point for my lucky purple shirt, I thought happily.

And I got even luckier because even though I had to say good-bye to Emma after home-room, Mia walked into the room. We had math together!

The morning just seemed to get better and better. My second-period class, Spanish, was just down the hall. Then I went to gym class, and I was so happy—Emma, Mia, and Alexis were there!

I should probably explain my history with gym, or "physical education," as teachers like to call it. I'm a pretty fast runner, but when it comes to most other sports stuff, I'm sort of a spaz. When we play volleyball and I hit the ball, I usually end up hitting the wall or the ceiling or a person. It's not pretty. And last year, I got teased pretty hard about it.

I *am* good at softball, though. I even made the school team. But I like playing for fun. I'm not competitive, and being on a team that always played to win stressed me out too much, so I gave it up.

This year, though, I would have my three best friends to back me up in gym class. And I knew I would need it, because I had the same gym teacher, Ms. Chen. She acts more like an army drill sergeant than a middle school teacher. Honestly, she scares me.

Since it was the first day of school, we didn't have to change into our gym clothes or anything. So before the bell rang, we were all just kind of hanging out on the bleachers. Some of the boys were running around and throwing basketballs at one another.

One of the balls bounced right up to where I was sitting with my friends. It rolled to my feet, so I picked it up, and George Martinez ran over to get it.

"Hey, Silly Arms! We're in the same class again," he said, smiling.

George started calling me Silly Arms last year, because of the way I play volleyball. I've never looked in a mirror while playing volleyball, but I guess I must look pretty silly. I never get mad because I know he's just teasing, like he always does. But then some other kids (like Sydney and her friends, for instance) started calling me that to be mean.

Before I could say anything to George, Eddie Rossi ran up behind him. Eddie is the tallest kid in our grade, and probably in our whole school. Last year he even grew a mustache. But I guess he shaved it over the summer, because his face looked clean-shaven again.

Anyway, this is what Eddie said: "Hey, leave her alone!"

"It's okay," George replied. "Katie's cool!"

Then he took the ball from me and tossed it to Eddie, and they both ran off.

My mouth was open so wide, you could probably have fit a whole cupcake into it.

"That was weird," I said.

"It's so obvious," Alexis said. "Eddie likes you."

"No way," I told her. "It makes no sense. Last year Eddie teased me just as bad as Sydney did. He used to call me Silly Arms all the time. Besides, he's a jock who likes popular girls, not girls like me."

"That doesn't mean he can't still like you," Alexis argued. "People change all the time. He doesn't even have a mustache anymore."

"Well, I think that Eddie and George *both* like Katie," Mia said.

I must have been blushing, because my face

felt hot. I am not the kind of girl who boys get a crush on, and especially not *two* boys at once.

Then Ms. Chen marched in, blowing her whistle, and for once I was glad to see her.

"Stand up and look alive, people! Just because it's the first day of school doesn't mean you can be slackers!"

I jumped to my feet pretty quickly. You definitely don't want Ms. Chen on your case. But I couldn't stop wondering about what happened with Eddie and George and if it meant I was still having good luck or not.

CHAPTER 3

This Means War!

𝓜s. Chen spent the whole gym period telling us the rules of gym and giving us advice about fitness. Finally, the bell rang.

"That was totally boring, but definitely better than being hit in the head by a volleyball," I told my friends as we left. Everyone laughed.

"Don't worry. I'm sure that will happen next week," Mia teased me.

"Hey, we can all go to lunch together," Emma realized.

"I'm going to stop at my locker first," I said. "This math book is pretty heavy. I don't want to carry it around all afternoon."

"No problem, we can all meet at our table, like always," Mia said.

I liked the sound of that. On the first day of school last year, I didn't know where to sit. Now I had three good friends to sit with. I would definitely call that lucky!

Last year I was convinced that my locker was an evil robot out to get me. It's one of those lockers where the lock is built into the door, and the school gives you the combination. I swear I always put in the right one, but that locker never wanted to open.

So I took a deep breath as I slowly turned the dial.

26 . . . 14 . . . 5 . . .

I pulled the handle, and the door wouldn't open.

Oh no! It's happening again! I thought. My heart began to beat faster. I took another deep breath and turned again.

26 . . . 14 . . . 5 . . .

Click! I pulled the handle, and the door opened up.

"Thank you, lucky fingernails," I whispered.

Then I noticed the two girls at the lockers next to me. They were talking pretty loudly.

"It's true! Sydney really moved!" one girl said.

"Does this mean no more PGC?" the other girl asked.

As I headed to the lunchroom, I heard more kids talking.

"I heard the PGC broke up."

"I heard that Sydney left Maggie in charge."

"I wonder if they'll let me join now."

I kind of couldn't believe how many people were talking about Sydney. She was miles away, and she was still the most popular person in school. In a way, that's kind of impressive.

Mia, Emma, Alexis, and I ended up in the cafeteria together at the same time. We made our way to our favorite table, near the back of the room. Alexis and Emma put down their backpacks and went to get on the lunch line. Mia and I always bring lunch from home, so we opened up our lunch bags.

"Did your mom pack you a back-to-school cupcake?" Mia asked.

"Probably," I said. There's been a special cupcake in my first school lunch ever since I could remember.

But when I opened up my bag, I found a turkey and guacamole wrap, an apple, a bag of carrot sticks, and my water bottle—but no cupcake.

"That's weird," I said. "Maybe she forgot to put it in." I felt pretty disappointed.

Suddenly a strange hush came over the noisy

Cupcake Diaries

cafeteria, and Mia and I both looked up to see what was going on.

My former best friend, Callie, was walking through the cafeteria with Maggie and Bella, the other two members of the PGC. Even though they all look different—Callie is tall with blond hair and blue eyes; Maggie is kind of short with crazy, curly brown hair; and Bella (her real name is Brenda) has dark hair and tries to look like that girl from those vampire movies—they were all dressed kind of the same. They each had on short-sleeved sweaters, plaid skirts, dark tights, and ankle boots.

"Those outfits are straight out of last month's *Teen Style*," Mia observed.

"Isn't it kind of warm for sweaters?" I wondered. "It's still officially summer, you know."

The three of them casually walked to the PGC's usual table, but you could tell they knew everyone was looking at them. Then Alexis and Emma came back to our table with their lunch trays.

"Well, I guess the PGC is still going strong," Alexis remarked.

"*Everyone's* talking about it," Emma said as she sat down.

"I know," I told them. "It's kind of crazy."

"Anyway, I have way more exciting news than

296

that," Alexis said. "We haven't even gotten our flyers out yet, but I booked a job today. Ms. Biddle stopped me in the hallway. She wants some cupcakes for a birthday party in a couple of months."

Ms. Biddle was our science teacher last year, and one of our first customers. She's really cool.

"Awesome," I said. "I wonder what kind she wants?"

"Before we talk about that, we should talk about this year's school fund-raiser," Alexis said. "I so want to win again."

I took a bite of my turkey wrap and nodded. At the start of the year, the school has this big fair right before the first school dance, and school groups have booths and try to raise money for the school. Last year our cupcake booth raised the most money, and we won. The PGC did this awful makeover booth, and it felt kind of good to beat them.

"Last year we did the school colors and went with vanilla cupcakes," Alexis reminded us. "I'm thinking that we need to switch it up this year."

Mia nodded. "Yeah, we can do something really creative."

We all got excited thinking of what we could do.

"How about a big tower of cupcakes?" Emma suggested.

"Cool!" I cried. "Or maybe we could do the world's biggest cupcake and sell pieces of it."

"Then we would need the world's biggest oven," Alexis pointed out.

"Maybe we could think of a theme, and then we could decorate the booth in the theme and do cupcakes to match," Mia said.

We really liked that idea. "But what kind of theme?" I asked. "It should have something to do with school, right?"

We were so busy talking that I didn't notice when Callie walked up to the table, followed by Maggie and Bella.

"Hey, Katie," she said, and I jumped a little at the sound of my name.

"Oh hey, Callie," I said, although what I really wanted to say was, *What on Earth are you doing at our table?*

"So, I was just wondering if you guys are going to do cupcakes for the fund-raiser this year," she said.

Alexis looked straight at her. "Well," she said, "we're the Cupcake Club. It's kind of a given."

Callie ignored her. "Well, we were thinking of doing cupcakes this year."

I almost choked on my carrot stick. The PGC

could *not* do cupcakes! That was copying! I was about to start freaking out when Mia spoke up in her usual calm, cool way.

"I guess may the best cupcake win, then," she said.

Callie got a look on her face, like maybe she wasn't expecting that answer. Like maybe she *wanted* us to freak out. I was glad Mia spoke up first.

"Well, then, I guess it's on," she said, tossing her hair. (And when did she start doing that, anyway?)

Then she turned and walked away, and Maggie and Bella followed her, just like they used to follow Sydney.

"They can't even come up with their own idea!" Alexis fumed.

"'It's on'?" Emma repeated. "What is she even talking about? I thought Callie wasn't as bad as Sydney. She might be worse!"

Mia nodded. "I guess it's clear who the new leader of the PGC is."

I didn't say anything. I couldn't. I felt terrible. It wasn't just the PGC declaring war on the Cupcake Club. It was *Callie* declaring war on *me*. That's what it felt like, anyway. This was the girl I learned to ride bikes with, who I had a zillion sleepovers with, who knew my deepest secrets. I never did anything to make her stop being friends with me, and she dumped me. That was bad enough. But this . . . this really hurt.

I looked down at my rainbow-painted fingernails.

So much for my lucky day, I thought.

CHAPTER 4

What's Up with Mom?

Even though I was pretty upset by my encounter with Callie, I have to admit that the rest of the day was okay. After lunch, Mia was in my next two classes (which was good, because Callie, Maggie, and Bella were in them too). For fifth period we had social studies with Mrs. Kratzer. She's short, with short hair and round glasses, and she seems really friendly. Then we had science with Ms. Chandar, who's way more serious than Mrs. Kratzer, but she seems nice, too.

In seventh period I had an elective class, and I chose drama for this semester. Even though the idea of getting onstage terrifies me, I didn't have to worry about that in this class. I thought it might be fun to study drama without having to be in a real play, you know? The teacher's name is Mr. Brent, and he looks really young, like he could be in college or something. Anyway, the class looked like it might be fun.

Finally, I had English. English is my favorite subject, so it's like saving the best for last. The teacher, Ms. Harmeyer, seems kind of quiet and shy, like somebody who likes to read books all the time instead of talking a lot. I guess maybe that's why she became an English teacher.

When school ended, I packed all my books into my backpack and went outside to catch the bus. Last year, Joanne, who works in my mom's office, would pick me up and take me to Mom's work until her day was over. Some days my mom gets off early, and some days she has to work late.

This year, Mom said I could take the bus home and stay at the house by myself. I almost couldn't believe it. My mom has always been super-protective, probably because she's had to raise me by herself. I figured she wouldn't let me stay by myself until I graduated college. But now I have my own key to the house, and it feels pretty cool.

When I got home I headed right for the kitchen and ate a banana. I forgot how hungry going to school makes me!

Then I remembered that I was supposed to call Mom the second I got in the door. Whoops! I was a little surprised Mom hadn't called or alerted the fire department when she didn't hear from me.

"Hi, sweetie!" Mom said when she picked up. "How was the first day of school?"

"Well," I said, unsure of how much I wanted to tell her about Callie, "mostly it was pretty good."

"Great!" she said. "Can't wait to hear all about it when I get home. Now please begin your homework, okay? I'll be home to start dinner soon."

I hung up. The house was quiet and empty, so I decided to go to my room and blast my iPod while I did my homework.

My room is kind of small, but it has everything I need in it. The furniture is this white bedroom set that was my mom's when she was a little girl, and Grandma Carole and Grandpa Chuck saved it in case Mom ever had a little girl of her own—me! A few years ago I started putting stickers on everything, and Mom got a little mad, but then Grandma Carole told her it was my set now, and it should reflect my personality. My grandma is pretty cool that way.

During the summer I used some of my Cupcake Club earnings to get stuff for my room that I saw in a catalog. Over my desk there's a big cupcake-shaped bulletin board that I can stick pictures on. There are two pink cupcake-shaped pillows on top of my purple-and-green bedspread too.

I try to keep my room neat, but mostly I end up sticking things in the closet. Then when I can't shut the door, I have to clean everything up before Mom sees it. Luckily, I had just done that before school started, so things were looking pretty nice.

I opened my backpack, put all my books on top of my desk, and then turned on the laptop Grandma Carole and Grandpa Chuck got me for my last birthday. Then I plugged my iPod into the dock on the nightstand next to my bed and turned it all the way up.

Mom never would have let me play music so loud during homework time, so it felt pretty daring. I didn't really have much to do anyway, since it was the first day of school. Ms. Harmeyer's assignment was to write a poem about one thing you did this summer. I think my poems always end up sounding corny, so I decided to wait until Mom came home to help me. She was really good at writing stuff. Instead I went online to look up some cupcake ideas for the fund-raiser.

I got distracted by all the ads for cupcake supplies that kept popping up, and before I knew it, it was five forty-five. I thought that was weird, because Mom always gets home by five thirty on the dot.

A few minutes later I heard Mom's voice calling up the stairs.

"Katie! Turn that down!"

I quickly ran to shut off the iPod and then bounded down the steps. Mom was at the bottom wearing jeans and a white blouse, which was also weird because she always wears her scrubs home.

"Hey, you're late," I said. "Did you have an emergency at work?"

"Katie, I told you, I didn't go to work today," Mom said. "I had to take Grandma Carole to the doctor again."

"Um, no, you did not tell me that," I said. "Is she okay?"

"We'll talk about it at dinner, Katie," Mom replied. "I ordered us a pizza. It'll be here soon."

I couldn't believe it. Mom and I had pizza last night. Normally, Mom won't even let us order pizza. She makes it herself, including the crust. And when we do order it in, she makes us get veggies on top of it. So delivery pizza two nights in a row was totally out of the ordinary.

"But we just had pizza last night," I reminded her.

Mom sighed. "I'm sorry, Katie. I forgot."

"How could you forget?" I asked. "Remember, we got eggplant and black olives for the very first time, and you said it was the best pizza yet."

Mom motioned me over to the couch. "Katie, let's talk now. You should know what's going on," she said. She sounded superserious, and I felt a little scared.

I sat down next to her.

"Katie, it looks like Grandma Carole is going to have surgery for her heart," Mom said. "The doctors say she's going to be fine. She's in really good health. You know how active she is."

I nodded. "She's better at sports than I am."

"But she has a lot of doctor's appointments to go to, and Grandpa Chuck is still having trouble with his knees, so I'm going to take her," Mom explained. Grandma Carole lives, like, an hour away, so I knew that wasn't going to be easy. "And then, when she goes in for her surgery . . ."

The doorbell rang—it was the pizza guy. While Mom paid for the food, I thought about what she had just said. It sounded serious, but Mom said Grandma was going to be okay. Moms don't lie about that stuff, do they?

I set the table, and soon we were eating broccoli pizza and salad. It was so delicious, I didn't mind we were having pizza for the second day in a row.

"This is sooo good," I said, swallowing a bite of pizza. "I was starving after school today."

Mom threw down her napkin. "Oh, Katie, I almost forgot! How was the first day of school?"

"It was pretty good," I said. I told her most of the stuff that happened. I left out the part about Eddie and George, because that was kind of embarrassing. And I didn't tell her about Callie, because I didn't want her to get upset. I also left out the part about the missing cupcake, because now I understood why she forgot about it.

"Well, it sounds like you're off to a good start," Mom said with a smile, and then her look got serious. "Katie, we still need to talk about the surgery. I'm going to have to stay with Grandma Carole a few days while she's recovering. Mrs. Rogers is going to stay with you."

Mom announced it in that fake-happy voice adults use when they are trying to convince you that what they are saying is good when they really know it isn't. I almost groaned out loud.

Mrs. Rogers is the woman who took care of me when I was a little kid and Mom had to work. She still babysits me sometimes when Mom goes out late, and the annoying thing is that she still treats me like a three-year-old. The last time she was here, she actually checked my toothbrush before I went to bed to make sure I had brushed my teeth. My mom is a dentist! Of *course* I brushed my teeth!

"Mom, not Mrs. Rogers, please," I begged. "She treats me like a baby. Can't I go with you?"

"Absolutely not," Mom said. "You need to stay in school."

I bit my lip. "But, Mom, it's not fair!"

"Katie, I really need your cooperation here," Mom said, and I could tell I had upset her. "I don't want to worry about you while I'm taking care of Grandma. So no complaining, okay?"

It was really, really hard not to say anything back, but I kept quiet. I knew Mom was right. I would just have to deal with Mrs. Rogers for a few days. Thank goodness for school.

But I was still feeling kind of bad. Then I remembered something from Ms. Chen's boring fitness lecture that actually made me feel better.

"Mom, the lights on the high school track stay

on until nine," I said. "Can we go for a run?"

The worried look on Mom's face relaxed. "Why not? Let's wait a little bit. It's not good to go running right after you eat. But I think a run would do us both good."

So a little while later I changed into my running clothes, and Mom and I went down to the track. There was a chill in the air, but it wasn't too cold—perfect weather for running. As we ran around and around in circles, I stopped feeling worried and sad and guilty.

It just goes to show you that sometimes it pays to listen to boring lectures in school!

CHAPTER 5

The War Begins

The second day of school was pretty good, especially since it was Friday, and there was a three-day weekend to look forward to. Two days of school, three days of break. Why can't it be like that year-round?

During lunch I tried not to think about Callie too much, but she and the PGC girls were making this big show of whispering and then looking over at us.

"That is *so* immature," Alexis said.

"Totally," Mia agreed. "It must have really upset them when we beat them last year."

"We should have another club meeting," I said. "We need to come up with something really amazing. Tonight we'll be busy baking for The Special

Day." Our friend Mona had a standing order with us, and we baked for her on Fridays.

"How about tomorrow afternoon?" Alexis suggested. "Mia and I have a soccer game in the morning, but we could do something around two."

"Sounds good," Emma said. "I have three dogs to walk in the morning, but I'm free in the afternoon."

"Hey, maybe I'll come watch your game," I said to Mia and Alexis. "I'll get my mom to drop me off."

"Then it's set," Alexis said. "We can meet at my house. Everyone should come with ideas."

I felt better knowing that we had a plan in place. I was not about to just sit back and let Callie beat us in a cupcake war!

The rest of the day was pretty good—until English class. Ms. Harmeyer asked everyone to hand in their poems. I had completely forgotten about it!

It is totally not like me to forget to do my homework. I got a sick feeling in my stomach. After class, I ran up to Ms. Harmeyer's desk.

"Ms. Harmeyer, I forgot to do my poem," I said. "I was waiting for my mom to help me and then things got . . . I just forgot. Can I do it over the weekend?"

Ms. Harmeyer shook her head. "I'm sorry, Katie. You're in middle school now, and my homework policy is very strict."

I felt like crying. "Okay," I said. "I won't forget again."

"I'll be offering an extra-credit assignment soon," she said.

I nodded. "Thanks," I said. "Have a nice weekend."

Things got much better once school was over. When I got off the bus, Mom was home, and she was cooking a Mexican-style chicken casserole—from scratch. Dinner was delicious, and at the end, Mom told me to close my eyes. When I opened them, she held out a plate with a perfect cupcake on it. The icing was blue, and there was a chocolate-covered graham cracker sticking up on top that looked like a chalkboard. A tiny white piece of candy next to the board looked like a piece of chalk. And Mom had written in icing on the board: "Back to School."

"I meant to make this for you on your first day, but I forgot," Mom said, and her eyes were a little teary. "I'm so sorry, Katie. I've got a lot on my mind lately."

"It's okay." I got up and gave her a hug. "This

is an awesome cupcake! I've got to take a picture."

I took out my cell phone, snapped a photo, and sent it to my friends.

Alexis replied first:

Nice! Good idea for contest maybe.

That reminded me. "Mom, can I go to a Cupcake Club meeting tomorrow? And there's a soccer game in the morning, too."

Mom nodded. "Sure. As long as your room is clean."

I could still close my closet door, so I knew I was okay.

"Yup," I answered.

The next morning was one of those hot September days that still feels like summer. By the time the soccer game was over, I was dripping with sweat—and I didn't even play! So I was glad we had our Cupcake Club meeting in Alexis's nice, air-conditioned kitchen.

When we arrived, Emma and her little brother, Jake, were already there. I happen to think that Jake is adorable, but I know he gets on Emma's nerves sometimes. Even though she has two older brothers, Emma gets stuck babysitting Jake a lot.

"Katie! Katie! I have a lizard!" Jake yelled, running toward me. He had something bright yellow and wiggly in his hand. For a second I thought it might be real, but when I got closer, I saw it was made of rubber. Still, I pretended to be scared.

"Oh no! A lizard!" I cried. "Is it slimy?"

"He's not slimy. His name is Charles," Jake said. "Here, feel him."

Jake put the rubber lizard in my hand. "He feels nice and smooth," I said.

Emma looked at me. "Sorry. Mom had to work the Saturday shift at the library."

"No problem," I said. I slid into my seat and pulled Jake onto my lap. "Jake can help us design our cupcakes. What kind of cupcakes should we make, Jake?"

"Lizard cupcakes!" he cried.

Mia laughed. "Now that's a winning idea."

"We need to get serious, guys," Alexis said. "We can't just *try* to win this fund-raiser. We *have* to win it *big-time*."

"Alexis is right," Emma agreed. "It would be terrible if the PGC beat us. It could really hurt our business."

Alexis flipped open her laptop. "I'll take notes,"

she said. "Katie, what do you know about Callie's baking skills?"

"She's pretty good," I admitted. "Her mom and my mom are friends, and they're the ones who taught me and Callie how to bake. I know Callie's mom will help her if she asks."

Alexis looked thoughtful. "I don't know about Maggie and Bella, but I'm pretty sure Bella doesn't bake. Vampires don't like to eat cupcakes, right?"

"I've heard Maggie say that her family goes out to restaurants all the time," Mia added. "So I bet Maggie doesn't know how to bake either."

"That definitely works in our favor," Alexis said, typing furiously. "We have a whole year of baking experience as a club."

"Hey, don't we have to register or something?" I remembered.

"I'll check the school's website," Alexis said, typing some more. After a few clicks, she stopped and raised her eyebrows. "Well, this is interesting."

I looked over her shoulder. "What?"

"There's a list of clubs that have entered already," Alexis said. "See this one? The BFC: the Best Friends Club. Callie Wilson, Maggie Rodriguez, and Bella Kovacs."

"They changed their name?" I asked.

315

"I don't get it," Alexis said, sitting back. "So what are they declaring? That they are now not popular?"

"Oh who cares?" I asked, suddenly feeling cranky. "I am so sick of them!"

Honestly, it felt like another direct blow from Callie. Like she was saying that Maggie and Bella were her best friends and not me. Which was true. But it felt personal. Like she was rubbing it in.

Alexis ignored my crankiness. "I mean, it makes no sense," she said. "Aren't they worried this will hurt their popularity? It seems risky."

"I don't know, it's kind of nice," Mia said. "When they called themselves the Popular Girls Club, it was obnoxious, right? But there's nothing obnoxious about being best friends."

Unless you dump your old best friend to get new ones, I thought. But I didn't say it.

"Maybe Callie is trying to make the PGC—I mean, the BFC—more friendly," Emma suggested.

"Whatever," I said. "Shouldn't we start planning our cupcakes?"

"Oh, before I forget, is everyone coming to our Labor Day barbecue on Monday?" Emma asked.

"Of course," Alexis replied.

"Me too," said Mia.

I cringed. I totally forgot to ask my mom about it. Every year we have this tradition of going to Callie's house on Labor Day. But being around Callie was the absolute last thing I wanted to do.

Mom will just have to understand, I thought. *I want to be with my* real *friends.*

"I still have to ask," I said. "So, anyway, we were talking about cupcakes. . . ."

"Lizard cupcakes!" Jake said, and everybody laughed.

CHAPTER 6

Think Fast, Katie!

When I got home from the Cupcake meeting, Mom was vacuuming the living room. I figured if I wanted to get out of Callie's barbecue, it wouldn't hurt to get on her good side, so I grabbed a broom and started sweeping the kitchen floor. Then I emptied the dishwasher.

"Thank you, Katie," Mom said, giving me a hug when I was done. "How was your Cupcake meeting?"

"It was good," I said. "Emma reminded me of something. She invited all of us to her house for a Labor Day barbecue on Monday."

"Labor Day!" Mom smacked her forehead with her palm. "Things have been so crazy that I never told Barbara if we were coming to the Wilsons' barbecue or not." (Barbara is Callie's mom, and my mom's best friend.)

"Do we have to go there?" I asked. "I'd rather be with my friends."

Mom sat down and bit her bottom lip, which she always does when she's worried or thinking.

"I need to get some shopping done for Grandma Carole's hospital stay, and I was hoping to cook some food and freeze it, so she won't have to cook while she's recovering," she said. "I suppose I could drop you off at Emma's while I get things done. I'm sure Barbara will understand."

"That would be great!" I said. "And I'll help you cook for Grandma and Grandpa if you want."

Mom smiled. "That would be fun. We can make a dish for you to bring to the barbecue, too."

So on Sunday we ended up cooking together, which was fun. I wanted to make an enchilada casserole for Grandma Carole, but Mom thought it might be too spicy for her. So instead we made a big pot of chicken soup. There was enough for us to have for dinner, with grilled cheese sandwiches on the side. *Yum!*

"We still need to make something for your barbecue," Mom said. "How about a pasta salad?"

"How about a *Mexican* pasta salad?" I suggested. (Can you tell yet that I am on a Mexican-food kick?)

"That sounds interesting," Mom said. "How would you do that?"

I thought about all of my favorite Mexican ingredients that we used in my cooking class. "I could put in black beans and tomatoes, and maybe some shredded cheese and some corn even. And avocados, of course!"

Mom nodded. "That sounds good. And you could put lime juice in the dressing. That could be tasty."

Because we've been cooking a lot of Mexican food, we had everything we needed in the house. Mom helped me cook the pasta—I used one of those squiggly shapes—and then when it cooled down, I mixed everything except the avocados together. I kept adding stuff and tasting it, and it was pretty good. Mom told me to wait to add the avocados until tomorrow, or else they would get brown.

So the next day at noon I was sitting in Mom's car with the bowl of Mexican pasta salad in my lap. When we pulled up we could already see a bunch of people at Emma's house. Her two older brothers,

Matt and Sam, were playing basketball in the driveway with a couple of their friends.

Both of Emma's brothers are nice. Matt is one grade above us, and he likes to tease all of us Cupcake Club members a lot. Sam is in high school, and he never teases us like Matt does. And even though they both have blond hair and blue eyes (just like Emma and Jakc), I think Sam is cuter.

"I'll come get you around four," Mom said, leaning over to give me a kiss. "Have a good time. Call me on my cell if you need me, okay?"

"Sure, Mom," I said. Then I got out of the car, balancing the bowl as I tried to close the door.

"Think fast, Katie!"

A basketball whizzed past my face, and I looked up to see Matt grinning in the driveway. Sam ran to retrieve the ball as it bounced down the sidewalk.

"My hands are kind of full here!" I told Matt.

"Sorry," Matt said sheepishly. "I didn't know."

Sam ran up to me and tossed the ball to Matt. Then he peered into the plastic wrap–covered bowl.

"What is that?" he asked. "It looks good."

"It's, um, Katie's Mexican Special Salad," I said. "I just invented it."

"Well, if you made it, then it must be good," Sam said, and I could feel my face getting hot.

"I'd better bring it over to your mom," I said, and then quickly walked away.

I found Emma, Mia, and Alexis in the kitchen.

"Yay! Katie's here!" Emma said.

I held out the bowl. "I brought a Mexican pasta salad."

"Thanks," Emma said. "Let's bring it outside."

Emma's family has a big backyard, which is perfect for them, because they all like to play sports. The Taylors had set up a canopy for the party, and I put my pasta salad on a big picnic table that was covered with a blue flowered tablecloth. There was lots of food on the table already—pickles, green salad, cut-up veggies, potato salad, deviled eggs, and a plain pasta salad. I was glad I had made my pasta salad a little different.

Outside the canopy, Mr. Taylor, Emma's dad, was grilling chicken. On the grassy lawn beyond, Mrs. Taylor and some other adults were sitting in lawn chairs and talking.

Jake hurried over to us and shoved a Wiffle ball bat into my hands. "Katie, play baseball with me!"

There was no way I could disappoint a cute kid like Jake. Emma, Jake, and I decided to be on one team, and Mia and Alexis were on the other. We didn't play for real. We mostly just pitched the ball to one another and ran around.

Then all the boys came into the backyard.

"We want food!" Matt yelled.

"Matthew, whatever happened to 'please'?" called back Mrs. Taylor.

"Please!" Matthew said. "Give me some food!"

Mr. Taylor carried a big platter of barbecued chicken to the table. "No pushing, people. There's enough for everybody."

Emma rolled her eyes. "We'd better get over there if we want to eat. When there's food around, my brothers act like a school of angry piranhas."

"Don't call me a piranha!" Jake said. He looked mad.

Emma hugged him. "Not you, Jakey. *Those* two."

We walked over to the picnic table, and we could see that Emma was not exaggerating. The boys were piling their plates with humongous mountains of food. Sam was spooning my Mexican pasta salad onto his plate.

"Dude, save some for the rest of us!" Matt complained.

"Maybe," Sam said. "It's too good."

Then Matt punched Sam in the arm, and Sam almost dropped his plate. Luckily, Mrs. Taylor appeared just in time.

"All right, boys, that's enough," she said. "We've got hot dogs coming up next if you're still hungry."

There was still plenty of food left, so the Cupcakers got our plates together and then went to sit on a blanket Emma had spread out for us under one of the trees in her yard. For a minute, I couldn't help but think of all my past Labor Days, which I spent hanging out with Callie at her house. It was a little weird to be somewhere new, but I had my three best friends with me. And that felt good.

Even better, we didn't talk about Callie or the BFC or even the fund-raiser. We talked about teachers and that new cooking contest reality show on TV, and Alexis complained about her older sister, Dylan, and Mia complained about her stepbrother, Dan.

"My grandma Carole's going to have heart surgery," I blurted out during the conversation. I'm not sure why I said it, but I guess I wanted my friends to know.

"Oh no! Is she going to be okay?" Emma said.

"My mom says she will be," I answered.

"Your grandma is supernice," Alexis said. "Maybe we should make her some get-well cupcakes. Free of charge, of course."

I smiled. Alexis may be all about business sometimes, but she has a big heart, too.

"I hope everything goes okay, Katie," Mia said. "I'm going to make your grandma a get-well card."

"You guys are the best," I said, and I meant it. Then I leaned back on the blanket and looked up at the blue sky that peeked through the leaves of the tree. For that moment, everything was perfect.

I really like it when that happens.

CHAPTER 7

I Can't Believe She Did That!

The next day we had school again, and now that Labor Day was over, it felt more real. Like summer was definitely over, even if it was still kind of hot out.

The teachers were taking it seriously too, and on Tuesday, I got slammed with homework in every class. I didn't want to mess up like I had with my English homework last week, so I made sure to write down everything in my assignment book.

Something else happened on Tuesday too. That's when Callie started acting totally different. Well, not *totally* different, but she wasn't acting like the Callie I knew. The BFC Callie was acting even worse than the PGC Callie.

Let me give you some examples. On Tuesday the Cupcake Club was eating lunch when Sophie and Lucy came over to our table. They're mostly friends with Mia, but they're nice to everyone.

"Congratulations, Mia, you made the list," Sophie said. But she didn't say it in an excited way. She sounded more sarcastic.

"What list?" Mia asked.

Lucy nodded over to the BFC table. "Callie, Maggie, and Bella invited us to eat lunch with them today. So we said yes, and while we were there, they started making a list of who has the best hair today and who has lame hair. Can you believe it?"

"That is so rude," Alexis exclaimed, fuming.

"Yeah, you and Katie are both on the lame-hair list," Sophie told us.

That made me mad, but I decided to make a joke about it instead.

"Oh no! I guess my dreams of being a famous hair model are over," I said, and everyone laughed.

Alexis stood up. "I should go over there and tear that list to pieces."

"Don't do it," Mia said. "We can't show them that it bothers us."

"Why should it bother you? You're on the good list," Alexis said.

"It bothers me because you guys are my friends," Mia said.

327

"I must be invisible," Emma said, twirling a strand of her blond hair. "I'm not even on the list at all. I think that's even more insulting."

"Just thought you should know," Sophie said with a shrug, and the two girls walked off.

Alexis didn't look mad anymore. She looked thoughtful. "Interesting," she said. "I wonder why they invited Sophie and Lucy to sit with them."

"Maybe they're recruiting new members," Emma suggested.

"They probably just want to find somebody to make their cupcakes for them, so they don't have to do the dirty work," I said, feeling cranky again.

"I don't know," Mia said. "The PGC was always so closed off. Maybe Callie is trying to open things up and be a little friendlier."

Alexis snorted. "Right. The 'new and improved' BFC led by the 'new and improved' Callie."

So the hair thing is one example. Then there's the whole flirting thing. In social studies, Callie and Maggie were whispering to each other before the bell rang. Then Tyler Norstrom, this tall boy on the basketball team, walked into the room. When he walked past Callie's desk, I noticed she did this thing where she tossed her hair over her shoulder. Then she looked straight at Tyler and batted her eyelashes at him.

You know, Callie is really pretty, and I guess she can pull off that kind of stuff if she wants to. But this hair-tossing person was not the Callie I grew up with. Now she was becoming more like Sydney every day.

After school on Tuesday, I went right home and started on my mountain of homework. I decided to do my English first, so I wouldn't forget it. I scanned the instruction sheet. We had to write about the assigned book we read over the summer. There were all these choices on what to write, and I picked writing a letter about the book. I wrote a really good letter, giving all the details of the book, and it was one page longer than Ms. Harmeyer asked for. I was pretty satisfied when I was done, because I knew it would impress her.

The next morning I saw Callie in the hallway. She was at her locker with Maggie and Bella. Then my friend Beth Suzuki from Spanish class walked by. Beth has a kind of funky fashion style, like Mia. She was wearing black leggings and a black top, with a black-and-white scarf around her neck and red high-tops.

I actually heard Callie say, "Red sneakers?

Seriously?" It wasn't a particularly funny or clever thing to say, but both Bella and Maggie laughed. I don't think Beth heard them, though.

And those examples aren't even the worst. At lunchtime, I was in the hall, walking to the cafeteria, when Callie came over to me.

"Hey, Katie," she said. "Do you want to eat lunch with us today?"

I felt like a bus hit me. What was Callie up to? I was really surprised. Then I realized she was waiting for an answer. Well, whatever her plans were, I wasn't about to give her any satisfaction.

"No, thanks," I said. "I always sit with my *friends*."

Callie flinched, like she was shocked by my answer. "What gives?" she asked me. "I'm trying to be nice here."

"You mean nice, like when you put me on your lame-hair list?" I asked.

Callie's face turned a little red. "Maggie did that."

"Right. Because *her* hair is so awesome," I said. I knew that was childish, but I couldn't help it.

"We were just goofing around," Callie said. "Come on, sit with us."

On a scale of one to ten, my annoyance level with Callie was at a hundred.

"If you're trying to make things up to me, it's a little late," I said. "And don't expect me to jump when you ask me to do stuff, like Bella and Maggie do."

"Wow, and I thought you were my friend," Callie said, acting hurt.

"I *was* your friend. Your best friend," I replied. "And then you dumped me for Sydney. You let Sydney say mean stuff about me, and you didn't stick up for me. Half the time you acted like you didn't know me. So don't tell *me* I'm not a good friend. I never did anything like that to you."

I could feel my eyes stinging, and I saw a few people staring at us as they walked by.

Do not cry, I warned myself. *You will never live it down.*

"You—you don't know how much pressure I'm under," Callie stammered. "I just wanted to be popular. . . . When Sydney asked me to join the PGC last year, I couldn't say no. I asked her to stop teasing you in gym class, but she wouldn't listen."

"Then you should have stopped being friends with her," I said flatly. "I wouldn't be friends with somebody who was mean to you."

Callie shook her head. "You don't understand.

It wasn't that simple. But Sydney's gone now, anyway. So I thought—"

"Sorry, Callie," I interrupted. "My friends are waiting for me."

I turned and walked into the noisy cafeteria. My heart was pounding really fast. I felt hurt and sad and mad and good, all at the same time.

I had wanted to say that stuff to Callie for months.

CHAPTER 8

A Totally Groovy Theme

At lunch, I didn't tell my friends what happened, because I was feeling kind of rattled. But I was in the mood to talk about it that night, when Mom and I were eating Chinese take-out. And yes, if you're counting, that's take-out again. What can I say, Mom was on a roll? But I love Chinese food, so I wasn't complaining.

"So, Mom," I said, twirling a lo mein on my plate. "Something weird happened in school today. Callie asked me to eat lunch at her table!"

"That's nice, honey," Mom said.

"No, it is *not* nice!" I insisted. "You know Callie has been ignoring me for a year so she can hang out with girls who are mean to me. And just because Sydney's gone, she thinks I'll just run over and sit with her. Can you believe that?"

While I was talking, Mom was texting someone on her cell phone.

"Mom! Are you listening?" I asked.

Mom put down the phone. "It sounds like she's trying to make things up to you. I'm not sure why you're so upset."

"Forget it," I said, and Mom picked up her phone again. Now I was upset about Callie *and* Mom. Why was everyone acting so weird?

On Thursday night we had a Cupcake Club meeting at Mia's house. Mia wasn't going to be around for the weekend, because she stays with her dad in New York City every other weekend. Her parents are divorced, like mine, only I don't get to see my dad. I think Mia's pretty lucky, even though she has to sort of live in two different places. But she doesn't seem to mind.

Anyway, Mia's house is fun, because she has two little fluffy dogs, Milkshake and Tiki. Plus, Mia's mom and her stepdad, Eddie, let us have a dinner meeting.

We ate pizza (with no veggies!) in the dining room as we tried—once again—to come up with plans for the school fund-raiser. But first I was finally ready to tell my friends about my face-off with Callie.

"No way!" Alexis said when I was done with the story. "Who does she think she is?"

"It's kind of weird she doesn't realize how much she hurt your feelings before," Emma said.

"I know, right?" I said. It felt good to have my friends back me up.

"I don't know," Mia said cautiously. "I mean, it sounds like she tried to make up with you."

"She probably just wants to convert Katie to the BFC, so that she can bake the cupcakes," Alexis said.

I hadn't thought of that. But it was possible that Alexis was on to something.

"Well, that will *never* happen," I promised. "Cupcake Club forever!"

Alexis opened up her laptop. "Well, there might not *be* a Cupcake Club if we lose the fund-raiser," she said dramatically.

"Hey, Alexis, what happened to your notebook?" I asked.

"In the Future Business Leaders of America we're encouraged to use our laptops," she said. "It's more efficient."

"Maybe we could google some cupcake ideas," Mia suggested.

"I like that back-to-school cupcake that Katie's mom made her"—Alexis flipped the laptop around to show the photo that I sent everyone—"but we might need to charge a lot for it to cover our overall production costs."

"Let's start with a design," Mia suggested. "Then we can pick a flavor that goes with the design."

"We have to think of something everybody likes," I said. "What about the beach? Everyone likes the beach, right? Maybe we can do a tropical cupcake, and we can decorate the booth with beach balls and stuff."

"That's fun, but it doesn't feel like school, or fall," Mia pointed out.

I sighed. "I know."

Alexis was furiously surfing the Web. "You know, it's the fiftieth anniversary of Park Street Middle School this year. Maybe we could do something with that."

"Like cupcakes with a big 'fifty' on them?" Emma asked.

Alexis thought for a moment. "Hmm . . . so the school opened in the 1960s. Maybe we could do a sixties theme."

"Like a groovy peace-and-love kind of theme?" I asked.

"That would be so cool," Mia agreed. "We could do tie-dyed icing! And T-shirts to match!"

"And we could decorate the cupcakes with peace signs," Emma added.

I really loved the idea. Anytime I get to wear rainbow colors, I'm happy.

"If we do tie-dyed icing, we should keep the flavors simple," Alexis said. "Chocolate or vanilla. Most people like simple flavors, anyway."

"How do we make tie-dyed icing?" Emma asked.

Mia shrugged. "I'm not sure. But I bet we could figure it out."

"I'll see if there's anything online," Alexis said, and started typing.

"Mia, do you think your mom would mind if we baked?" I asked.

Mia shook her head. "Nope. She even bought extra eggs and milk, just in case we wanted to."

"Then let's clean up the pizza and get started," I said. "I have an idea."

By now I think the Cupcake Club has baked thousands of cupcakes. Okay, maybe not thousands, but at least hundreds. So we can whip up a dozen vanilla cupcakes in no time.

After about a half hour we had a pan of cupcakes

baking in the oven. Mia's stepdad, Eddie, came into the room and smelled the air.

"Mmm, I love when you girls have Cupcake meetings at this house," he said.

"This is just a test batch, so you'll definitely get some," Mia promised him.

Eddie smiled. "It's my lucky day!"

While the cupcakes baked, we mixed powdered sugar, butter, a little milk, and some vanilla together to make a basic vanilla frosting.

"Mia, do you have food coloring?" I asked.

"Sure." Mia went to the cabinet and came back with a package that contained five little bottles of liquid food coloring. First, I put in a few drops of yellow. Then I swirled it around with the tip of my knife.

"Ooh, pretty," Emma said. "Can I try?"

I nodded, and Emma put in some blue and then swirled it around the yellow. Then Mia did the same thing with red, and Alexis added green.

"It looks pretty good," I said. "Now we just have to see how it looks on the cupcakes."

After the cupcakes were done baking and we'd let them cool, we tried spreading the tie-dyed icing on them. But when we did that, the colors started blending together, and the color ended up looking like a depressing purplish brown.

I frowned. "Sorry, guys."

"No, we almost had it," Mia said. "I think it'll work if we ice the cupcakes *first*, and then do the swirly food-coloring thing."

Emma frowned. "That will take forever, won't it?"

"It might, but we want to win, don't we?" Alexis pointed out.

"It won't be so bad," I said. "Besides, I think if we use the gel food coloring, the color will be easier to control."

Eddie came back into the kitchen and made a face. "What kind of icing is that?"

"Ugly but delicious," I told him.

Mia handed him one. "You can taste test it for us. I know you love to do that."

Eddie peeled away the cupcake liner and took a bite. "It *is* delicious!" he said. "But I need some milk."

Eddie took five cups out of the cabinet, got the milk out of the refrigerator, and put everything on the table. "Won't you ladies join me?"

We all sat down. Mia poured the milk, and we all happily ate our cupcakes and drank our milk.

"There's nothing like cake and milk," Eddie said. "It reminds me of being a little boy."

"Eddie, you were a little boy in the sixties, right?" Alexis asked.

Eddie nodded. "That's right. Why do you ask?"

"I've got an idea," Mia said. "We could sell milk to go with our cupcakes, just like in the old days."

"Old days? Hey, I'm not that old," Eddie protested.

"You know, my mom and I get our milk from this place that sells it in old-fashioned glass bottles," I said. "We could pour the milk from those and then recycle the empty bottles. We can donate that money to the school too."

Eddie nodded. "It sounds like you girls have a good idea."

I grinned and made a peace sign with my fingers. "It's not just good. It's totally groovy!"

CHAPTER 9

Ugh! Another Poem

The next day was Cupcake Friday. We started calling it that because that's the day one of us brings in cupcakes for lunch. This week it was Mia's turn.

"Ta-da!" she said, opening up the small box she had brought. Inside were four perfect cupcakes. The icing on top was light blue and green, and it was piped on, so that it looked like ocean waves, or feathers, even.

"They are so pretty," I said.

"They're plain vanilla, but I'm practicing with those new decorating tips I got," Mia said. "Once you get the hang of it, it's easy."

"If you put candy fish on top, it could look like the ocean," Emma suggested.

"We need to keep a database of these ideas,"

Alexis said. "Maybe someone will ask us to do a pool party or something. These would be perfect. We just have to remember."

"I have a file of stuff at home," I said. "It's full of recipes and pictures of cupcakes from magazines."

Alexis nodded. "We should scan all that in onto my laptop. Maybe we could do it this weekend?"

I shook my head. "We're spending the weekend at my grandma's," I said. Mom had told me last night.

"Oh, that reminds me," Mia said. "I made a card for her."

Mia dug into her backpack and pulled out a card made of folded scrapbook paper. On the front she had drawn a robin, Grandma Carole's favorite bird, and surrounded it with lots of flowers.

"I remembered the robin from when we made that birthday cupcake cake for her," Mia said.

"Mia, it's so beautiful!" I said. "She'll love it."

"Katie, Emma and I were going to make a card for her this weekend," Alexis said.

"You guys can sign this one," Mia offered.

Everyone signed the card. Then I put it away, so it wouldn't get cupcake icing on it.

"Oh, by the way," Alexis said. "In French class

today, Maggie and Bella were whispering really loudly about the BFC cupcakes. They kept saying it was a huge secret and everyone was going to be blown away."

"They can try," I said. "But our cupcakes are going to be awesome."

The rest of the afternoon went pretty slowly, probably because it was Friday and I couldn't wait for school to be over. The last class of the day was English, and at the start of class, Ms. Harmeyer handed back our homework from earlier in the week. I was excited, because I knew I did really well on the assignment.

So you can imagine how I felt when I got my paper back and saw a big red C on it. I was totally shocked. I was dying to ask Ms. Harmeyer about it, and it was torture to wait until the end of class. When the bell rang, I ran up to her desk.

"Ms. Harmeyer, um, I have a question," I said. "I thought I did a really good job on this. I even wrote extra. So . . ."

"It was very well written, Katie," Ms. Harmeyer said. "But you didn't follow the instructions. You were supposed to write the letter from the point of view of one of the characters in the book. So I had to lower your grade because of that."

I couldn't believe it. I was sure I had done everything just right! My eyes got hot. What was up with me lately? Everything was making me want to cry.

Ms. Harmeyer lost the serious expression she usually wore. "Katie, I understand you did exceptionally well in English last year," she said. "But you seem to be struggling so far this year. Is everything all right?"

"I guess," I said. "I mean, my grandma needs to have an operation, and my mom's really worried, and then there's this whole thing going on with this girl I used to be friends with. . . ."

Ms. Harmeyer nodded. "I thought it might be something like that. I do think you need to focus more on your schoolwork if you can, Katie. But I'll give you a special extra-credit assignment, okay?"

"Really?" I asked. "Thank you sooo much!"

"I'll make it easy," she said. "Write me a poem. It can be about anything you want. It's due next Thursday."

I made a face. "A poem?"

"What's the matter?" the teacher asked. "Don't you like poetry?"

"It's okay," I said. "But it's hard to write. It's like I know what I want to say, but then I can't make it rhyme or put the right number of beats on each line. So it comes out all wrong."

"Not all poetry has to rhyme," Ms. Harmeyer told me. "I'll tell you what. You spend the weekend thinking of what you want your poem to be about. On Monday I'll bring in some examples of different types of poetry, and we can look at them together. Then maybe you'll feel better about poems."

"Okay," I said, nodding. "Thanks."

I dreaded showing Mom the C I got on my homework, but when she saw it that night, she said basically the same thing as Ms. Harmeyer.

"I know you have a lot on your mind, Katie," Mom said. "I'm sorry if I haven't been acting like myself lately. I'm sure it will all calm down after Grandma's surgery. Can you hang in there for me?"

"Don't worry, Mom. It's okay," I said. "Plus, Ms. Harmeyer gave me an extra-credit assignment, so I can make up the grade."

That night, we packed our bags, and the next morning we headed out to Grandma Carole and Grandpa Chuck's house. We live in the same state, but they live near the ocean, in one of those places where the houses are all owned by old people— or senior citizens, as my mom always tells me to say. (For some reason, old people do not like to be called old.)

On the ride down we listened to the radio, and I stared out the window at the trees. I tried to think of an idea for my poem. I could write about cupcakes. Or maybe I could write a poem about how awesome my grandma Carole is. That would be nice.

Suddenly, as I was thinking about Grandma Carole, I got sad. What if this was the last time I got to see her, ever? Mom said she was going to be okay. I had to believe that.

When we finally got to Grandma and Grandpa's little yellow house, Grandma Carole was standing by the open front door with a big smile on her face. I totally stopped worrying. She looked just like she always does. Her white hair was cut short, and she wore a blue T-shirt with white exercise pants, and sneakers.

"I'm so lucky! I get both of my girls this weekend!" Grandma said, hugging us.

"How are you feeling?" I asked her.

"Not bad, Katie, not bad," Grandma said. "I'll feel better when the surgery is over with. But between my doctors and Grandpa Chuck and your mom, I'm in very good hands."

"Hey, I need some hugs too!" Grandpa Chuck called out. He was in the living room, his feet resting on an ottoman.

"Hope you don't mind if I don't get up," he said as I bent down to hug him. "Doctor says I need one of those new-fangled bionic knees. But that won't happen until your grandma is back on her feet."

"That won't take long at all," Grandma promised.

"Grandma, I have something for you," I said. I reached into my overnight bag and got out the get-well card that Mia had made and we all signed.

"Oh, how beautiful!" Grandma said, and her eyes got teary (maybe that's where I get it from).

Normally, when we visit my grandparents, we go out and do stuff. We drive to the beach and then walk around, or play tennis, or go to the driving range to hit golf balls. But I guess Grandma wasn't supposed to do that stuff, because all morning, Mom and Grandma Carole were doing paperwork, and Grandpa Chuck and I were watching TV. It was kind of boring.

Then I helped Mom make lunch, and I got an idea.

"Mom, do you think Grandma would make cupcakes with us?" I asked. "Maybe we could bring them to the nurses at her doctor's office."

"That's a lovely idea," Mom said. "But we've got to do all the dishes, okay?"

"Of course!" I said.

So for the rest of the afternoon we looked through Grandma's old recipe book and picked out a recipe for banana cinnamon cupcakes. Then we made them, and Grandpa Chuck put on his favorite country music CD. We sang and joked around, and I didn't worry about Grandma Carole one bit.

That's the good thing about making cupcakes. While you're doing it, it's hard to worry about other stuff. And at the end you get something delicious to eat. Maybe if everyone baked more cupcakes, the world would be a happier place.

CHAPTER 10

A Bad Day

ℐ ended up having fun visiting Grandma Carole and Grandpa Chuck, but I was glad when we got home on Sunday. I had lots of homework to do, and by Monday morning I was really eager to see my friends.

Since I knew I had to focus on work, I decided I had to ignore Callie as much as possible. Mostly, it was easy to do because Callie didn't seem interested in talking to me (or even looking at me), either. Sometimes it was harder to do, especially because we had a few classes together. But Mia being in the same classes too made it okay.

Then, when I needed her most, Mia had to leave school, because she had a bad toothache. She left in the middle of social studies. I felt bad for her, but since Mia's dentist is my mom, I knew she would be okay.

The next class was science with Ms. Chandar. That day, we were doing a lab where we had to mix some chemicals together in a beaker and then watch the reaction. Normally I'm pretty good at this kind of thing, because it's sort of like baking. Plus, with Mia as my lab partner, it would've been easy.

But without Mia, I was on my own.

"It is a simple experiment, Katie," Ms. Chandar said. "You can do it without a partner."

We went to get our ingredients for the experiment, which was a container of blue stuff and a container of clear stuff. I listened carefully as Ms. Chandar told us how to measure out the blue stuff and then pour it into the clear stuff. I carefully began to pour—and then I sneezed.

I don't know where it came from. It was one of those random sneezes. It took me by surprise, and I dropped the beaker. The blue stuff spilled all over the lab table in front of me.

Ms. Chandar didn't notice, so I had to raise my hand.

"I had an accident," I told her, which is a pretty embarrassing thing to have to say in front of the whole class.

Ms. Chandar sighed. "The towels are in the cabinet at the back of the room."

As I headed for the towels, I noticed that my hands were bright blue. And, of course, I had to walk right past Maggie and Bella's table to get to the towels.

"Way to go, Katie," Maggie said, giggling.

"Is that how you make your cupcakes, too?" Bella asked.

I ignored them and got the towels. Then I had to walk past them again.

"Look! Katie has Smurf hands!" Maggie said, and now a bunch of kids were laughing.

"She's Clumsy Smurf!" Bella said, and then they both started cracking up.

My face turned red, but I just kept walking. You won't believe what happened next. Eddie Rossi walked up to Maggie and Bella.

"Cut it out, guys," he said. "It was just an accident."

Maggie and Bella quickly stopped laughing. I know they think Eddie is cute, and they both looked kind of embarrassed.

Thank you, I mouthed to Eddie, and then hurried to my desk and started wiping up the mess.

Weird, right? I mean, normally Eddie would have started cracking up too and calling me Smurf Face or something.

Maybe Alexis and Mia are right, I thought. *Maybe he does like me.*

Which was even weirder, because, well, I don't think of Eddie like that. But it was definitely interesting.

When I got home from school, I wanted to talk to Mia about it, but I didn't want to bug her if her tooth was still hurting her.

When Mom came home from work, the first thing I asked was "How's Mia?"

"She's got a cavity, but she's feeling better already," Mom said. "I'm seeing her again tomorrow after school, to go over her X-rays. One of her permanent teeth is growing in a little bit strange."

"I'm glad she's okay," I said. I took out my cell phone to text her, but then Mom kept talking.

"Katie, I need to discuss something with you," Mom said. "Mrs. Rogers's daughter's baby came early, so she can't come stay with you this weekend."

"Hooray!" I said. "So I can stay at Mia's, right?"

Mom shook her head. "Just on Friday night, when you're making cupcakes. But you'll be going home with the Wilsons after the fund-raiser. I won't be home until late Tuesday, and I want to make sure you're in good hands while I'm gone."

I was completely shocked. "No way!" I protested. "You can't expect me to go over to Callie's! She's, like, my mortal enemy now!"

Mom sighed. "Katie, it's decided. This is not up for discussion."

"But it's not fair!" I yelled, and I was definitely crying now. "I can't stand being around Callie! Why can't I just stay at Mia's the whole time?"

"Because it's a lot to ask for you to stay with someone for that long. Barbara is my best friend, and I don't want to have to worry about you while I'm worried about Grandma and everything else," Mom said in a rush. "End of story."

"You don't understand!" I wailed. "You can't do this to me!"

"Katie, enough!" Mom yelled, which is something she almost never does. "I know you've been having problems with Callie for a while now, but Grandma Carole is a lot more important than your silly dramas with your friends. You're going to stay at Callie's, and you're just going to have to deal with it. Now go to your room until you cool off."

I ran out of the living room and stomped up the stairs as hard and as loud as I could. Then I went into my room, slammed the door behind me, and fell facedown onto my bed.

I cried for a while, and then I texted Mia.

Mom says I have 2 stay with Callie for 4 days while she is gone! How am I supposed to do that?

I'll ask my mom if you can stay here, Mia texted.

It's no use. She's best friends with Callie's mom, so she doesn't care that Callie and I are enemies now, I typed.

Maybe it won't be so bad, Mia said.

I don't even want to breathe the same air as her, I wrote back.

The next message I got from Mia was a photo of an astronaut.

U can wear this, she wrote.

LOL, I typed, and I really was.

Mia can always make me feel better. Then I remembered—Mia needed to feel better too.

How is your tooth? I asked.
Better, she replied. Ur Mom is nice.
Aaaaaa! Only sometimes! I wrote.

Now, I know that wasn't exactly true. She is nice most of the time. But right then I was superangry with her.

After I said good-bye to Mia, I went to my desk and turned on my laptop. I knew exactly what my poem was going to be about.

CHAPTER II

Now I'm Confused Again

There is a black cloud in my heart.
When it rains, I cry.
Nothing is fair.
Nothing is fair.
Why do people get sick?
Why do friends fight?

I won't write the whole poem here now, because it's kind of long, but you get the idea. Once I realized I didn't have to rhyme, then it was kind of easy. I just concentrated on my feelings. Plus, I made sure to put in some metaphors and similes, to make Ms. Harmeyer happy, so I could get a good grade.

I have to admit that I actually felt better after I wrote the poem. Kind of like my angry feelings left me and attached to the paper or something. Running makes me feel better too, but in a different way. When I run, worries and other feelings leave my body, but I guess with poetry, those feelings float away into the air.

The next day, it was hard to even look at Callie, though, because my stomach flip-flopped every time I thought about having to stay with her. Thank goodness for my friends. At least they understood.

"That's just awful!" Emma said when I told her and Alexis about it during lunch. Mia sat next to me and nodded sympathetically.

"You could stay at my house," Alexis offered.

"Or mine," Emma added.

I shook my head. "Thanks, but I already tried seeing if I could stay at Mia's. Mom's being totally unfair about it."

"It'll go by fast," Mia said.

"Bring headphones with you," Alexis suggested.

I sighed. "I'll just be glad when this is over."

"Hey, Mom said we could do the test batch at our house tonight," Emma said. "Is seven okay?"

Everyone said that would be fine.

"Mom and I bought the ingredients over the weekend," Emma continued.

"I hope you saved your receipt," said Alexis.

Emma rolled her eyes. "Of course! I know you would never let me forget it if I didn't."

I suddenly felt nervous. "It feels like we still have a ton of things to do," I said. "What about the decorations and everything?"

"I made a tie-dyed tablecloth for us at Dad's last weekend," Mia reported. "Ava helped me."

"And my dad's going to get the milk for us on Saturday morning," Alexis said. "He's going to donate the milk, since it's for a good cause."

"Oh, and we found the cutest striped straws to put in the cups of milk!" Emma reported. "They're rainbow colored, to go with the tie-dyed theme."

"And we're going to wear aprons that we can decorate with peace symbols and stuff," Alexis said.

"Wow," I said. "You guys did all that?"

"We were texting all weekend," Alexis said. "We didn't want to bother you at your grandma's."

For a second I didn't know if my feelings should be hurt, but then I decided they shouldn't be. I'm glad I spent the weekend with Grandma Carole instead of worrying about the fund-raiser.

"Thanks for doing all that," I said.

"Besides, Katie, we're counting on you to make the cupcakes as groovy as possible," Mia added.

I nodded. "I'll feel better after we do the test batch."

Mia frowned. "I've got to go back to your mom after school today. I hope I can still get my homework done, or I might not be able to come."

"Don't worry about it," Alexis said. "It's just a test. Friday night is when we'll need all four of us to really work."

I made a fake-sad face. "Now I have to ride the bus by myself again!"

"Well, at least you won't have metal tools in your mouth," Mia said.

"Good point," I agreed.

I still had four classes to go before the bus, and at least I had Mia with me for social studies and science. When we got to science class, I whispered the story of what had happened with Eddie the day before. Mia nodded.

"I *told* you he likes you!" she whispered back.

I shook my head. I still couldn't believe it.

Then in drama class we learned some interesting stuff about the history of theater in ancient Greece, and in English class I handed in my poem to Ms. Harmeyer. This time, I was *sure* I had done a good job. I couldn't wait to get it back.

When school was out, I slid into my usual seat

on the bus: the sixth row from the front. Then something very surprising happened. George Martinez sat next to me!

"Hey," he said.

"Hey," I said back. I felt a little nervous all of a sudden. What could George want?

"So, with that social studies homework, are we supposed to answer all those review questions or just the fill-in ones at the top?" he asked.

All right, I thought. *He's just asking about homework. That's cool.*

I took out my assignment book and looked through it. "All of them," I told him.

George sighed. "Man, I hate those questions on the bottom. They take so long to do."

"I know," I agreed. "Do you think Mrs. Kratzer even reads all those answers?"

"I bet she does," George says. "She looks like she loves to read. I bet her house is full of books."

"Just because she wears glasses?" I asked.

George shrugged. "I don't know. It's just . . . that's how she looks."

That reminded me of something. "We were watching this old TV show at my grandparents' house, and there was this episode where this guy loved books, and then the world ended or something. But he was happy, because he could read all the time. And then his eyeglasses broke!"

"The Twilight Zone," George said. "My dad loves that show. He has them all on DVD. That was a good episode."

I shuddered. "That show is supercreepy. I'd rather see a funny show."

"Did you see that new cartoon about the chicken that's trying to rule the world?" George asked.

I nodded. (Yes, I still watch cartoons sometimes.) "That show is hysterical. Like when he tried to attack the city with that giant omelet?"

"'More onions! More onions!'" George yelled, imitating the chicken, and we both started cracking up.

Then I realized something. George and I were having an actual conversation, just like I would have with Mia or Alexis or Emma. We weren't just goofing around or teasing each other. It was kind of nice.

I was laughing so hard that I almost missed getting off at my bus stop.

"Hey, Katie!" the bus driver yelled. "You're up."

I grabbed my backpack. "See ya," I told George. As the bus drove past, George waved to me through the window. I couldn't help thinking about what Mia had said on the first day of school.

I think they both like you!

It was all so strange. I definitely didn't know how I felt about Eddie liking me, if he did. But when I thought about George liking me, I decided I didn't mind so much.

Aaaaah! My face was getting red just thinking about it.

CHAPTER 12

Spectacular!

*L*ater that night, Alexis, Emma, and I did a test batch of the cupcakes (Mia couldn't make it after all), and this time the icing came out perfectly. So when Friday rolled around, we were ready for a marathon baking session. First we'd bake our cupcakes for Mona and then work on our contest cupcakes.

My mom dropped me off at Mia's at four o'clock. Our car was packed with stuff: my sleeping bag; a big duffel bag full of my clothes; my school backpack; four cupcake pans; four cooling racks; a box of stuff for the booth; and a Crock-Pot filled with veggie chili and a basket of corn bread, because Mom felt bad that Mia's mom and stepdad had to feed us dinner again.

"You didn't have to do this, Sharon," Mrs.Valdes said as she and Mia helped us unload the car. "I know you've got so much to do these days."

"I don't mind," Mom said. "I wish I could help out more. Thanks so much for hosting the girls tonight and for letting Katie sleep over. Did you get the phone numbers I sent you?"

Mia's mom nodded. "We'll take good care of Katie, we promise. I hope everything works out all right with your mother."

Mom smiled. "Me too," she said with a sigh. "Thanks."

After we got everything into Mia's house, I walked with Mom back to the car.

"Now, don't forget. Mrs. Wilson is going to bring you home after the fund-raiser tomorrow," Mom reminded me.

"I know," I said glumly.

Mom hugged me. "I love you," she said. "Don't worry. Everything will be okay."

I knew Mom was talking about Grandma, and that made me feel good. But Mom still didn't really understand, or didn't really care, how I felt about staying with Callie. That definitely did *not* feel okay.

I went back inside, and Alexis and Emma

showed up a few minutes later. We all gathered in Mia's kitchen. It's nice and big, with an island in the middle, so it's a good space to make a ton of cupcakes.

"Okay, troops, it's time for battle!" Alexis announced. "We've got a lot to do if we're going to beat the BFC."

I saluted. "What's the plan, General?"

"First, we bake," Alexis said. "While the cupcakes bake, we'll make the icing. When the cupcakes cool, I was thinking you and Mia could ice them while Emma and I work on the aprons."

Emma held up a plain white apron. "I brought some fabric pens, so we can draw peace signs and stuff on them."

"Awesome," I said. "I'll start loading the cupcake tins."

Between the four of us, we had eight cupcake tins. I lined them up on Mia's kitchen table. Mia came over with a paper bag.

"Look what I found at that fancy bake shop," she said. She pulled out two packs of cupcake liners with a tie-dyed pattern.

"Oh my gosh, they're perfect!" I cried. "But wait a second. This is a fund-raiser, right? How are we paying for all this?"

"Well, my mom and dad donated the baking supplies," Emma said.

"And my dad's getting the milk," Alexis reminded them. "We'll have to pay for the aprons and cupcake liners out of our general fund. But I like to think of it as advertising. We could get a bunch of customers out of this." Then she frowned. "Rats! I made a flyer for us to hand out, but I forgot to print it. Let me text my mom."

Pretty soon we were in our usual cupcake-making groove. We made a batch of batter in Mia's stand mixer. We filled the tins. Then we made a new batch. We kept baking until we had two hundred and four cupcakes cooling on the table—that's seventeen dozen!

That's when Mia's mom came in. "I think it's time you girls had a break," she said. "Dinner's ready in the dining room."

We washed up and then headed into the dining room, where the table was set for seven: the Cupcake Club; Mrs. Valdes; Eddie; and Mia's stepbrother, Dan. Besides Mom's chili and corn bread, there was a big salad on the table.

"You girls are busy bees in there," Eddie said, and he started scooping the chili into bowls.

"We have sooo much left to do," I lamented.

"I think you girls are doing great," said Mia's mom. "It's not even seven o'clock yet."

"When do we get to taste them?" Eddie asked.

"Soon," Mia promised. "We already made one batch of icing. Then Katie's going to do her swirly tie-dyed magic on the cupcakes."

"It's easy," I said. "You'll be able to do it too."

Dan didn't say much—he never docs. But maybe that's because he was busy eating. He ate three bowls of chili and four pieces of corn bread. I glanced at Mia after Dan went for his fourth bowl.

She shrugged. "He's working out a lot lately. Getting ready for basketball season."

Dan nodded. "Besides, this stuff is awesome."

Dan was still eating when we got up, cleared our plates, and got to work on icing the cupcakes. Mia put a smooth coat of vanilla icing on the first cupcake and then handed it to me.

I was armed with a box of toothpicks and several tubes of gel color. I put a tiny drop of yellow onto the icing and then swirled it with a toothpick. Then I swirled on a drop of green and then a drop of blue.

"Awesome!" Mia said. "That looks perfect!"

"See? You can so do it," I told her.

Mia nodded. "I'll ice and you swirl, and then we'll switch."

Mia and I got busy with the icing, and once the dining room table was clear, Alexis and Emma used it as their work space to do the aprons. We had four dozen cupcakes done by the time Emma walked in wearing one of the aprons. It had peace signs and flowers with big round petals all over it.

"Wow, that's fantastic!" Mia said.

"Spectacular!" I agreed. "Our booth is going to look very groovy."

Alexis joined us. "You know, we forgot to talk about how we're displaying them. I guess we can just use our round plastic trays." The trays are our go-to display method. They're supercheap to buy, and we can use them again and again. But thanks to Mom, I had something better.

"I almost forgot!" I said. I put down the cupcake I was icing and went into the front hallway, where I had dumped all my stuff. I came back into the kitchen carrying a box.

"You know how Mom likes to collect old things?" I asked. "Well, she has these vintage glass cake stands she said we could borrow. They're kind of sixties looking, right?"

"They're perfect!" Alexis said happily.

"I like how they're all different heights," Mia said. "That'll look cool when we set up the cupcakes."

Hearing that made me feel good, because now I felt like I had contributed something to the booth besides the cupcake design.

"We'll be done with the aprons in a little while," Emma said. "Then we'll come help you ice the cupcakes."

About an hour later, almost all the cupcakes were done and stored away in the plastic containers we use to keep them fresh and to transport them. Eddie and Dan came into the kitchen as we were finishing up.

"Got any for us to taste?" Eddie asked.

We actually learned early on that it's a good idea to taste our cupcakes before we serve them. Sometimes mistakes can happen that you can't see with your eyes—like not putting in enough sugar or adding too much salt, for example. So it's always good to have cupcake tasters on hand. For some reason, fathers and brothers seem to be very good at this.

Mia handed Eddie and Dan one cupcake each. Then we were all quiet as we watched them both take a bite.

Eddie grinned. "These are very good."

"Just very good?" Alexis asked. "Would you say they were award-winning cupcakes?"

"They're excellent!" Eddie said.

"Excellent isn't good enough," Mia said. "We need them to be spectacular."

"Well, they taste excellent and they look spectacular," Eddie said.

That seemed to satisfy everyone but Alexis, who turned to Dan.

"What do you think?" she asked him.

Dan shrugged. "What Dad said."

"Then I think we're good," I said. "Come on, let's finish up these last ones."

It was almost ten o'clock when we finally had everything cleaned up. Alexis's mom came to pick up Alexis and Emma. Alexis was furiously checking her to-do list as she was heading out the door.

"Cupcakes. Aprons. Milk. Straws. Tablecloth. Sign . . . sign!" she cried. "Oh no! We forgot to make a sign for the booth."

"Katie and I will do it," Mia promised.

Alexis sighed. "I'll see you guys in the morning."

She and Emma left, and I yawned. "We have to get up so early!"

"The sign won't take long," Mia reassured me. "I have all the stuff."

We changed into pj's and brushed our teeth, and then I dragged my sleeping bag up to Mia's room. Mia put a big piece of poster board on the floor and then brought out a shoe box filled with markers. I let Mia do all the drawing, because she's awesome at that, and then I helped color in all the bubble letters and flowers.

"Do you think we'll beat Callie and the BFC?" I asked, yawning.

"I don't know," Mia replied. "But we've done all we can. We'll have to wait and see."

I thought about what it would feel like to lose— and then have to go home with Callie after that.

"I really hope we win," I said.

I fell asleep in my sleeping bag on the floor, surrounded by a rainbow of markers.

CHAPTER 13

Some Very Suspicious School Spirit

The fund-raiser officially started at noon, but we decided we wanted to get to the school by ten thirty, so that we would have plenty of time to set up. Eddie made Mia and me a breakfast of omelets and toast. ("Because you worked so hard on those spectacular cupcakes," he told us.) Then Emma's mom drove up in their minivan at ten, with Emma and Alexis, and we loaded everything into the back.

There was no sign of Callie, Maggie, or Bella when we got to the fund-raiser. It was held in the school parking lot, and there were blue canopy tents, with tables underneath them, set up all over the lot. Each table was labeled with the name of a club, and we found the Cupcake Club table pretty quickly.

"We're near the front again," Alexis remarked. "That's good for business."

We got to work getting the booth ready right away. Mia's tie-dyed tablecloth looked fabulous on the table. I arranged Mom's cake platters, and Mia was right—the different heights looked cool. We put on our aprons and then worked together to carefully place the cupcakes on the stands. It's hard to do without getting icing on your fingers, and it's even harder to do without licking your fingers, which wouldn't be very hygienic.

Mr. Becker showed up around eleven thirty, wheeling a big cooler filled with milk bottles.

"Your table looks very nice, girls," he said.

"Thanks for getting the milk for us," I told him.

"I'm happy to support you guys," Alexis's dad replied. "You're all very ambitious. I have some other things for you too."

He unstrapped a cord that was wrapped around the cooler and gave Alexis a cardboard box.

"I had those flyers copied for you this morning," he said.

Alexis hugged him. "You're the best," she said. "When I'm CEO of my own company, you can be my assistant."

Mr. Becker laughed. "I don't think I would want

that job. I have a feeling it wouldn't be easy."

After he left, we all took a look at the flyers Alexis had made.

Having a Party or Special Event?
Serve Your Guests the Best Cupcakes in Town
Made Especially for You
by the Cupcake Club!
We have lots of different flavors and designs!

Underneath the words, there were pictures of some of the cupcakes we've made, and Alexis's cell phone number and the e-mail address we use for the club.

"This is great," I proclaimed. "We'll definitely get new business from this."

The last thing we needed to do was to put up our sign. We poked holes in the corners and then used string to hang it from the canopy poles behind the table. Then we stepped back to admire our work.

PEACE OUT!
Have a Groovy 50th Anniversary, Park Street!
Old School Cupcakes $2.00 • Milk $1.00
The Cupcake Club

The sign was decorated with flowers and peace signs, just like the aprons, and it looked really great. Then Emma's mom walked up with Jake.

"Wow, girls, this is wonderful!" she said. "Let me get a picture!"

Mia and I stood on one side of the table, and Alexis and Emma stood on the other, so we could make sure the cupcakes got in the picture. Of course, Jake ran over at the last minute, so he could be in it too. But he's short, so he didn't block the cupcakes.

"Okay, great," Mrs. Taylor said. "You girls had better get behind the table. You're going to be swamped soon."

She was right. People started swarming into the parking lot. Next to us, the Chess Club was charging people to challenge them at chess. On the other side of us, the school band had set up a funny photo booth. There wasn't any other food nearby, so the hungry people headed right for our cupcakes.

One of our first customers was Principal LaCosta. Even though it was Saturday, she was still dressed like a principal, in a navy blue suit and a pale yellow blouse. Her wavy brown hair was held in place by lots of hairspray, like it always is.

"Ah, the Cupcake Club!" she said. "I'm glad to

see you girls are still at it. And it's great to see that you're celebrating our school anniversary."

She bought one cupcake and one cup of milk. Alexis had a big smile on her face as she deposited the money into the cash box.

Other people liked the theme, too, especially parents.

"Tie-dyed cupcakes. Very groovy!" said one dad. Lots of people said stuff like that, or they flashed a peace sign at us.

We were really busy selling cupcakes for a while, and then I thought of something.

"Hey, we don't even know what kind of cupcakes the BFC has," I said, suddenly feeling worried again. They might be doing even better than we were.

Alexis frowned. "Maybe you and Mia should go check it out. Emma and I can handle this."

Mia and I made our way through the crowd. It wasn't hard to find the BFC booth, because it was the loudest booth in the place. They had a drummer, a trumpet player, and a flute player in front playing football fight songs.

As we got closer, we saw Maggie and Bella dressed as cheerleaders, waving blue-and-yellow pom-poms outside the booth.

"Get your school spirit here!" they were yelling.

Callie was dressed like a cheerleader too, and she was selling the cupcakes behind the BFC table. The cupcakes had white icing and maybe some cinnamon sprinkled on top.

"They didn't even do blue and yellow for school spirit," I remarked to Mia.

Beth Suzuki was walking by, and she heard me. "That's not the kind of school spirit they're talking about."

"What do you mean?" I asked.

"Some kids are saying the cupcakes taste like they have, you know, *spirits* in them," she said. "The kind that makes you drunk."

"That's ridiculous!" I sputtered. "Callie would never do that."

Beth shrugged. "Whatever. That's just what I heard." She walked away, and then we heard Maggie and Bella talking to Eddie Rossi, Wes Kinney, and some other boys about the cupcakes.

"Our cupcakes have lots of *spirit*," Maggie said, emphasizing the last word, and then she winked.

"I'll have ten!" Wes cried, and then he ran to the table.

Mia looked at me, and her eyes were wide. "I can't believe they're doing this!"

Then it hit me. "Wait, I recognize those cupcakes. Mrs. Wilson makes them for Christmas every year. She calls them rum ball cupcakes, but she uses imitation rum extract. I know because my mom told me. I've been eating them since I was little. They taste like rum, but there's no alcohol in them."

"Maybe. But they're trying to make everyone *think* there is," Mia pointed out.

"We'd better tell Alexis and Emma," I said, and we made our way back to the booth.

Emma and Alexis were shocked after we reported what the BFC were doing.

"So *that's* their secret plan," Alexis said. "They must think they'll sell tons of cupcakes if everyone thinks there's alcohol in them."

"Well, it's working," Emma said, glancing at their booth. "Look!"

There was a long line at the BFC stand, mostly made up of boys.

Alexis shook her head. "This is so unfair."

"I guess, but they're not really doing anything wrong, are they?" I asked. "We knew they were going to do something big. So we've just got to try harder, that's all."

"Katie's right," Mia said. She cupped her hands around her mouth. "Get your groovy cupcakes here! Tie-dyed cupcakes! You've never seen any-thing like them!"

I joined in. "See how delicious peace can be!" I yelled. "Give peace a chance!" I knew I sounded silly, but I had to say something. I wasn't going to let the BFC win!

CHAPTER 14

Big Trouble for the BFC

$\mathcal{F}$or the next hour I stayed focused on selling. I poured milk. Mia and Emma handed out cupcakes, and Alexis worked the cash box. I tried not to think of all the great business the BFC was getting, but it was hard not to. Those marching band kids kept playing the same school spirit songs over and over.

"That music is making me crazy!" I cried. "I wish we had our own band. Then we could drown them out."

"Hey, I have an idea," Mia said. She took out her cell phone and then nodded to Emma. "Be right back."

A few minutes later Mia came back with a big smile on her face, but she didn't say what she was planning. After about fifteen minutes her stepdad showed up with one of those boom-box docking stations. He popped in an iPod.

"Where do you want this, Mia?" Eddie asked.

"On the end of the table," she said. "And crank it up!"

Eddie nodded and then turned on the iPod, and a song by the Beatles started playing.

Mia grinned. "Eddie has a whole playlist of sixties songs. Perfect, right?"

"Glad I could help," Eddie said. "How are your sales going?"

I glanced at the table. A lot of cake stands were empty.

"We've sold one hundred and thirty-two cupcakes, but we've got to sell them *all* if we're going to meet our total from last year," Alexis reported.

"Don't forget the milk," Emma reminded her.

"Oh, that's right!" Alexis said. She looked down at her notepad. "We've sold fifty-nine cups of milk."

I looked in the cooler. "We're almost out of milk," I reported. "And we still need to recycle the bottles before the end of the fund-raiser."

Eddie gave us a funny little bow. "At your service, ladies. I'm going to walk around. Give a yell when you want me to take them back to the store for you."

As Mia's stepdad started to walk away, he stopped and did a goofy dance to the music. Mia groaned and rolled her eyes. "Stop! Please! You're going to drive away all our customers!"

Eddie smiled and danced away. He might have been goofy, but the music got the attention of more of the parents. Pretty soon the booth was nice and crowded again.

George even came to the booth with his friend Ken. George started doing this wacky dance to the music, waving his arms in the air and everything. I was cracking up.

Then he walked up to me. "All that dancing made me thirsty. Can I have some milk, please?" He held out a crumpled dollar bill.

"Sure. You need to pay Alexis," I told him as I handed him a cup of milk and a straw.

George took a long, loud slurp of milk. "Mmm, milky!" he said. Then he was quiet for a little bit, like he was going to say something. Finally he said, "So, Katie, you're going to the dance, right?"

I nodded. "Yup."

"Cool," he said. "I guess I'll see you there, then."

And then he paid Alexis, and he and Ken walked away.

Mia looked at me and wiggled her eyebrows.

"Do *not* say it!" I warned her.

Then Emma tapped me on the shoulder. "Hey, look over there!"

Principal LaCosta and Mr. Hammond, the school's vice principal, were marching toward the BFC booth, and they looked angry. The marching band kids stopped playing, but we still couldn't hear what anyone was saying. Principal LaCosta was talking to all the customers, and then all the customers started walking away! Then Maggie and Bella and Callie were talking to Principal LaCosta. Everyone looked very upset. Callie even looked like she might start to cry. I saw Principal LaCosta shaking her head and frowning. She said a few more words to the girls and pointed to the booth. To our amazement, Callie and the BFC started packing up their cupcakes!

The marching band's flute player walked by our booth, so I quickly approached her.

"Hey, what happened to the BFC booth?" I asked.

"Principal LaCosta said the theme of the booth was inappropriate," the girl told me with a shrug. "I thought it was just school spirit. But I guess some kids think there's alcohol in the cupcakes."

I turned back to my friends. "Whoa. Can you believe it?"

"Of course I can," Alexis said. "It doesn't matter if there's alcohol in the cupcakes or not. You can't promote alcohol at a middle school fund-raiser. I'm sure they're in big trouble."

I looked over to the booth and saw Principal LaCosta and Mr. Hammond leading the girls into the school, probably to the principal's office. I felt a twinge of sympathy for Callie . . . but that quickly went away when the BFC's cupcake customers came to our booth instead. It was amazing. We were slammed, and we were sold out of cupcakes in about fifteen minutes.

"This is fantastic!" Alexis said, counting the money. "We made four hundred and sixty-seven dollars—that's more than last year! And that's not even counting the money from the recycled bottles."

"I'll get Eddie!" Mia said, and she sped off to look for him.

I was feeling pretty excited. It looked like we were going to win—again! And then Mrs. Wilson walked up to the booth.

"There you are, Katie," she said. "Listen, I'm afraid we need to leave a little early. I got a call from Principal LaCosta about Callie."

"I know," I said, awkwardly averting her eyes. I felt kind of embarrassed for Callie.

"I have to go get her, and we'll come pick you up on the way to the car, okay?" she asked.

I nodded. "Sorry, guys," I said, turning to Emma and Alexis. "I'll clean up as much as I can before she gets back."

It turns out I had plenty of time to clean up. Principal LaCosta must have had a lot to say to everybody. Mrs. Wilson came back to the booth with Callie about four feet behind her, ignoring us. Her eyes were red, and I could tell she had been crying.

"Ready, Katie?" Mrs. Wilson asked.

"Sure," I said. I went behind the table and grabbed my overnight bag and backpack. Then I followed Mrs. Wilson and Callie out of the parking lot. I packed my stuff into the trunk and slid into the backseat. Callie was in the front seat with her mom, which was a relief. I sat back and tried to act invisible.

"Mom, this is so unfair," Callie wailed. "You know there's no alcohol in those cupcakes."

"I do know that, Callie, but as Principal LaCosta said, that's not the real problem," Mrs. Wilson told her. "The problem is that you tried to make kids *think* there was alcohol in them."

"It's not my fault if people thought that," Callie replied. "I can't control what other people think."

"Principal LaCosta says you and Maggie and Bella were the ones spreading the rumor," said Mrs. Wilson.

"And you believe *her* and not your own daughter?" Callie cried indignantly.

I knew Principal LaCosta was right, because I had seen it myself. But I didn't say anything. Callie was in big enough trouble as it was.

Mrs. Wilson sighed. "That's enough, Callie. We'll talk more about this with your father."

Callie started to cry again, and now I felt *really* awkward. I felt like I should say something to comfort her, but I figured anything I said might just make her mad. So I kept quiet.

Boy, this is going to be a really fun weekend! I thought.

CHAPTER 15

Believe It or Not, Things Get Worse!

few minutes later we pulled up in front of Callie's house. Callie quickly got out of the front seat and slammed the door behind her—hard. Then she walked through the front gate and slammed that behind her. Then she walked through the front door and—you guessed it—slammed that behind her too.

Mrs. Wilson did not look happy as she opened the trunk for me.

"Um, where should I put my bags?" I asked as she walked in the house.

"In Callie's room," she replied. "We pulled out the daybed for you this morning."

I'm sure I turned as pale as vanilla icing when I heard that. Callie's room! Mrs. Wilson actually expected us to stay in the same room! *Ugh!*

Maybe Mrs. Wilson didn't realize how bad things were between me and Callie. Or maybe, like my mom, she was choosing to ignore it. I think they still thought of us as little girls who had sleepovers together. I didn't even bother to argue with her.

I sighed and then walked to the staircase as Mr. Wilson came out of the kitchen wearing a big apron. (Only a big apron would fit him, because he kind of reminds me of a grizzly bear.)

"Katie! Where have you been? You look like you've grown a foot over the summer!" Mr. Wilson said. Then he gave me a big hug.

Remember I told you how Callie and I have known each other since we were babies? Well, that means I've known her parents for that long too. Mr. Wilson was always kind of like a father to me, which was nice, because I never see my natural father. But since Callie dumped me, I never get to see my second father either. That's another reason why what Callie did hurts so much.

I started to answer him, but Callie's mom interrupted us. "Joe, we need to talk," she said in a serious voice.

Mr. Wilson nodded. "See you later, Katie. I'm

making my famous spaghetti for dinner. Hope you're hungry!"

Normally I love Mr. Wilson's spaghetti, but the thought of having to stay in Callie's room made me lose my appetite. I slowly dragged my bags up the stairs and knocked on Callie's door. She didn't answer at first, so I knocked again.

"What do you want?" she finally asked.

"Your mom says I'm sleeping in here," I said.

After a minute, Callie opened the door and then walked back over to her bed without saying a word to me. She was furiously texting someone on her cell phone—Maggie and Bella, I'm sure.

"So, I guess I'll just put down my stuff," I said, and Callie ignored me again.

I placed my bags on the daybed, which had been pulled out from under Callie's bed and was closer to the floor. I didn't know what to do, so I pulled out my cell phone to text my mom.

How's grandma? I texted. Is she out of surgery yet?

Not yet, my mom texted back. I'll let you know the minute I hear anything.

I put down my phone and looked around Callie's room. She still had lots of posters on her walls, mostly of cute boys from magazines. Then I noticed the picture of me and Callie from when we were kids was missing from the top of her dresser.

That made me mad and sad at the same time. I needed to hear from one of my *true* friends.

Help me! I texted Mia.

I turned my back to Callie's bed, to make sure she couldn't see.

I'm trapped in Callie's room! I have to sleep here!

Everyone is talking about the BFC, Mia texted back. They really messed up.

I know, I replied. Can you believe it? Callie is worse than Sydney!

Then Mr. Wilson called down to us. "Girls! Time for spaghetti!"

I quickly shut my cell phone. Callie climbed down from her bed and almost stepped on me as she headed out. I slowly followed her.

Downstairs, the kitchen table was set for four. There was a big bowl of salad, a bigger bowl of spaghetti, and a basket of bread.

"Let's dig in!" Mr. Wilson said.

"Where's Jenna?" I asked. Callie's older sister is a senior in high school.

"She's working at the mall," Mrs. Wilson told me. "She got a job in that clothing store that sells all the jeans."

"Cool," I said, and I sat down.

Mr. Wilson took my plate and piled it high with food. It smelled delicious, but I still wasn't that hungry. To be polite, I started picking at it with my fork. Callie wasn't even trying. She just sat there with her arms crossed. Mr. Wilson sighed. "Callie, I think we need to talk about what happened today," he said.

"Not in front of Katie," Callie said, glaring at me.

"I can, um, eat somewhere else," I said.

Callie's dad sighed again. "No, let's eat. Callie, we can talk after dinner."

Now Callie glared at him. She didn't eat a bite, but I have to admit that the delicious smell got to me. I ate at least half of the giant mound of spaghetti on my plate.

"Thanks, Mr. Wilson," I said when I was done. "That was really good."

"Katie, why don't you go upstairs and get ready for the dance?" Mrs. Wilson suggested.

"Sure," I said.

I headed upstairs, and the first thing I did was brush my teeth, because I am the daughter of a dentist. (Besides, who wants spaghetti breath?) Then I went into Callie's room and opened up my overnight bag.

Last year, Mia went to the mall with me to help me pick out the perfect dress, which became my favorite purple dress. But my purple dress was too short, and I totally forgot to go out and get a new one.

In case you didn't already know, I don't really know much about fashion. I put stuff on, and if I like it, I leave it on. When I packed, I kind of just grabbed a bunch of stuff. One of the things I grabbed was my second-favorite dress—this dress I wear in the summer. It has straps instead of sleeves and a kind of orange-and-pink tie-dyed pattern. Since it was still hot out, I thought it might be okay to wear. But now I worried that maybe it was too summery.

I sighed and put it on. It was the only dress I packed. But I had no idea what else to wear with it.

I wish Mia were here! I thought.

Then I had an idea. I took a picture of myself and texted her.

Help again! I said. What should I wear with this?
Mia didn't hesitate. Do u have ur white flats?

I quickly checked my bag. Yes! I had them.

Yes! I said.
Good. Wear those. Any sweaters? Mia asked.

I looked through my bag again.

Green with short sleeves or white with long sleeves,
I wrote.
Try the green, Mia texted back.

I wasn't sure if the green would go with orange
and pink, but then again, I love to wear lots of colors together. I tried it on, took another picture, and
texted Mia. I had to admit that it looked pretty
good.

Great! she replied. Will bring a necklace 4 u that'll
look great with your outfit.

Then my phone started to ring. It was my mom.

Gotta go, I texted, then I answered the phone.

"Hi, sweetie, how's it going?" Mom asked.

"How's Grandma?" I asked her back.

I heard Callie's footsteps on the stairs, so I quickly left her bedroom. I went into the bathroom and then closed the door behind me.

"She's doing great!" Mom said, and she sounded happy and relieved. "She's awake and alert. The doctors say the surgery went well, and she can go home in a few days."

"That's great!" I said. I suddenly felt a lot lighter, as though a huge weight had been lifted from my shoulders. I didn't realize how much I had been secretly worrying about Grandma until Mom said she was going to be all right.

"So how did the fund-raiser go?" Mom asked.

"Well . . . ," I began, and then I told her the whole story.

"That's terrible!" Mom said. "You and I know that Callie would never put alcohol in cupcakes."

"I know, Mom," I said. "But I guess they're in trouble because . . . well . . . it's complicated."

"Did you tell Principal LaCosta that you make those cupcakes with her every year?" Mom asked.

"No," I said.

"You could vouch for her, Katie," Mom said. "That's what friends do."

"But we're not friends anymore, Mom," I said, and my voice was angry. "I keep telling you that!"

Mom was quiet for a minute. "Well, you used to be," she finally said. "I'm surprised at you, Katie. Keeping quiet is the same thing as not sticking up for someone. You would want her to do the same thing for you."

"But *she* wouldn't!" I said, and I know my voice was really loud—that's how upset I was. "She's changed, Mom! She's mean and terrible, and she wouldn't stick up for me. Ever!" Why couldn't she just understand?

Mom sighed. "Just because Callie isn't behaving nicely, doesn't mean that you shouldn't."

"I guess," I said, but I did not feel like being nice to Callie right now. She got herself into this mess— and now she'd have to deal with it.

CHAPTER 16

Everybody's Talking

When I opened the bathroom door, Callie was standing there. I felt scared for a second. Had she heard what I said to my mom?

"Are you done yet?" Callie asked in a really snotty voice.

"Yeah," I replied, and I quickly went down the stairs.

Mr. and Mrs. Wilson were waiting in the living room.

"Katie, you look so pretty!" Callie's mom exclaimed.

"Thanks," I said.

Mr. Wilson shook his head. "I can't believe how fast you girls are growing up. When Callie comes down, I'll take a picture of you both."

So we waited for Callie to get dressed. And we waited. Finally, Mrs. Wilson yelled up the stairs.

"Callie, are you ready yet?" she called out.

Callie stomped down the stairs wearing sweatpants and a T-shirt.

"I'm not going," she said, flopping down on the sofa. "It was unfair, and we aren't going to win, so what's the point?"

Mr. Wilson shook his head. "You're not being a good sport, Callie."

"Honestly, Callie, I had to plead with Principal LaCosta not to ban you from the dance," Mrs. Wilson said. She sounded really frustrated. "And now you're not going to go?"

Callie shrugged. "You can't make me."

Mrs. Wilson looked at her husband, and they must be telepathic or something, because the next thing I knew, Mr. Wilson said, "Okay, Katie. Looks like it's just you and me. I'll give you a ride."

Riding to the dance without Callie was pretty awkward, but I was also relieved to be away from her for a while.

"I'm sorry about Callie's behavior tonight," Mr. Wilson said. "She just hasn't been herself this year."

"Yeah, I know," I agreed. And then the next

thing just slipped out. "Or last year, either."

Mr. Wilson nodded. "Callie's having a hard time figuring out where she belongs," he said. "She's still the same Callie, though."

I didn't agree with him, but I didn't say anything. I was really glad when he pulled up in front of the school.

"Your mom arranged for Emma's mom to drop you off after the dance," he said. "See you later, and have a good time!"

"Thanks," I said, and then I headed inside the school gym.

The place was packed with middle school kids and the parents who were chaperoning. This year, there was a big blue-and-yellow balloon archway over the dj table that looked really cool. Blue-and-yellow crepe paper was strung all across the ceiling.

I spotted Emma, Alexis, and Mia over by the watercoolers. Emma had a pink headband in her hair, and she wore this really cute white dress with tiny pink flowers on it. Mia looked superfashionable, as always, in a dress with a big red-and-purple pattern. (She told me later it's called color blocking.) And Alexis's curly hair was straightened, and she had on a black dress, and her heels were kind of high.

"Let me guess," I said. "Dylan got to you."

Alexis nodded. "I couldn't escape."

"Well, I think you look nice," I said. "You look like you're in high school."

Alexis blushed. "Thanks!"

"You all look nice," I said.

"You do too," Emma told me.

I looked at Mia. "Thanks to you. If I didn't have my own personal fashion consultant, I'd be lost."

Mia laughed. "Hey, you're my first client! And here's the necklace I promised you." She put it on me, and she was right—it was perfect.

As we were talking, I got that weird feeling someone was looking at me. (Has that ever happened to you?) When I turned around, I saw that Maggie and Bella were sitting at a table, and they were surrounded by a bunch of girls. The girls were pointing and whispering.

I frowned. "What's that about?" I asked my friends.

"They've been talking to anyone who'll listen," Alexis said. "They keep saying the whole contest was fixed."

"That's crazy," I said. "They ruined things for themselves."

Then I heard Maggie get really loud. "Principal

LaCosta just didn't want us to win," she said. "We were beating the Cupcake Club, and she didn't want to see her teacher's pets lose."

"I wouldn't be surprised if those Cupcake girls were the ones who told on you," said one of the girls at the table.

I was getting really mad. "That is ridiculous!" I said.

"They can talk all they want," Alexis said. "We raised almost five hundred dollars. We're definitely winning."

But the idea of winning didn't seem so important anymore—especially if people didn't think we deserved it. I spotted Principal LaCosta over by the food table, and I decided to do something, right then and there.

"Be right back," I told my friends.

Usually I would be afraid to talk to Principal LaCosta, but I guess I was just feeling tired of all the rumors and lies and stuff.

"Principal LaCosta, can I talk to you, please?" I asked.

She turned and saw me. "Oh, hi, Katie. Of course."

"It's about the Best Friends Club's cupcakes," I said. "I used to make those cupcakes with Callie every year, and I know there's no rum in them. She uses imitation rum extract. So maybe you could let them back in the contest. I know they sold a lot of cupcakes, and if they sold the most, then they deserve to win."

"It's nice of you to stand up for your friend," Principal LaCosta said. "But the girls' parents already told me about the imitation rum. That's not the issue here. The issue is we simply can't have students promoting alcohol use, even if they're just joking about it. Do you understand?"

I nodded. Mrs. Wilson had said the same thing.

"Thanks," I said, and then I felt nervous for real, so I walked away. I noticed Maggie and Bella staring at me, and I wondered if they had heard.

I hoped they did, but it didn't matter. I stood up for Callie, and I felt a lot better.

Then Mia ran up and grabbed my arm. "I love this song!" she cried, and then we were all dancing, and suddenly things were fun again.

CHAPTER 17

One Mystery Is Solved

There's a funny thing that happens at a middle school dance. When it starts, most of the girls stay on the left side of the gym, and most of the boys hang out on the right side of the gym. The girls dance with girls, and the boys dance with boys. Then, as the night goes on, everyone starts dancing with one another, boys and girls together. And sometimes boys even ask girls to dance.

About halfway through the dance, I was standing around talking to my friends. Sophie and Lucy were with us, and Beth came over with some girls who I think are all into art, because they were dressed really funky, like Beth. Anyway, we were just talking and laughing and having a good time when the subject turned to boys.

"We need more cute boys in this school!" Sophie was wailing.

"I think Eddie Rossi is cute," admitted Lucy, and Sophie looked shocked.

"He's, like, two feet taller than you!" Sophie squealed.

"Eddie has a crush on Katie," Alexis blurted out, and I felt my face get red.

"Alexis! He does not!" I protested.

"Well, I think George Martinez has a crush on Katie," Sophie said.

I wished I could turn invisible. "How do you know that?" I asked her.

"Because he's waving at you," Sophie said, pointing across the gym.

I looked, and Sophie was right. George was walking toward us, and he was smiling and waving at us.

Mia grabbed my arm. "Oh my gosh! He's going to ask you to dance!"

"He is not!" I said, but secretly I hoped she was right. Or wrong. I'm not sure! I was so nervous.

Before George could get there, Eddie Rossi walked up from the other direction. And he was walking right toward me.

My friends were stunned. Mia was practically pulling off my arm. I could tell she was dying to say something, but thankfully everyone kept quiet.

"Hey, Katie," Eddie said. "I . . . I've been meaning to talk to you about something since school started."

My heart was pounding so fast. "Oh?"

Eddie nodded. "Yeah, it's kind of hard to explain, but . . . well, I want to apologize to you."

That was definitely not what I thought he was going to say!

"Apologize for what?" I asked, confused.

"For the way I made fun of you last year in gym class," Eddie said. He took a deep breath. "I went to camp this summer with my little brother, and he got teased a lot. It was hard to see. And then we had this whole meeting where we learned about bullying and stuff, and I realized that I did it too."

I was shocked by Eddie's confession. I didn't think people could change like that.

"I'm sorry your brother got bullied," I said.

"Thanks. And I'm sorry too," Eddie said. "For the stuff I said to you. That's one of the things they told us. That it's never too late to apologize."

"Everything's cool," I told him. "I really appreciate how you've been sticking up for me lately."

"I'll have your back from now on," Eddie promised.

I smiled. "Thanks. I could use it!" I was totally relieved that he didn't like me in the way everybody thought. He was just trying to make up for his past behavior.

From the corner of my eye, I saw George turn around and walk away. I was going to call out to him, but then Eddie said, "See ya, Katie," and he was gone too.

I turned to Mia. "What just happened?"

"Maybe George thought Eddie was asking you to dance," she said.

"But he wasn't," I said. "Eddie doesn't even like me. He's just nicer now, that's all."

That's when I realized that I was disappointed. And *that* meant I *wanted* to dance with George. Wow. Scary.

Then the microphone next to the dj table was turned on, and Principal LaCosta started to talk. The gym got quiet.

"Hello, Park Street Middle School!" she cried, and everyone clapped. "Today's fund-raiser was a big success. We raised almost three thousand dollars!"

Everyone cheered really loud at that.

"And the club that raised the most money . . . for the second year in a row . . . is the Cupcake Club!" she announced.

We all started squealing and hugging one another. I couldn't believe it. We had done it again!

We ran up to the dj booth, and Principal LaCosta handed each of us a blue-and-yellow Park Street Middle School blanket. Last year we got sweatshirts. I guess she's trying to keep us warm.

I wore my blanket like a cape and started spinning and twirling on the dance floor.

"Hey, Supergirl!"

It was George. He started spinning around like I was. We kept dancing like that and laughing. I'm sure we looked totally goofy.

Bella and Maggie walked by.

"It's so unfair," Maggie said, loudly enough for me to hear. "Definitely not a fair fight!"

I could have said something back, but I didn't. Instead, I just kept on spinning with George.

CHAPTER 18

A Sweet Ending

By the time the dance was over I was super-exhausted and happy. I wrapped my winning blanket around me as I rode back to Callie's in the back of Emma's car. Alexis and Mia were squished in with me.

"I wish you could go home with me," Mia said.

"Me too," I said. "But it's just a few more nights."

"Text me any time, okay?" Mia said.

"Me too," added Alexis.

"And me," said Emma.

"You guys are the best!" I said with a yawn.

"Okay, Katie, this is your stop," Mrs. Taylor announced.

"Thanks, Mrs. Taylor!" I said, and I climbed out of the car.

The porch light was on, and Mrs. Wilson was waiting for me with the door open.

"How was the dance, Katie?" she asked.

"It was good," I said.

"Callie's up in her bedroom," she told me. "I'm not sure if she's awake or not, so you might want to be quiet."

"Okay," I said. It would perfect if Callie was asleep. Then I wouldn't have to talk to her.

But I was not so lucky. Callie was in bed with the lights off, but she was sitting up with her cell phone on.

"Oh, hey," Callie said.

"Hey," I said back. I started digging in my bag for my pajamas.

Callie turned on the little lamp on her night-stand. She looked like she had calmed down a lot from how she'd been before the dance. Because I've known Callie forever, I know she doesn't usually stay mad for very long. At least the *old* Callie didn't stay mad for very long. A few moments went by, and then she started asking questions. I knew she was dying to find out what happened at the dance.

"So, what dress did Mia wear?" she asked.

"It was color blocked," I said, glad that Mia had told me so I had something to say. "Purple and red."

Callie nodded. "Cool. Did Jeremy Paskowski dance with anybody?"

I shrugged. "I don't know him."

"He's that tall blond-haired kid on the basketball team," Callie said.

I could sort of picture him. "Um, I don't think so."

Then Callie blurted out, "I know why you didn't stick up for me."

"I *did* stick up for you," I told her. "I explained to Principal LaCosta tonight that those aren't really rum cupcakes. I asked her to include the sales you made in the contest. But she said no."

Callie looked surprised. "Why did you do that?"

"I'm not sure," I confessed. "But it was the right thing to do. We used to be good friends."

We were quiet again, until Callie spoke up.

"You won, right?" she asked.

I nodded. "Yes."

"Peace Out was a good theme," Callie said.

"So was school spirit," I told her. "It was cool that you had a band and everything."

More silence.

"I'm really sorry about how things turned out," Callie said finally.

I wasn't expecting that. Callie was apologizing?

I wasn't sure what to say. It turns out that was okay, because Callie kept talking. "I'm sorry I didn't stick up for you to Sydney, and I'm sorry I didn't treat you like a friend."

"Okay," I said, because I still didn't know what else to say.

"Sydney had all these rules about who we should talk to and who we shouldn't, but I think that's stupid," Callie went on. "I can talk to or be friends with whoever I like. And I don't have to be mean to other people in order to be popular."

That was interesting. But I guess it made sense. That's probably why she changed the club name after all.

"But you're going to stay in the club?" I asked.

"Well, sure!" replied Callie. "I like it."

I didn't know what to say. But letting Callie do all the talking was working out pretty well for me so far, so I just nodded.

"Things are just different," Callie said after a while. "I changed the name of the club because I realized Sydney was pretty horrible. I liked the idea of the club, but not what the club was. It will be different this year."

I sighed. I really wanted to believe Callie, but with all that hair flipping and stuff, she didn't seem that much different from Sydney to me. And I didn't really like Maggie or Bella all that much. And their whole club was pretty silly.

But Callie had apologized. That was pretty big.

"Truce?" Callie asked.

"Truce," I agreed.

Callie held out her hand. "Shake on it," she said. "So we can Peace Out."

I laughed, and we shook hands. Then I grabbed my pajamas.

"I'm going to get changed," I told her.

As I brushed my teeth, I thought about everything that had happened. What a crazy day! The Cupcake Club won the contest. I figured out the mystery of Eddie Rossi. I danced with George, kind of. Grandma Carole was okay. And the war with Callie looked like it was over. . . . And that all happened without my lucky purple dress or lucky purple shirt or even my lucky nail polish. I felt relieved. I felt, well, peaceful. I guess that theme worked out well in more ways than one.

I smiled at my reflection in the mirror.

Maybe this was going to be my best, grooviest middle school year after all!

KB | ET

AB | MV

cute!

Want another sweet cupcake?
Here's a sneak peek
of the tenth book in the

CUPCAKE DIARIES

series:

Mia's
boiling point

A Middle School Miracle?

"Oh my gosh, it's a cupcake plunger!" my friend Katie squealed.

I don't think I've ever seen Katie so excited. We were in a shop in the mall called Baker's Hollow. They sell baking supplies, and inside are all these fake trees with built-in shelves and the supplies are displayed on them.

Katie and I were at the cupcake tree, which has pretty, fake pink cupcakes "growing" in its fake branches. The shelves are filled with cupcake baking pans, cupcake decorations, and tons of different kinds of cupcake liners.

Katie was holding up a metal tube with a purple top on it. She pulled on the top, and it moved up and down, like a plunger.

"This is so cool!" she cried. "You stick this in the top of the cupcake and plunge down halfway, and a perfect little tube of cake comes out. Then you fill the hole with stuff and then put the cake back on top and frost it. Just imagine what you could put in here! Whipped cream! Pudding!"

She turned to me, and her brown eyes were shining with excitement. "You could even do ice cream! Can you imagine biting into a cupcake and there's ice cream inside? How awesome would that be?"

"Totally awesome," I agreed. "Plus, it's purple. Your favorite color."

Katie dug into her pocket, took out some crumpled bills, and started to count.

"It's only six dollars. I could get it and still have enough left over for a smoothie," she said, and then she sighed. "I am so glad they opened this store, but I am going to go broke spending all my money on cupcake supplies. I'm obsessed!"

"I know how you feel," I said. "I am totally obsessed with shoes lately. I'm trying to find the perfect pair of neutral heels. I want them dressy, but not too dressy—maybe a shiny patent leather, with a high heel. But not too high. I don't want to fall flat on my face! I can picture them in my mind, but I haven't seen them anywhere for real yet."

Katie looked down at her sneakers, which were decorated with rainbows drawn on with Magic Marker. "I don't think I'll ever wear heels. They're too uncomfortable."

That's the difference between Katie and me—she doesn't care about fashion at all, and I pretty much live for it. Today, for instance, Katie was wearing a purple hoodie, jeans, and sneakers. Which is perfectly adorable on her, but not dressed up enough for me. You never know who you could run into at the mall! So I had on skinny black jeans, my furry black boots, a white lace cami, and a sky-blue cardigan on top. The beads in my hoop earrings matched my cardigan, and the boho style of the earrings worked perfectly with my boots.

But even though Katie doesn't care much about fashion, she's my best friend here in Maple Grove. I moved here a year ago after my parents got divorced. Katie was the first friend I met.

"Okay, I'd better get on line before I buy something else," she told me.

A few minutes later we left the shop, and Katie was happily holding an adorable little paper shopping bag with a picture of a cupcake tree on it.

"That's such a great logo," I said. "I wish I had thought of that for the Cupcake Club."

"I bet you could think of an even better logo if you wanted to," Katie said.

That made me feel pretty good. I love to draw and would love to be a fashion designer or maybe a graphic designer one day. Or maybe one of those designers who does displays in store windows in Manhattan. How cool would that be?

As we walked toward the smoothie shop, the smell of chocolate distracted us. Katie and I didn't even need to discuss it. We walked right into Adele's Chocolates and headed for the counter.

This is a "must-go-to" shop at the mall. Adele makes all the chocolates herself, and the flavors are amazing.

"Mmm, look," I said, pointing to a glistening morsel of chocolate in a gold paper cup. "Salted caramel. That sounds so good."

Katie pointed to a piece of dark chocolate sitting in a pale purple cup. "Dark chocolate infused with lavender. I wonder what that tastes like?"

"That would make a good cupcake," I said, and Katie nodded. We talk about cupcakes a lot because we're in the Cupcake Club with our friends Alexis and Emma. It's a real business. People hire us to bake for their parties and other events.

Katie had a pained look on her face. "Soooo tempting. But I think I really need some smoothie energy right about now. Mom says chocolate makes me loopy."

I grabbed Katie's arm and pretended to drag her out of the store. "Resist! Resist!" I said, and we both started laughing like crazy.

"We should go right to the smoothie place," I said when we calmed down. "No more distractions."

"Right," Katie said. She stood up straight, like a soldier, and saluted. "To the smoothie place!"

It was Saturday, so the mall was pretty crowded as we made our way to Smoothie Paradise. I used to hate the mall when I first moved here, because I was so used to shopping in New York City. But now I like it. It's never too hot or too cold, and when I'm done shopping I just have to carry the bags outside to Mom's car. It's definitely a lot easier than toting things home on the subway.

Even though the mall was full of people, the line at Smoothie Paradise was pretty short. Katie and I each ordered the same thing—a smoothie with mango and passion fruit—and then sat down at a small round table in the corner.

"This is my favorite kind of day," Katie said after taking a long slurp from her straw. "I got all my homework done last night, so I don't have anything to worry about."

I nodded. "Me too."

Katie sat back in her chair. "You know, middle school isn't so bad so far. I mean, it's not perfect, but I think it's easier this year."

"Definitely," I agreed. "It's, like, we know our way around. And besides school, other things are easier too. Like living with Eddie and Dan. That's not so weird anymore."

Eddie is my stepdad, and Dan is my stepbrother. They're both pretty nice.

"Is it getting any easier living in two different apartments?" Katie asked.

I thought about it for a minute. "Yeah, kind of," I admitted. "But mostly when I go to my dad's, I feel like I'm visiting." I basically go out to New York to see my dad every other weekend.

"You must miss him," Katie said.

I wasn't sure how to answer that. Katie's parents are divorced too, and she never sees her dad. He remarried, and I think he even has a whole new family. So as tough as my situation is, I think Katie's is even tougher.

I decided to be honest. "Sometimes I miss him," I said. "But he texts me and Skypes me and stuff during the week. So he's there if I need him."

Katie got a little quiet after I said that, so I changed the subject.

"We should go to Icon after this," I said. Katie knows that's my favorite clothing store. "They sell shoes there, too. Maybe they have my perfect heels."

We left the shop and headed for Icon. It's easy to find because you can hear techno music blasting from it even when the mall is noisy. The decor is really sleek and clean, with white walls and gleaming silver racks. I like it that way because the clothes are really highlighted.

That day I walked right past the clothes and headed straight for the shoes, which were displayed on white blocks sticking out of the back wall. They had chunky heels, wedge heels, and spike heels, but the perfect shoe, the one I could picture in my head, wasn't there.

While I was looking at all the shoes, Katie was giggling and wobbling in a pair of superhigh silver heels. I suddenly heard a familiar voice behind us.

"Hi, Mia. Hi, Katie."

It was Callie Wilson, Katie's former best friend and the leader of the Best Friends Club, which used to be the Popular Girls Club. Things have always been pretty tense between the Cupcake Club and the BFC. A lot of it had to do with Katie and Callie's broken friendship. But recently, they kind of patched things up, and so today Callie was smiling and friendly.

Katie, on the other hand, looked a little startled. She quickly slipped out of the silver heels, embarrassed.

"Oh, hey, Callie," Katie said.

"Hi," I added.

Maggie and Bella, the other two girls in the BFC, walked up behind Callie. Maggie has wild hair and can be pretty funny when she wants to be—and pretty mean, too. Bella is the quietest of the three. She's super into those vampire movies—like, so into them that she changed her name from Brenda to Bella, and she straightens her auburn hair to look just like the girl who loves the vampire.

"Shopping for shoes?" Callie asked, even though it was pretty obvious. I guess she was trying to make conversation.

"I'm trying to find the perfect pair of heels," I said. "But I think they only exist in my head."

"Ooh, I saw this adorable pair online," Maggie said. She whipped out her smartphone and started typing on the keyboard. Then she shoved the screen in front of my face. "See?"

"Those are totally cute, but the ones I'm dreaming of have a pointier toe," I told her. "But thanks!"

"Did you guys see those new wrap dresses they got in?" Callie asked. "Katie, there's a purple one that would look so cute on you."

"We'll definitely check them out," I replied.

"Yeah," Katie added.

Callie gave a little wave and then flipped her long, blond hair over her shoulder. "Okay, we've got to go. Later."

She walked away, and Bella and Maggie followed her. Katie and I stared at each other in shock.

"Did that just actually happen?" Katie asked.

"You mean, did we actually just have a normal conversation with the BFC, with no name-calling or teasing? Yes!" I replied.

Katie grinned. "It's a middle school miracle!"

The Shoes of My Dreams

On Sunday morning when I woke up, the house smelled like bacon. As far as I'm concerned, that is the absolute best way to wake up.

I got dressed and went downstairs to find Mom and Eddie in the kitchen. There was a big plate of bacon on the table, and Eddie was flipping pancakes at the stove.

"She's alive!" Eddie said, teasing me. I looked at the clock, and it was ten thirty.

"Hey, it's still morning," I said. "Besides, I don't see Dan."

Dan is in high school, and he sleeps way more than I do. I was pretty sure Dan must still be asleep.

I was right. "He's still sleeping," Mom said. She had her long, black hair pulled back with a big barrette. People say I look like my mom, but it's mostly my hair; I definitely have my dad's nose, and our faces are both oval. Mom's is more heart shaped.

"Too bad! That means more bacon for us," Eddie said cheerfully.

"Ed, that's not nice. We should save him some," Mom scolded.

Eddie put a platter of pancakes on the table and gave my mom a kiss. (Gross.) "Of course I will, *mi amore*. You know I have a soft heart."

"That's why I married you," Mom said, and I made a loud coughing noise.

"Excuse me! Child present!" I reminded them.

Eddie hugged my mom. "You'll understand one day, Mia, when you're in love."

"Okay, now I am seriously losing my appetite," I said. I like Eddie and everything, but deep down I still wish my mom and dad were together. So I don't need to see Mom and Eddie all lovey-dovey.

Mom gave Eddie a look, and he stopped hugging her and sat down at the table. "Pancakes, anyone?"

"Me, please," I said. "And bacon."

While Eddie piled the food onto my plate, Mom said, "Mia, I know I've been working a lot lately, so I was thinking maybe we could have a girls' day out today. Unless you have other plans with your friends."

I put down my fork. "Can we go to the city? Hang out in SoHo? And get Thai food? And go window shopping? When can we leave?"

Even though I stay with my dad in Manhattan every other weekend, I hardly ever get to go with my mom. I miss the things we used to do there together.

Mom smiled. "I don't see why not. We should leave after breakfast. We can take the ferry."

So less than two hours later we were standing on the top deck of a ferry crossing the Hudson River. It was a pretty chilly out, but I didn't mind because I got to wear a new fall jacket that one of my mom's designer friends had given her. It's cobalt blue, and it has a vintage-style collar that looks like two petals, and three big buttons in the front, and it's fitted around the waist, with a belt and a big buckle.

I wore it with black knit tights and this navy shirtdress I have, which was from another one of my mom's friends. Mom's a fashion stylist, so I am superlucky and can get great clothes for free.

Mom was going for the all-black look, which she does a lot. Black sweater, black knee-length skirt, black tights, black boots, black trench coat. I call it her spy outfit.

"Yes, but I can always accessorize," Mom loves to say, and she can make it look different every time with a bright red scarf or a big silver necklace or a belt or something. She's good at that.

When the ferry docked we took a cab to SoHo, a neighborhood in Manhattan that stands for "south of Houston," which is Houston Street (only people pronounce it "*how*-ston" instead of "*hyoo*-ston," like the city in Texas). There are other places to shop in New York City, like great department stores, but I think SoHo is fun because the streets are narrow and lots of designers have little shops there. New stores are always springing up, so you never know what you'll see.

We were extremely full from the pancakes and bacon, so we went window shopping first. A lot of the clothing boutiques had winter coats on display already. We admired a shop with some pretty cool faux-fur jackets and then moved on to the next store.

I froze. The window was filled with the most amazing shoes I had ever seen. The sign above the door read KARA KAREN.

"She must have just opened up the boutique,"

Mom said. "Everyone's saying great things about her."

I grabbed Mom by the arm. "We are going inside!" I informed her.

Mom didn't argue. A bell jingled as we walked inside the store, a clean, well-lit space with polished wood floors. The shoes were displayed on a round table in the center of the shop with different tiers, like a layer cake. My eyes scanned the display from the bottom, to the middle, to the very top layer, and that's when I saw them—my dream shoes.

The heel was high, but not too high. And it wasn't chunky, but not too spiky, either. The toe was nice and pointy, just like I wanted. The shoe itself was black, but kind of sparkly. Delicate straps crisscrossed the top of the shoe.

Mom must have noticed my wide-eyed look. Or maybe I was drooling.

"Those are great shoes," she said. "Impractical, but gorgeous."

I immediately started to appeal to Mom's fashion sense. "Mom, you know I need heels for special occasions. This is the perfect pair! They'll go with just about anything. And the heel's not too high."

Mom reached up and took the sample shoe off the stand. Then she looked at the price tag.

"How much?" I asked nervously.

"Too much," Mom said. The tag said: $212.

I was so disappointed! "I knew they were too good to be true," I said with a sigh. "I guess when I imagined my dream shoes, I should have imagined a cheaper price."

Mom was turning the shoe over in her hand, examining it with a thoughtful look on her face.

"I'll tell you what, Mia," she said. "If you can raise money for your half of the shoes, I'll pay for the other half." She laughed. "You buy one shoe and I'll buy the other!"

I immediately felt much better. "You mean we can get them now and I'll owe you?"

Mom shook her head. "No, you have to earn the money first. Then you'll appreciate them more."

I did some quick calculations in my head. I had some money saved from the Cupcake business, and I get allowance for helping around the house. I could see if maybe I could do some extra chores, and I knew the Cupcake Club had a big job coming up. It wouldn't take long . . . but just thinking about the wait was unbearable!

I took the shoe from my mom and hugged it dramatically. "I'll miss you! But I will come back for you, I promise!"

Mom laughed again. "Well, before you get carried away, we should at least try them on."

The saleswoman in the shop got the shoes in my size, and I put them on. They looked fabulous! I was a little wobbly when I walked in them, but I got the hang of it pretty quickly.

"It's that extra-pointy toe," Mom said. "But I have to admit, you're pretty good in them."

"It's in my genes," I said. When Mom walks in high heels, she's as graceful as a ballet dancer.

"We should get lunch soon," Mom said.

I looked at myself in the mirror one last time. Then I took off the shoes. I took a gazillion pictures of them with my phone camera. Then I sadly gave them back to the saleswoman.

"Good-bye," I whispered, gazing longingly at the shoes as we left the shop.

Yes, I was definitely in the middle of a shoe obsession!

$\mathcal{H}$ow about a

BONUS

CUPCAKE  DIARIES?

$\mathcal{E}$mma,
smile and say
"cupcake!"

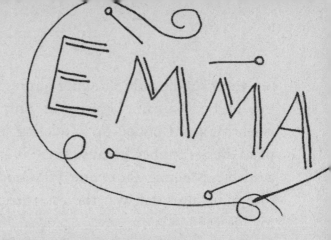

On Pins and Needles

I woke up extra early this Saturday morning to frost the mini cupcakes I was delivering to our number-one client, Mona, at The Special Day bridal salon. Well, the truth was, frosting wouldn't take long, but I wanted to wash and set my hair in my mom's big rollers before I went to the bridal salon. I would be modeling today for Mona's clients, and I wanted to try a new hairstyle and see what everyone at the shop thought.

It's kind of crazy how I started modeling for Mona. One Saturday morning I was making a regular cupcake delivery to the store (my friends and I in the Cupcake Club have a cupcake business, and Mona buys cupcakes from us for her Saturday brides each week), and an important mystery client was there for an early showing of dresses. It turned out to be Romaine Ford, our only hometown celebrity, and I ended up modeling junior bridesmaid dresses for her because there was no one else available. Meeting Romaine Ford and everything that came after that was the most exciting part of my life yet.

Since then, I've been modeling for Mona about once or twice a month for trunk shows, which is when specialty designers bring in their line for the day. It's fun. I get to dress up and sometimes have my hair styled (no makeup, though! It could ruin the dresses!) and hang out in a totally girlie environment for the morning, away from my three smelly brothers. Best of all, Mona pays me.

So this morning I showered, then put on my fancy jeans and a pretty turtleneck sweater, some tiny pearl stud earrings, and a belt. Then I rolled my hair and forgot all about it for a while as I finished up the cupcakes. Well, until my brother Matt walked into the kitchen and fell down on the floor laughing. I guess I looked pretty funny with my hair all in rollers, but there are times like these when I really wish I had a sister. Anyway, it only took about half an hour to frost and pack the cupcakes since they're minis, which are not much wider than a quarter. Mona loves them. Brides are always on diets, so they're hungry, which makes them cranky. These cupcakes are so tiny, no one can resist, and she says they make cranky brides friendlier. Isn't that funny?

Afterward, I ran the blow-dryer over my curlers to really set my hair, then I unpinned the rollers and swung my head from side to side. My hair is a very yellow blond on top, from the sun, but underneath it's a much darker shade. The curls made the colors all swirly and mixed together, and the style gave me a lot of height. I looked two inches taller! I laughed at the sight of it. It might be too much, but who cared? It was just an experiment, anyway. Well, my mom might care. She's always concerned about being "age appropriate."

My mom called up from the kitchen that we had to go or I'd be late, so I flipped off the bathroom light and took the stairs down, two at a time. As I swung around the banister and into the kitchen, my mom turned around and then did a double take.

"Oh, Emma! Your hair looks gorgeous!" she said with a gasp.

I grinned. "Thanks! You don't think it's too much?"

My mom laughed. "Well, maybe for soccer

practice or something, but under the circumstances, I think it will be a huge success!" She smoothed her own perky blond ponytail and laughed again, looking down at her Nike sweatpants and Under Armor top. "I am feeling very underdressed!"

"You look great, Mama," I said, calling her by my private baby name for her. "You're the prettiest mom in school." I grabbed my jacket off the hook in my locker in the mudroom, stepped over about five piles of sweaty boys' sporting goods, and headed out to the car.

"Thank you, lovebug, you do say the sweetest things, even if they're not always true!"

At The Special Day, Mona and her assistants were bustling around getting things set up for the day's trunk show.

The Special Day is just what you would imagine if you were trying to picture the most awesome, over-the-top, bridal store. It's like a magical castle, and someday that's where I want to buy my wedding dress. First of all, outside the store they have beautiful green trees, and topiaries in white wooden flower boxes, and a pretty white awning with white lanterns hanging on either side of the door. It looks like something from movies I've seen of Paris. Then, inside is white, white, white everywhere. A boy couldn't last one minute in there without ruining something, I tell you. There are thick white pile carpets, which make it really quiet; superplush white sofas and chairs that you sink into; low white marble coffee tables where tea is served in fine white china; and everywhere are white boxes of white Kleenex, because everyone cries when women try on wedding dresses. Once, I even saw Mona tear up when a young woman with cancer came in to try on her dress. She was bald from her treatment, but very brave and getting healthier, and Mona cried when she saw her in her beautiful dress.

Today, Mona's main assistant, Patricia, came striding over to help me with my cupcake carriers. "Oh, Emma! Your hair! You look incredible!" said Patricia.

I smiled. "Thanks. It was just an experiment."

"Well, it looks wonderful. Mona! Come see Emma's new hairstyle!"

Mona looked up from the rack of dresses she was arranging, and I saw her tilt her head and squint at me. "Emma!" she cried. (Mona is really dramatic, by the way. Did I mention that?) She raced across the store toward me, her arms outstretched. "Darling! You look divine! Simply divine!" She had her hands on my arms, and now she pulled me in for a European-style two-cheek kiss. I laughed.

Mona said, "Oh, Patricia, isn't she divine?"

Smiling, Patricia nodded and added, "Divine!"

(Did I mention that "divine" is Mona's favorite word?) But now Mona stopped gushing over me and patted her severe black bun. "Patricia!" she snapped, all business now. "I have an idea!"

"Yes, Mona? What is it?" asked Patricia. Patricia is very patient, but I guess I don't need to mention that either.

Mona circled me, looking at my new hair with her arms folded, tapping her chin, slightly bent at the waist. "Mm-hmm. Mm-hmm. Yes. Yes!" After what felt like an eternity, she looked up at Patricia with a gleam in her eye. "Call Emma's mother and ask if we can photograph her today, and if so, could we use it in the paper. Then if she says yes, call Joachim and get him over here on the double. I'd like to run another ad!"

I raised my eyebrows at Patricia and she raised hers back at me, and we smiled like coconspirators. An ad?! Holy smokes! *Wait until I tell my friends,* was all I could think! I prayed my mom said yes. Sometimes my parents can be funny about stuff like that—they always are nice when people tell them

I'm pretty, like if we're out to dinner or something, but they always tell me after that looks don't last and that schoolwork and teamwork are more important than appearances. I know what they mean, but I still like it when people say I'm pretty. Especially because I don't think I'm pretty all the time; only when I try a little and, like, wear something fancy or do my hair. Otherwise I think I just look normal.

I went with Patricia to sort through the dresses I'd wear today while she dialed my mom's cell on the cordless phone. Today's dresses were by Jaden Sacks, a famous designer from New York City. The line is superchic and exclusive. She usually only sells in her boutique on Madison Avenue. I know this because Mona told me the week before. She was very excited to be able to carry the dresses in the store. The junior bridesmaid dresses were gorgeous, made of incredible materials—thick, slippery satin that pooled in my hand and slid through my fingers like quicksilver; pleated sheer silk so light and thin, it was like cotton candy on my skin; and lace that was somehow detailed and fancy on one side but cotton soft on the underside so it buffered me from the scratchiness of the stitching. The designs were simple—fashion forward but not tacky or overdone. Jaden Sacks is famous for using the finest supplies and craftspeople. Mona also told me that, but I looked it up on the Internet, too. Her dresses for brides are not traditional puffy "wedding cakes" with lots of layers, but rather columns or sheaths or mermaids with trains. Very glamorous and understated. Her dresses for junior bridesmaids don't really look like bridesmaids dresses. They aren't too poufy or lacy or anything, and they don't look like mini brides, but they still look what my mom would call "age appropriate." Which is good, because when it comes to modeling, my mom is all over being age appropriate. Mona has to show Mom all the dresses I'll wear beforehand, so she can okay them. It's kind of crazy. I mean, how can a bridesmaid dress be too sexy? But Mona says you'd be surprised.

Patricia whispered to me as she waited for my mom to pick up the phone, telling me that Mona was hoping Jaden Sacks might consider letting her carry the dresses for good, selling the line as a regular attraction at the store. Mona had already run a number of ads in the local paper about today's trunk show, and she was expecting a big crowd—not just brides but local fashionistas who were curious to see the exclusive line on their home turf. (I already knew that one of my best friends, Mia, and her mom, Mrs. Valdes, who were major fashionistas and were clients of Mona's, were coming today to inspect the line and cheer on Mona. I couldn't wait to tell Mia about the potential ad!)

I could hear Patricia speaking to my mom.

"Oh, Mrs. Taylor! Hi! It's Patricia at The Special Day! No, everything's fine. She's here. Everything is wonderful." There was a pause. "No! The hair is divine! That's actually why I'm calling you. Mona loved it so much that she had an idea to shoot photos of Emma today to run in an ad in the paper, and she wanted to know if that would be okay with you. We'd pay her extra, of course." There was another pause. "Yes, I totally understand. No, it's not a problem at all. Okay, talk soon. Bye!" Patricia clicked the off button on the phone and set the receiver on the bench in the large fitting room. I waited for Patricia to give me the scoop. When she didn't immediately say anything, I had to ask.

"What did she say?!" I couldn't contain my excitement any longer.

"She said it sounded like fun, but she wanted to talk it over with your father before she gave her permission."

"What? That is such a bummer!" I complained. I knew it was babyish, but I didn't care. How could my mom even think of saying no to an opportunity like this? My mom was protective, but oh boy, my dad was even more protective of me. There's no way he'd say yes.

"Hey, modeling is a big deal," Patricia reminded me gently. "You're talking about putting your photo out there for all the world to see. It might seem like fun for you, but maybe your parents are worried it will give you an image that's not consistent with what they want for you. I completely respect your mother's response. Trust me"—Patricia rolled her eyes—"in the fashion business you get plenty of mothers who are just the opposite—pushing their very young daughters at you, willing to sell their souls to the devil just to make some money off their child's looks before they change or get braces or whatever. It's a tough business."

"One ad doesn't mean I'm in the modeling business!" I protested.

Patricia smiled a wry smile. "It might," she said. "I'm calling Joachim, just in case, and telling him to stand by." She grabbed my hand and squeezed, then handed me my first dress and motioned that she was leaving.

I beamed at Patricia and held up my crossed fingers as she left. Then I began to get ready. I hate changing in front of other people, so Mona got me a slip to wear under the dresses—it's kind of like a long stretchy nude-colored camisole, and it makes me feel more comfortable, in case someone accidentally barges in. But Patricia always leaves me alone to get the slip on and get started, and she calls in to make sure I'm ready before she comes back. We have a good routine now, and we totally get each other. It's kind of weird to think that one of my friends could be forty years older than me and working full-time in a bridal salon, but I'd have to say that's the case with me and Patricia.

The first Jaden Sacks dress was just so gorgeous. It had a high square neckline and what Patricia called "tulip" sleeves, which were capped kind of midway down my upper arm with overlapping petals of fabric. Then a high plain waist with a pale blue ribbon to define it, and a floor-length skirt of satin that swished heavily as I walked. The best part was it had a very light tulle underskirt in a pale blue that matched the ribbon and peeked out only when I moved. I loved it.

I called Patricia, and she came back in, the phone pressed to hear ear, nodding. Whoever she was talking to wouldn't let her get a word in edge-wise. I hoped it wasn't my mom!

I watched her face in the mirror as she bent her knees and clutched the receiver between her shoulder and chin so she could tie my ribbon with both hands. Then she leaned to the side to look at me in the mirror and gave me two thumbs-up and a wink. That meant I looked great. But who was on the phone?

"Uh-huh. Yes. Yes. Okay. Right." Patricia was nodding again.

I knitted my eyebrows together and mouthed, *My mom?* I was on pins and needles waiting to hear. But Patricia shook her head and covered the receiver with her hand. *Joachim,* she mouthed, and she rolled her eyes for the second time today. "Right. Well, listen, Joachim, that's all great. I think your vision sounds wonderful, and we will have all the snacks on hand that you requested, as well as a space roped off for your shoot, and total privacy. Yes. I understand it will be a Sunday rate because it is so last-minute. I will confirm as soon as I hear back from the model. Thank you."

Patricia sighed a deep sigh and sat down heavily on the bench. "This is going to be a really long day," she said.

Are you an
Emma, a *Mia*, a *Katie*, or an *Alexis*?
Take our quiz and find out!

Read each question and circle the letter
that best describes you.

(If you don't want to write in your book, use a separate piece of paper.)

1. You've been invited to a party. What do you wear?

A. Jeans and a cute T-shirt. You want
to look nice, but you also want to be
comfortable.

B. You beg your parents to lend you
money for the cool boots you saw
online. If you're going to a party, you
have to wear the latest fashion!

C. Something pretty, but practical. If
you're going to spend money on a new
outfit, it better be one you'll be able to
wear a lot.

D. Something feminine—lacy and floral.
And definitely pink if not floral—a girl
can never go wrong wearing *pink*!

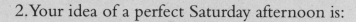

2. Your idea of a perfect Saturday afternoon is:

A. Seeing a movie with your BFFs and then going out for pizza afterward.

B. THE MALL! Hopefully one of the stores will be having a big sale!

C. Creating a perfect budget to buy clothes, go out with friends, and save money for college—all at the same time—and then meeting your friends for lunch.

D. Going for a manicure and pedicure.

3. You have to study for a big test. What's your study style?

A. In your bedroom, with your favorite music playing.

B. At home, with help from your parents if necessary.

C. At the library, where you can take out some new books after you've finished studying, or anyplace else that's absolutely quiet.

D. Anyplace away from *home*—away from your messy, loud siblings!

4. There's a new girl at school. What's your first reaction?

A. You're a little cautious. You've been hurt before, so it takes you a while to warm up to new friends.

B. You think it's great. You welcome her with open arms. (Maybe you can share each other's clothes!)

C. If she's nice *and* smart, maybe you'll consider being friends with her.

D. You'll gladly welcome another friend—as long as she really wants to be friends with you—and not just meet your cute older brothers!

5. When it comes to boys . . .

A. They make you a little nervous. You want to be friends first—for a long time—until you'd consider someone a boyfriend.

B. He has to be tall, trustworthy, sweet—and of course, superstylish!

C. He has to be cute, funny, and smart—and he gets extra points if he likes to dance!

D. He has to be loyal and true as well as good-looking. You look sweet, but you're tough when you have to be.

6. When it comes to your family . . .

A. You come from a single-parent home. It's hard for you to imagine your parent dating, but you will try to get used to it.

B. You come from a mixed family with stepsiblings and a stepparent. At first it was overwhelming, but you're starting to get used to having everyone in the mix!

C. You get along okay with your parents, but your older sister thinks she's queen of the world. Still sometimes you ask her for advice anyway.

D. You live in a house with many brothers—dirty, sticky, smelly boys! You love them all, but sometimes would give anything for a sister!

7. Your dream vacation would be:

A. Anyplace beachy. You love to swim and also just relax on a beach blanket.

B. Paris—to see the latest fashions.

C. Egypt—you'd love to see the pyramids and try to figure out how they were constructed without any modern machinery.

D. Holland—you'd love to see the tulips in bloom!

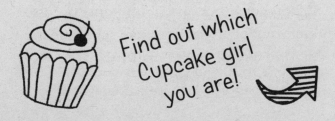

Find out which Cupcake girl you are!

Which Cupcake girl are you?
What your answers mean:

Mostly As:
You're a Katie! Your style is easy and comfortable.
You always look good, and you always feel good too.
You have a few very close friends (both girls and boys),
and you like it that way. You don't want to confide
in just anybody.

Mostly Bs:
You're a Mia! You're the girl everyone envies at school
because you can wear an old ratty sweatshirt and jeans
and somehow still look like a runway model. Your
sense of style is what everyone notices first, but you're
also a great friend.

Mostly Cs:
You're an Alexis! You are supersmart and not afraid to
show it! You get As in every subject, and like nothing
more than creating business plans and budgets. You love
your friends but have to remember sometimes that not
everyone in the world is as brilliant as you are.

Mostly Ds:
You're an Emma! You are a girly-girl and love to wear
pretty clothes. Pink is your signature color. But people
should not be fooled by your sweet exterior. You can
be as tough as nails when necessary and would never
let anyone push you around.

A Little Sweet Talk!

There are 22 words in this puzzle, and they all have something to do with your four favorite Cupcake girls! Can you find them all?

(If you don't want to write in your book, make a copy of this page.)

WORD LIST: AGENT, BROTHER, CAMP, CHARM, CONFIDENCE, CUPCAKE, DRESS, FRIENDSHIP, FLUTE, HIKE, JAKE, MODEL, PERFORM, POISE, POOL, SING, SISTER, STAR, STYLE, SWIM, TALENT, WEDDING

#1

D	R	E	S	S	M	R	A	H	C
P	A	J	B	Y	O	J	A	K	E
O	D	G	H	M	D	P	M	A	C
I	R	S	E	F	E	L	Y	T	S
S	T	A	R	N	L	M	I	W	S
E	P	O	O	L	T	E	K	I	H
C	O	N	F	I	D	E	N	C	E
J	G	C	U	P	C	A	K	E	S
G	N	I	D	D	E	W	N	D	I
F	L	U	T	E	G	N	I	S	S
B	R	O	T	H	E	R	A	M	T
R	E	T	N	E	L	A	T	G	E
P	E	R	F	O	R	M	D	E	R
F	R	I	E	N	D	S	H	I	P

There are 16 words in this puzzle, and they all have something to do with your four favorite Cupcake girls! Can you find them all?

(If you don't want to write in your book, make a copy of this page.)

WORD LIST: ACCESSORY, BLUSH, CAKE, FAIRY, FROSTING, GOOFY, HAIR, INVOICE, LOCKER, MAKEUP, PARTY, PROFIT, PRICE, REPUTATION, STYLISH, WIG

#2

```
R E P U T A T I O N
C O E C I O V N I K
F Z P R I C E D F G
A B S T Y L I S H Y
I W L Y T R A P N C
R Z I U G O O F Y P
Y G I W S C A K E R
L J L L M H A I R O
M A K E U P I S H F
R E K C O L O M E I
A C C E S S O R Y T
G N I T S O R F A B
```

All Mixed Up!

Mia gave Emma a shopping list, but Jake scrambled all the words. Can you figure out what the words are supposed to be? Write each word correctly on the lines. Then write the circled letters in order, on the lines on the bottom of the page. You'll have the answer to a cupcake riddle!

(If you don't want to write in your book, make a copy of this page.)

COCHOTELA   _ _ _ ⃝ _ _ _ _ _

AUSRG   _ _ _ _ ⃝

RACAMLE   _ ⃝ _ _ _ _ _

MAERC   ⃝ _ _ _ _

LIMK   _ _ _ ⃝

ESGG   ⃝ _ _ _

STARDUC   _ _ _ _ _ _ ⃝

NOMANNIC   _ _ _ ⃝ _ _ _

DANCY   _ _ _ ⃝

NOCCOUT   _ ⃝ _ _ _ _ _

LOUFR   _ ⃝ _ _ _

KEAC   _ _ ⃝ _

RIDDLE: Why did the cupcake laugh at the egg?

RIDDLE ANSWER:

Because the egg _ _ _ _ _ _ _ _   _ _ _ _ _ _!

The words below were used in *Alexis Cool as a Cupcake.*
Unscramble each word, and write the correctly spelled
words on the lines. Then write the circled letters in order,
on the lines at the bottom of the page.

#2

You'll have the answer to a silly cupcake riddle.

(If you don't want to write in your book, make a copy of this page.)

UBSESSIN Ⓞ＿＿＿＿＿＿＿

KEACPUC ＿＿＿＿＿＿Ⓞ

YEALD ＿＿＿Ⓞ＿

TORTU Ⓞ＿＿＿＿

WEO ＿Ⓞ＿

WHEENALLO Ⓞ＿＿＿＿＿＿＿＿

PEICRE ＿＿＿Ⓞ＿＿

DERAPA Ⓞ＿＿＿＿＿

FESSPROION Ⓞ＿＿＿＿＿＿＿＿＿

TUMECOS ＿＿＿＿＿＿Ⓞ

DIEINGRENT ＿＿＿＿＿Ⓞ＿＿＿＿

RIDDLE: Why did the cupcakes think the cook was mean?

RIDDLE ANSWER: Because she ＿ ＿ ＿ ＿ the eggs

and ＿ ＿ ＿ ＿ ＿ ＿ ＿ the cream!

ANSWER KEY:

A Little Sweet Talk!

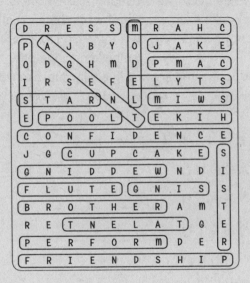

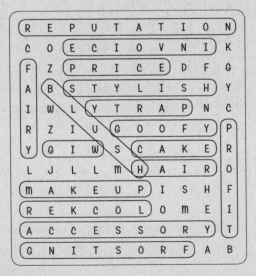

All Mixed Up!

#1

COCHOTELA	C H O Ⓒ O L A T E
AUSRG	S U G A Ⓡ
RACAMLE	C Ⓐ R A M E L
MAERC	Ⓒ R E A M
LIMK	M I L Ⓚ
ESGG	Ⓔ G G S
STARDUC	C U S T A R Ⓓ
NOMANNIC	C I N N Ⓐ M O N
DANCY	C A N D Ⓨ
NOCCOUT	C Ⓞ C O N U T
LOUFR	F L Ⓛ O U R
KEAC	C A Ⓚ E

RIDDLE: Why did the cupcake laugh at the egg?
RIDDLE ANSWER: Because the egg CRACKED A YOLK!

#2

UBSESSIN	Ⓑ U S I N E S S
KEACPUC	C U P C A K Ⓔ
YEALD	D E L Ⓐ Y
TORTU	Ⓣ U T O R
WEO	O Ⓦ E
WHEENALLO	Ⓗ A L L O W E E N
PEICRE	R E C Ⓘ P E
DERAPA	Ⓟ A R A D E
FESSPROION	Ⓟ R O F E S S I O N
TUMECOS	C O S T U M Ⓔ
DIEINGRENT	I N G R E Ⓓ I E N T

RIDDLE: Why did the cupcakes think the cook was mean?
RIDDLE ANSWER: Because she B E A T the eggs
and W H I P P E D the cream!

Want more

CUPCAKE DIARIES?

Visit **CupcakeDiariesBooks.com**
for the series trailer, excerpts, activities,
and everything you need for throwing
your own cupcake party!

Simon
Spotlight

Still Hungry?
There's always room for another Cupcake!

Emma all stirred up!

Alexis cool as a cupcake

Katie and the cupcake war

Mia's boiling point

Emma, smile and say "cupcake!"

Alexis gets frosted

Katie's new recipe

Mia a matter of taste

Emma sugar and spice and everything nice

Alexis and the missing ingredient

Katie sprinkles & surprises

Mia fashion plates and cupcakes

Coco Simon always dreamed of opening a cupcake bakery but was afraid she would eat all of the profits. When she's not daydreaming about cupcakes, Coco edits children's books and has written close to one hundred books for children, tweens, and young adults, which is a lot less than the number of cupcakes she's eaten. Cupcake Diaries is the first time Coco has mixed her love of cupcakes with writing.

If you liked

CUPCAKE  DIARIES

be sure to check out these

other series from

Simon Spotlight

sew zoey

Zoey's clothing design blog puts her on the A-list in the fashion world . . . but when it comes to school, will she be teased, or will she be a trendsetter? Find out in the Sew Zoey series:

If you like reading about
the adventures of Katie, Mia,
Emma, and Alexis, you'll love
Alex and Ava, stars of the
It Takes Two series!

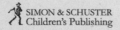